BLIND PURSUIT

ROB SINCLAIR

Boldwood

First published in Great Britain in 2026 by Boldwood Books Ltd.

Cover Design by Head Design Ltd

Cover Images: iStock

A CIP catalogue record for this book is available from the British Library.

Paperback ISBN 978-1-83703-213-6

Large Print ISBN 978-1-83703-212-9

Hardback ISBN 978-1-83703-211-2

Trade Paperback ISBN 978-1-80656-358-6

Ebook ISBN 978-1-83703-214-3

Kindle ISBN 978-1-83703-215-0

Audio CD ISBN 978-1-83703-206-8

MP3 CD ISBN 978-1-83703-207-5

Digital audio download ISBN 978-1-83703-209-9

This book is printed on certified sustainable paper. Boldwood Books is dedicated to putting sustainability at the heart of our business. For more information please visit https://www.boldwoodbooks.com/about-us/sustainability/

Boldwood Books Ltd, 23 Bowerdean Street, London, SW6 3TN

www.boldwoodbooks.com

1

BUCHAREST, ROMANIA

Given the choice, Lea would have dressed more for the weather. The heat had risen steadily over the morning, hitting over ninety degrees in the shade by midday and a hell of a lot more in the fierce sunshine. Which was exactly where she found herself at the cafe table, waiting. Her jeans felt heavy, sticking to her clammy legs. Sweat rolled down her spine, the wet patches on her T-shirt at least hidden from the people around her by the jacket she still wore. Although keeping her dignity wasn't the only reason she'd leave the jacket on.

She again wiped her brow with a napkin, then checked her watch.

Nearly twelve-thirty. She'd originally arrived in the area before 7 a.m., which was one of the reasons for her heftier than needed clothing, as she'd expected to be finished and at the train station for eight, out of the country on an air-conditioned carriage before now. Yet here she still was, waiting.

She picked her phone up from the table and called Denis. Again.

'Still no sign?' she asked.

'No. But I'm sure he's near.'

'I've been sitting here for more than an hour,' she said, briefly glancing around the other half-dozen tables outside, four of which were taken. No one paid her any attention, but it'd still been too long sitting here, out in the open. 'Five more minutes and I'm moving somewhere else.'

'Please, don't. Wait there. It's where he's headed. We've already changed the location three times, we—'

'Because he's several hours late.'

'He'll be there soon. Hold out.'

Easy for him to say; he'd been sitting in the cool of his car, air-con probably blasting the whole time. He ended the call before she could say anything more. She wiped her brow again, called the young waitress over and paid cash for the two sparkling waters she'd had. The woman gave her an apologetic look, perhaps noting her hot and flustered demeanour. Perhaps the youngster thought she'd been stood up by a date or something.

The waitress glanced curiously – suspiciously – to the helmet on the table for a second before wandering off. Lea reached out and lifted the corner of the helmet just a little to see the edge of the brown envelope underneath. Still there. As if it could have moved itself. Or as if the waitress or anyone else could have snaffled it away without Lea realising.

The phone buzzed on the table.

'He's nearly there,' Denis said. 'Dark grey Range Rover, approaching from your north.'

'You have a visual?' Lea asked.

'Yes.'

From his drone. In the alley he was parked in, he'd have no natural line of sight of their 'guest' or his vehicle at all. Not even when he approached Lea at the cafe.

She looked off to her left, the wide road leading north. Above the dense tree-line rose the top of the *Casa Presei Libere*. House of the Free Press. Once the tallest building in the Romanian capital. The looming structure had been built during the communist era, apparently a close mimic of the main building of the Moscow State University and was intended to house all of the country's printing presses and news staff. House of the Free Press. A grand misnomer if ever there was one. The sheer size of it only added to the contradiction, indicating just how much effort had gone into controlling propaganda and the minds of the public during the communist era. It had worked, but not for long here before the eventual uprising of the public wanting change. Romania was a very different place post-communism, but even in the modern world governments across the world strived for control of the public discourse for their own benefit.

Just look at the reasons why Lea and Denis were there in the first place.

'You see it yet?' Denis asked.

'Yeah, I see it,' Lea answered, her eyes now on the Range Rover a couple of hundred yards in the distance as it travelled with the other traffic in the two lanes facing her direction.

'OK. See you soon.'

She put the phone on the table, then moved her hand to her side to feel the bulge under her jacket. Another of the reasons why she'd kept the outer layer on despite the heat.

The Range Rover came to a stop across the street from her. Not a parking area. A man got out of the back – forty yards away but she could tell simply from his stature that it wasn't the man she was expecting.

She grabbed the phone and dialled Denis.

'It's not him,' he interjected before she could get a word out. So he'd spotted the obvious from the drone too.

'No,' Lea confirmed, a little unnecessarily really, she thought after the word had left her lips.

'Just stick to the plan.'

The call ended. The Range Rover remained in place at the side of the road, traffic already backing up behind it as the man made his way across the street to her.

Lea studied him. He was casually dressed in jeans and a linen shirt, a little under six feet tall with a moderately broad frame. Probably in his forties judging by his greying and receding hair. No sign of him carrying a weapon. Just an ordinary-looking guy in every sense.

'You're Lea?' he asked as he reached her table.

'Yes,' she said.

She indicated the chair opposite. He scanned the vicinity before pulling it out and taking it. His eyes fell on the helmet.

'Where's Yuri?' she asked. 'It was supposed to be him meeting me here.'

'In the car.'

'And Anderson?'

A mischievous smile crept up the man's face.

'In the car too. Do you have it?' he asked.

'It's in the car,' Lea responded with her own smile, and the man's dropped away.

He took out his phone and rattled off something in Romanian. Lea knew the basics, but spoken at speed and with his hand over the receiver to muffle his voice, she could make out next to nothing.

Not that she needed to. She understood what he would be relaying. His unhappiness that the swap wouldn't be anywhere near as simple as it could and should have been, but they'd played their part in that too. All to be expected, really. Although Lea certainly wasn't trying to screw these people – she just wanted to make sure all parties got what they'd been promised, and hopefully without events going south.

She reached out and lifted her helmet from the table. The man looked a little put out when he saw the brown envelope underneath. He quickly slid it towards him and onto his lap.

'A small gesture,' Lea said.

The man opened the top of the envelope and pulled a few of the papers a couple of inches out before scanning them and then sliding them away again. He pulled the phone to his ear once more. Another muffled conversation followed.

'Can I speak to him?' Lea asked, halting the phone conversation. 'To Yuri. But I want to know you really have Anderson in there too.'

Silence from the man for a few seconds before he was doing the talking again, but a few seconds later he held the device out to Lea. She took it and pressed it to her ear.

'Yuri?' she asked.

'Yes. Look at the car.'

She glanced that way. The car rolled forward, a few yards closer. The passenger window slid down to reveal a man's face. Lea's heart thumped her ribs a little harder. Anderson. Behind him a more shadowy face peered over, phone to his ear. Yuri.

'Satisfied?' he asked, the window already gliding up.

'Yes.'

She handed the phone back to the man. He killed the call.

'Where's the car?' he asked her.

'Too far to walk,' Lea said. She stood up from the table, helmet at the ready. 'Follow me.'

She didn't wait for a response before she turned and headed to her motorbike parked by a bollard not far away. The man had initially stayed put but by the time she had her helmet on and was stepping onto the bike he was at the SUV. As she turned the key he was inside, and the Range Rover pulled out and took a right towards her.

She sighed. Long and hard. The heat of the helmet one reason, relief that this hadn't yet gone awry another. Trepidation that they still had the biggest hurdle to come another.

She moved out into the road, took things slow and steady. The reality was that Denis was actually pretty nearby, really. Less than a quarter of a mile in a straight line from the cafe, although the route on the mostly one-way streets was a mile and a half.

She soon turned the final corner to the alley and pulled the bike up to the side of the building, Denis's car ten yards in front. The Range Rover stopped just behind her, blocking the exit that way. The engine remained rumbling.

She got off her bike and made her way over to Denis's car. He stepped out as she reached it, his manner stiff, poised.

'We good?' he said to her quietly.

She nodded in response, though they both knew this was the most dangerous part of the exchange. He opened the car boot and they stood on either side.

The same man emerged from the Range Rover first, but he didn't come forward. Instead, he pulled Anderson from the back while Yuri got out the other side.

An unseen figure still behind the wheel.

Yuri walked towards Lea and Denis, hesitant as hell, while his accomplice stood guard with Anderson. Yuri's head and his gaze shifted left, right, up, down.

'Just you two?' he asked.

'Just us,' Denis confirmed. The truth. Although Lea didn't really mind so much if Yuri didn't believe them. Perhaps it gave them that little bit more security if Yuri thought they had more backup here.

'This isn't what we agreed,' Yuri said.

'No,' Lea said, 'it isn't. Because you were supposed to be here at seven.'

'I explained to him why that wasn't possible,' Yuri said, nodding to Denis.

'Doesn't matter now,' Denis said. 'Let's just finish things.'

Yuri continued forward, Denis and Lea standing firm. Yuri stopped a couple of yards from the car and looked inside the boot.

'That's it?' he said.

'The money's in the holdall,' Lea said. 'Everything else you were promised is in the satchel.'

She held the satchel towards him, but he didn't take it.

'Count the money if you want,' Denis said.

'Take it out for me,' Yuri said.

Lea nodded to Denis and he reached into the boot...

Yuri's hand slipped behind him.

'Denis!' Lea shouted.

Bang.

Not Yuri firing. The guy by the Range Rover.

Lea dove for cover at the side of the car.

Bang. Bang.

A body crumpled down, head smacking onto the ground right by her. She expected to see Denis's lifeless eyes staring at her.

No. Yuri.

Although the twisted snarl on his face showed he was still alive. For now.

'Get out of here!' Denis yelled, tossing the satchel to her before letting off a volley of gunfire at the Range Rover.

But as she got up a bullet sank into her ankle. She gritted her teeth and roared with anger and pain and stumbled to the ground. She rolled over onto her back, lifted her gun out to fire back towards the Range Rover...

Except the SUV was already moving. Gunning towards her, Denis, his car. Denis flung himself to the side and Lea could only turn over and cower before the Range Rover ploughed into the back of the car. Metal and plastic crashed and snapped, glass shattered, twisted and broken debris filled the air and splatted down onto her.

Lea blinked, blinked, blinked as she lay on the ground, cheek to the concrete, eyes and mind refocusing. She didn't move her gaze from the satchel a few feet from her grip.

A piercing siren filled the air. More than one. Police. A coincidence?

No such thing.

She bounced to her feet, ignoring the pain in her ankle. Denis, groggy but conscious – was he shot? – looked over at her.

'Go!' he shouted.

She scooped the satchel from the ground as she moved. Ignored the shouting behind her. Whoever was still alive from the Range Rover. The police too who'd just arrived en masse. She jumped on her bike. The Range Rover backed away from the crumpled car and then gunned for her as she tugged on the throttle. She swung the bike around and sped off back the way she'd come, the SUV's tyres screeching as the driver tried to follow her move.

A quick glance in the side mirror. The Range Rover had turned to follow her out of the alley. A bigger, more powerful, faster machine than hers. On open roads. So she had to do everything she could to avoid them.

She took a left, tilting the bike wildly, her knee not far from the road. Sirens multiplied above the whine of her bike and the growl of the Range Rover. She took a right. Backed-up traffic at the next junction forced her left. Not the best choice entering the wide multi lanes of Calea Moșilor. Busy at least. Which meant she could bob and weave the bike between traffic. A flashing blue light whizzed past on the other side of the divide. More up ahead. On her side of the road. She flung a right onto a narrower road. Hoped to see empty space open up behind her. No. The Range Rover. A motorbike. Not police. Just a regular motorbike. No – not regular. More powerful than hers, and not alone. A second slid into the street behind it and soon both had overtaken the Range Rover. One of the riders pulled a snub weapon – Uzi? – up to fire at her...

She skidded around another corner before the rider could unleash, this time a left, aimed to take a quick right after to keep her on the narrower back streets, but a police car, lights flashing, screeched towards her. She tugged the throttle to clear it before a smash and then took the next right instead.

Another multi-lane road, the grand fountain at Bulevardul Unirii in the near distance.

She was at full pelt, nothing left to give, the two bikes behind her closing in fast. She jerked on the handlebars to move off from the road onto the grassy verge of the park that surrounded the fountain in the centre of the huge junction. Pedestrians shouted and screamed and dove for cover.

A police car raced alongside her on the road a few yards away. Up ahead two more headed directly for her. The two motorbikes, the Range Rover behind. All working in unison to get her?

It made no sense.

She twisted the brake as sharply as she could and the bike violently slowed. She dug her heel into the ground to help it further and to swing the bike around, momentarily forgetting about her injured ankle and she did her best to ignore the agonising pain. The closest of the motorbike chasers sped past, too much speed, braking too late, and from nowhere a police car bounced over a thicket and smacked the tail-end of the bike, sending the rider somersaulting into the water spraying from the fountain.

Lea wrenched the throttle and took off again, the road ten yards ahead. She'd head straight across the lanes of traffic. Back into the old town. She had to get away, get some space, call this in, get some help.

Five yards to the road. A clearing opened up. She could see right across the lanes to the other side.

Went for it.

Didn't see the car until the front tyre was already on the tarmac.

It swiped across the wheel, sending her and the bike into a terrifying spin. Lea's body flopped and skidded along the road, her body bouncing and scraping across the surface for several yards.

Dazed, she was barely aware of the chaos around her, the injuries she'd already sustained, the screams of bystanders and the screeching of tyres.

The only thing that her brain processed was the satchel on the ground next to her, the papers poking out of the torn fabric, covered in her blood...

And the sight of the truck just beyond it, hurtling towards her, so close, so big that it filled her whole world in those final split seconds before it ploughed right into her.

2

BRISTOL, ENGLAND

The police station in central Bristol looked like a regular office block from the outside, and pretty much the same inside. At least to the part Callum Murphy was taken to. No holding cells here, no barred windows or interview rooms with one-way mirrors. But then he wasn't a criminal, he hadn't been arrested. In fact, he didn't fully understand *why* he was there at all. But in his dumbfounded state back at the construction site he'd simply agreed to the officers' suggestion that he come here to talk to them.

Mr Murphy. I'm sorry to say that... your wife... She's dead.

A bad day had become infinitely worse in that moment. He'd been in the midst of a heated argument with the project manager and the building inspector about a mistake that was undeniably of his making, even if it was entirely unintentional. His mind was more concerned at that point about the state of his late mentor's business, with Callum now thrust to the front to take the reins, than with making any excuses for his failures.

But then the police had arrived.

Moments later his world had shattered, even if none of it made any sense.

He'd followed the police here. A woman in clean-cut office wear – she looked like an accountant as much as a police officer – had showed him to this room fifteen minutes ago, and since then he'd been on his own.

The room was bright, clean, functional. More of a meeting room than an interview room. The desk in front of him had electrical outlets, USB ports, and there was a window with a pretty crappy view of the overcast city.

He jolted when the door opened and two people walked in. Man, woman. Not the same woman as before, although it could well have been a relation given the similar features, similar manner, similar plain clothing. The newcomers wore bland business casual attire, both were probably mid-thirties with seriously stern – sombre? – faces. Whether that was for Callum's benefit or not, he couldn't be sure.

'Mr Murphy,' the woman said as they both took a seat opposite Callum. 'I'm DCI Gladstone, this is my colleague DI Poulter.'

Callum said nothing in return. Gladstone and Poulter shuffled a little, as though not knowing who was supposed to say what next.

'Is this normal?' Callum asked.

'Excuse me?' Gladstone said.

'I mean... I've never had to go through this before. But I expected... a knock on my door at home. A liaison officer, or whatever they're called, to come inside and make me a cup of tea in my own house or something. But... instead I'm here... with two detectives?'

They glanced at each other.

'I'm very sorry, Mr Murphy, it will become apparent why, but firstly... I'm so sorry for your loss. From what we understand from our colleagues overseas, your wife was involved in a motorbike accident in Bucharest this morning.'

'Bucharest?'

'Romania.'

'No, I know where Bucharest is. But Lea wasn't in Bucharest. She was in Prague. A conference with her employer, BTS? It's... a consulting company. That's what she does.'

Gladstone held her hands up, shook her head. 'I'm sorry, Mr Murphy, I don't know anything about that. Only what we've been told.'

'A motorbike accident? As in... she was knocked over, or what?'

'I believe she was driving. She was involved in a collision with a truck.'

Callum snorted, his hackles rising. He hadn't expected to come here feeling like this. In the car over here, he'd felt numb more than anything else. Not even distress or sadness. That had only crept in as he'd sat in this room, calling Lea over and over, hoping she'd pick up and he'd find this was all a horrible mistake.

Except she hadn't picked up, and so the worry – the guilt too, though he wasn't sure why – had grown and grown...

Until these two had arrived and started talking.

Now he was feeling mad more than anything, because none of this made any sense.

They *weren't* talking about Lea.

'We've been together the best part of three years,' Callum said. 'She's never ridden a motorbike once. She hates anything fast. So why the hell would she be doing that, in Bucharest, when she's in Prague? Which is what I already told you.'

He took out his phone again, dialled her number, his initially thudding heart losing its rhythm a bit more with each beat as ring after ring went unanswered. The detectives said nothing, just held their now more sympathetic gaze on him as they waited for him to concede.

The beep for voicemail sounded out in Callum's ear. He thought about leaving a message. *Wanted* to leave a message, and for Lea to pick it up and then call him back and laugh at him down the phone for acting so insane and believing what he was being told.

Instead, he hit the red button as her voice message played once again and then placed the device softly on the table.

'I know this is hard for you,' Poulter said. 'But we've already had your wife's body identified... It's definitely—'

'Identified by who? Isn't that my role, as her next of kin?'

No answer.

'I want to see her.'

Silence from the detectives.

'*I* want to see her. I—'

'We'll have someone else talk to you in due course about repatriating her remains—'

'No. I want to go there. If you're saying she's in Bucharest, I want to go there *now*. I need to see her. I need to show you two that this is—'

He stopped when Gladstone pulled out the glossy photos from her stack of papers. She slid a couple across the table. Callum's eyes cast on them. And after that he couldn't look away.

'Mr Murphy, the accident was bad. I'm not saying you can't go there, but I will say it probably won't help you. An identification from you or any other family member won't be necessary. I understand her identity was confirmed through her fingerprints. And... you recognise this tattoo on her wrist?'

He stared at the photo. The black of a road below tainted skin. The black of a road speckled with red. A hand, fingers twisted and gashed. A ring on the third finger. The ring that a little over a year ago he'd put there. Just above the wrist was the sleeve of a jacket he didn't recognise, torn and bloodied. Below the wrist, among the blood, was the small tattoo she'd already had when he first met her. Two Chinese characters, she'd told him. Hope and light, or something like that.

He couldn't even properly read his native language for God's sake, but he loved those two Chinese characters. The intricate patterns, swirls.

Hope and light.

There wasn't much of either of those right now.

Not for her or for him.

'Mr Murphy, that is your wife, isn't it?' Poulter asked.

'Yes.'

'I could show you more, but I really don't think... it's necessary. I'm sure you understand why.'

Callum pushed the photos back across the table. He wanted to erase the images he'd seen. Even more, he wanted to erase the even gorier images that he *hadn't* seen, of the rest of her. Images that, now swirling in his mind, would likely torment him forever.

He noted the tremor in his hand as he pulled it back to his body.

'Would you like some water?' Gladstone asked.

'Y-yes,' Callum replied and Poulter got to his feet and left the room. 'Why am I here?'

'It's quite normal when dealing with an incident like this on foreign soil. A lot of different parties become involved. And this isn't anything like a formal interview, but we do have some questions we need to ask you.'

'About what?'

'It's just to understand the situation better. So we have everything on record. At this end and in Romania.'

'You said it was an accident... Is that... Could there...' He put his head in his hands, tried to hold his emotions in check. Sooner or later, he'd fail. 'I don't even know what I'm trying to say.'

'Could the truck driver face charges? Is that what you're asking?'

'I guess. Could they?'

'I'm not close enough to it. But trust me that someone will be.'

Poulter came back into the room holding a little plastic cup with a measly amount of water inside. He placed it on the table, but Callum didn't touch it.

'So, after your questions, I can go?' Callum said, his voice monotone, robotic, the nothingness taking over inside him once more.

'Yes,' Gladstone said.

'Then ask.'

'When did you last speak to your wife?'

'Last night. Just after 9 p.m. I called to see how she was, how her day was. She said it'd been long and boring. Too much listening to other people talk. She'd already been out to dinner with a group of colleagues and was back in her hotel room. In Prague. It was a video call. She showed me the bloody room!'

Although Prague, Bucharest? Thinking back, the room he'd seen on the call could have been in fucking Bristol for all he really knew.

Maybe it'd have been obvious to someone else.

Forrest Gump.

Only minutes before the police had arrived that's exactly what that prick Wilson, the outsourced project manager on the old factory site, had called him.

Yeah, Wilson, with his degree in something or other and a professional qualification in something-or-other-else-fancy-sounding-thing that he'd earned entirely in a classroom and not the real world was pretentious, obnoxious, but perhaps he was right about Callum.

'You said your wife worked for—'

'BTS. She has done since before I met her. In fact, it's *how* we met. Kind of.'

'You worked for them too?'

'No.'

'So what is it you do?'

Callum paused before answering that one.

'I'm just a builder. I work for Worthington Construction.'

A couple of nods to that. Perhaps they'd heard of the small firm before, given the reputation of its founder, George, an expert in his field who'd overseen some of the most impressive developments in the area over recent years. Until his untimely death nine months ago from a heart attack while walking his dog on the estuary.

I'm just a builder.

Really, Callum was supposed to be much more than that now, but the events of the morning were just the latest stark example of his limitations being brutally exposed.

'So when you met her—'

'We were both travelling. Her on business, me for pleasure. We happened to be in the same hotel. I'm sorry... why is any of this important?'

'Like I said, we just need to tick some boxes. Make sure we understand her last movements.'

'Yeah. Now I'd really like to do that. Because last night she was in Prague and now you're telling me this morning she was killed in a motorbike crash in Bucharest.'

Poulter and Gladstone both held their tongues a few seconds as though aware Callum was teetering, that if pushed the wrong way he might explode, either with anger or despair.

'As far as you're aware, was your wife in any trouble? Was she afraid that anyone might want to hurt her?'

Callum balled his fists, channelling the building anger. 'Are you saying there's a chance someone did this to her deliberately? You told me it was an accident.'

'We honestly don't know,' Poulter said. 'But we're asking *you* if you think that's a possibility.'

'When she left home three days ago...' Callum trailed off, shaking his head, eyes welling, remembering that uneventful morning. A hug, a bland kiss on the cheek as he ate his cereal. The last time he'd ever see, touch his wife. 'There was nothing wrong. Nothing wrong at all.'

Poulter leaned over to Gladstone and the two of them exchanged hushed words for a few seconds.

'OK, Mr Murphy. I think we've taken up enough of your time,' Poulter said.

'That's it?'

'That's all we need for now.'

'Once again, I'm very sorry for your loss,' Gladstone said. 'Is there anyone we could call for you? A friend, a family member—'

'I just want to go home.'

'OK. Someone will be in shortly to take you out.'

They both left. Callum remained seated. For a few seconds at least. Then he got up and moved over to the window. Dusk outside. Streetlights were flicking on here and there. The heavy rain outside only compounded his downtrodden mood. He turned away, trying to keep his head clear of any thought. He moved to the door. Tried it. Locked?

He turned and looked around the room. Eventually found the camera up in one corner. He stared at it, as though expecting to see something there, answers to the myriad questions he now had.

The door opened and he instinctively swivelled and stepped back as though to protect himself from whoever was on the other side...

The same woman who'd brought him here in the first place.

'Mr Murphy. You're ready to go?'

'Yes.'

'Follow me.'

* * *

The stop-start journey home gave him plenty of time to dwell. Too much time. He tried calling Lea again. Stupid, really. But what if...?

No answer. He thought about who else to call. His parents? His brother? But he was too lost, too numb to do so.

What would he even say?

And what would be the point? Nothing would change the fact that his wife was dead.

He simply didn't have the strength to face reality right now anyway.

The first thing he'd do when he opened the door was rush to the drinks cabinet. Take out a whiskey. Drink until he passed out on the sofa. Angel's Envy. His favourite. A bottle Lea had first bought for him on a trip to the US. Memories spiralled in his head. Every fucking thing he looked at and thought of reminded him of her.

It'd be all of a couple of hours since he'd been told the news, and look at the mess he was in. How the hell could he do this? How could he cope?

But above all the trauma, something else swirled too. Unanswered questions. Why the hell was Lea in Bucharest at all?

His phone chirped as he turned onto his street. He looked at the screen. Willed to see her name and the little icon of her face.

No. It was work. He'd had several calls, voicemails, emails in the intervening time since he'd left the site. Some from Wilson, some from Gloria, George's widow, who still ran the office, a couple from his foreman too. No chance of him even attempting to figure out how to respond to those yet, even if perhaps carrying on with normality would be a good thing right now.

Normality? Nothing would ever be normal again.

He parked up on the drive. The house sat in darkness. He'd hoped to see a light on. To walk through the door and see her there, hear her pottering, smell her cooking.

He opened the front door and there was nothing. Just a damp chill and a lonely mustiness as though even the house itself was in mourning.

He flipped on the light in the hall, took off his shoes and jacket, the latter already dripping from the continued rain outside which drummed against the windowpanes.

He moved across the hall and reached for the living room light switch. Hadn't quite found it when he noted the droplets of water on the floor further along the hall, in the kitchen too. His finger flipped the switch as his brain scrambled to process.

He froze when he saw the figure in the armchair across the room.

'Callum, don't be alarmed,' the man said, his hands outstretched across the chair arms. 'I'm not here to hurt you.'

Fight or flight?

Initially Callum didn't do either.

'Who are you?'

Seemed like a good enough question if he was just going to stand there like a mug.

'I'm sorry about what happened to Lea,' the man said.

Anger now. Fight or flight? The first one was about to win out. He wanted to lash out. He'd charge across the room and tear this intruder from limb to limb.

'Please,' the man said, as though picking up on the threat. 'I'm not here to cause trouble. I'm only here to talk to you.'

'About what?'

'About Lea.'

'You knew my wife?' A nod. 'I've never seen you before.'

'I know. And I realise that this is going to be hard to understand right now. At any time, really. Perhaps... Take a seat.'

'I'm good. Say what you've got to say. Or maybe I should just call the police.'

Callum reached for his phone.

'You don't need the police. You only need to listen.'

'Let me be the judge of that.'

Footsteps behind him. Callum spun to see a young woman in the kitchen doorway.

'It's OK, big man,' she said, raising her empty hands as if to show she wasn't about to attack. 'I'm with him.'

Callum switched his gaze from one to the other.

'I'll give you five seconds,' Callum said to the man. 'And then I'm charging at *you* first.'

'Mr Murphy, there'll be no need for that. But let me put this simply... Your wife wasn't the woman you thought she was.'

Dark thoughts burrowed, wrestling for control.

'In fact... I'm here to tell you that pretty much everything you thought you knew about her... was a lie.'

3

'My name's Warren Brandt,' the man said, before Callum could question, or protest or attack or whatever else. 'This is my colleague, Jenn Hinch.'

Callum took a moment to look them both over. Probably in their late twenties, wearing casual clothing, jackets – the woman's was brown leather, the man's thick fabric. She wore black heavy-duty boots, which together with her mop of short messy hair gave her a tomboyish no-messing look. The man was a little more innocuous with trainers, clean-cut face, though he had a glint in his eye that Callum couldn't quite describe. Confidence, but cold and calculated.

'Colleague from where?' he asked.

'We're getting to that. But we both worked with your wife.'

'At BTS?'

Brandt smiled. A little mockingly, as though he thought Callum were an idiot. Callum's anger only rose further, though he held it inside. 'Lea's job at BTS didn't really exist. It was a front. She worked for SIS.' Callum's brain was still deciphering that when Brandt helped him out. 'MI6.'

Callum shook his head. 'No. This is bullshit. What the fuck are you two doing—?'

'We're not lying to you,' Hinch said. 'We—'

'And you expect me to believe you're good guys? Breaking into my house. Waiting for—'

'Callum, I know this isn't going to be easy to understand right now, so let me just fill in some of the biggest blanks for you. Lea worked for SIS for years. Since before she met you. You don't need to know how it started, what she did, but I will be very clear with you. Her death in Bucharest has created a big headache for a lot of people.'

'Headache? You think my wife's death is a headache?'

Brandt shrugged. 'Lea was in Bucharest on an exchange deal.'

'With you two?'

'Actually no, but we know enough of the details. She and a colleague were passing intel to a Belarusian asset, in exchange for... one of our own.'

'One of... what?'

'An asset. A person.'

Callum's brain pounded. He heard all the words but struggled to make any sense of them.

'Are you saying... she was *killed*? There was no accident?'

'We don't know for sure. We know the exchange went bad. We know both assets ended up dead. And we know that the intel that was supposed to be part of the deal is now... missing.'

'Missing?'

Brandt said nothing more, just stared at Callum as though he expected a eureka moment.

But then...

'You mean, you think Lea took it? Hid it?'

'Honestly? We're still wading through the mess. Lea died in Bucharest, a traffic incident – but only after she'd fled a scene where three other bodies were found. And we have another agent, her partner over there, missing too.'

'Lea wouldn't... couldn't—'

'Let's just say right now you probably have no idea what your wife was capable of,' Hinch said, with a pretty hostile tone.

'But I'm not saying Lea killed those three,' Brandt said. 'Just that we don't know what led to that fight. Or to Lea running. Or to the intel she was supposed to be delivering going missing, along with her partner.'

'This is too much,' Callum said, moving further into the room and slumping onto the sofa, the idea of these two being a threat to him diminishing as his brain fog multiplied.

'It's possible she hid it over here,' Hinch said, now taking up the living room doorway.

'Hid it?' Callum said. 'What are we talking about? Papers? DVD? A hard drive?'

'Any or all of those things,' Brandt said.

'And you think...' Callum paused and slumped further. '*That's* why you're here? Not for my benefit or to help me understand the truth about my wife after years of lies, but because you think I know something.'

Neither of them said anything to that.

'Well, I can make this very clear for you. I know nothing. Nothing at all.'

'She might have lied to you, but she was still your wife,' Hinch said. 'You still knew her better than anyone.'

'Based on what you're telling me, I'm not sure I knew her at all.'

'But you can help us. I mean, did she ever talk to you about—'

'About how she was a spy leading a double life? Haven't you figured the answer to that yet? Of course she fucking didn't. I never suspected a thing. Which only goes to show what a fool I am.'

Which only reinforced what most people already thought of him.

'Nobody said that,' Brandt added. 'Seriously, Callum, this is really important. If there's anything, anywhere—'

'I don't know anything!' he shouted, the force of it enough to keep both Brandt and Hinch from responding straight away. 'You two should leave. I can't do this right now.'

He stood from the sofa, chest puffed up, confidence and defiance taking over. Brandt rose too. At first Callum thought it was to comply, or perhaps even to attack. But no. A look of concern had spread across his face. Callum looked at Hinch. Concern there too as she tilted her head slightly, finger to her ear as if to...

Earpiece. Which meant it wasn't just these two.

'We need to go,' she said to Brandt.

'What's happening?' Callum asked to no response. In fact, the other two didn't move a muscle despite Hinch's words. Because both were listening to the sounds from outside.

Vehicles arriving. Not high revs, armed raid style. Just two cars, engines humming, quietly coming to a stop on the road outside. Soft clunks as doors – two, three, four, perhaps – opened and closed.

'It's the police,' Brandt said to him. 'Just play it calm. Get them to go away. Nobody needs to get hurt.'

Perhaps those words were supposed to fill Callum with confidence. They really didn't. Why would the police turning up result in a fight here?

Only one obvious explanation…

Despite their claims, these two hadn't been truthful with him at all.

Hinch tiptoed past him, further into the living room, a moment before the doorbell rang. Three loud bangs on the door followed.

Callum caught Brandt's eye again. Not an imploring look from him, more a warning.

He made his way to the door. Stopped right by it.

'Who is it?' Callum shouted out.

'Mr Murphy, my name is DCI Jasper.'

He slowly opened the door a few inches, enough to stick his head out. He didn't recognise the woman who'd spoken. Not someone he'd seen earlier in the day. She flashed him a warrant card before he looked over the hefty uniformed officers who flanked her on either side, big utility belts on each of them. Hard to tell in the darkness… but…

'Is everything OK?' Jasper asked, her face not betraying her mistrust.

'Why wouldn't it be?'

'Mr Murphy, we really need you to come with us. To discuss… your wife.'

Why the pause? And the glance over his shoulder. She *knew* something wasn't right.

'Mr Murphy? Is there someone else here with you?'

'Just a friendly neighbour,' Hinch said, coming out of the living room, one hand behind her back, but a wide and easy-going smile on her face. She'd taken her leather jacket off now, shoes too, as though to make herself look more at home. She sauntered up to Callum and put her hand on his shoulder, but as she slipped it down he felt hard pressure in his lower spine. Not a hand or a finger. Metal. A gun. 'Is there a problem?' she asked.

'No problem, miss, we just need to speak to Callum.'

'It's been a horrible day for him,' Hinch said, her voice all soft and feminine now, none of her previous hard edge. 'For us all, really. Whatever it is you need him for, can't it wait until morning?'

'Actually, no. It really can't. I can explain more in the car, but I really do need you to come with us, Mr Murphy.'

'It's fine,' Callum said to her. 'Just give me a few minutes to get ready, yeah?'

Jasper didn't look impressed, particularly when he went to shut the door.

She stuck her foot in the way to stop it from closing.

'We'll be right here,' she said. 'Waiting.'

Hinch turned and moved back into the living room, no sign of the gun now but she'd made her point. Callum followed her, in two minds. Three minds. Four minds. He had so many conflicting options of what he should do.

Attack and run was the one which appealed the most.

But who the fuck was he supposed to attack? The two strangers in his home or the police outside?

He hadn't made a decision when he heard shouting from outside. He was about to turn when gunshots boomed from the street.

'Move!' Hinch shouted, dashing back out of the living room, firing her weapon at the front door.

'Come on!' she shouted, rushing off into the kitchen.

Brandt came out, grabbed hold of Callum to drag him towards the back but then they both paused and hunkered as a spray of bullets came their way. Brandt fired in return and then went to grab Callum again...

Except Callum didn't go with him this time. Instead, he rose up and sent his elbow crashing under Brandt's chin before he slammed him up against the kitchen door frame, knocking the wind from him. His gun spilled. Callum thought about going for it.

'Callum! You idiot!' Hinch screamed.

Callum took no notice as he turned and dashed for the front door, hands above his head.

'Don't shoot! Don't shoot!'

Hands grabbed him as he rushed out onto the front step.

'Callum!' came the angry shout from behind. Brandt.

But Callum was already being shepherded away.

A dark figure lay on the ground at the edge of the driveway. A man, gunned down. An armed officer stood over him.

'Get in the car,' a male voice demanded a moment before Callum was bundled inside a vehicle, his brain screaming that maybe he'd just made the biggest mistake of his life.

The car blasted off down the road as he writhed to pull himself up in the seat.

'It's OK, it's OK,' came the voice from next to him. A familiar voice that provided just a little bit of comfort. But not much. 'You're OK,' DCI Jasper said again.

Although as he looked over at her, the fear on her face suggested the opposite.

'What the fuck is happening?' Callum yelled at her.

'That's a damn good question.'

'Who were those people? Why were they at my house?'

No answer.

'Do you know them?'

Jasper shook her head. 'No. Not exactly.'

'Not exactly? W-what are you...?'

'I'm sorry. This is as new to me as it is to you.'

The next moment she was speaking into a radio, though she turned away and Callum couldn't follow the whole conversation. Up front a uniformed man sat in the driver's seat. An armed officer, his hefty weapon on the passenger seat next to him. Not the safest way to travel. Probably not protocol, but maybe because neither he nor Jasper had expected to be fleeing like they had.

Except the fact she'd turned up with an armed team in the first place...

'They got away,' she said when she'd finished and Callum wasn't sure if she was speaking to him or the driver.

'But we got the third one,' the driver said.

'We got a dead body,' Jasper said.

'Will someone tell me what the hell is going on!' Callum yelled.

Nobody did, though the driver caught Callum's eye in the mirror. A look he couldn't figure out but perhaps it was supposed to be some sort of answer.

'Perhaps by now you've figured out your wife wasn't the woman you thought she was,' Jasper said.

'Something like that.'

'I'm led to believe she had links to SIS.'

Links? A strange way of putting it.

Jasper stared at him as though expecting a response. So he gave her one.

'Those two in my house said the same thing. That they worked with her—'

'You think the people who just attacked police officers were the good guys?'

Good. Bad. Callum had absolutely no idea.

'I don't know *who* they were,' Jasper said. 'And that's the truth. I only know I got a call, a demand, to go pick you up with an armed response team and bring you back to London—'

'London?'

'We're from the Met.'

'But...' The comment or question never came out.

'All I know is that this is to do with your wife's death. Or... her job.'

Callum said nothing, his confusion too all-consuming.

The next moment the car slammed to a stop, sending Callum shooting forward in his seat. Not the other two. Apparently, they'd been ready for it.

The front passenger door opened, and another uniformed officer stepped in, carefully moving the driver's firearm out of the way. At the same time, Jasper opened her door to get out.

'We've got a drive ahead of us,' she said, turning back to him. 'Plenty of time for you to get your thinking straight. When we get to London? You're going to tell me *everything* you know, or thought you knew, about your wife. And I mean absolutely everything.'

She stepped out of the car and slammed the door shut. Not a moment later and Callum was pushed back in his seat as the car shot off down the road.

4

TOULOUSE, FRANCE

Three years ago

Grand Hôtel François Desrosiers sat nestled on a quaint old-world street in central Toulouse, not far from the Capitole – a huge neoclassical building that could have doubled as a luxury palace given its intricate facade and prominent position in a huge, open square. In addition to being the main administration building in the city – and a big tourist draw – the Capitole also housed the well-regarded Théâtre du Capitole de Toulouse, which naturally meant that the hotel itself was busy with tourists all year round. On evenings when the opera was running, every bar and restaurant in the area was jam-packed with smartly dressed men and women taking advantage of the supposedly special pre-theatre offers which were generally exorbitantly priced.

Lea had stayed here before on opera night. Luckily that wasn't tonight. Nothing for several weeks, actually, which meant the hotel was busy but not full to bursting, and there was no queue as Lea checked in. Denis milled about in the lobby, playing on his phone. Even though they'd travelled to the city together, they'd separated earlier and he'd arrived at the hotel twenty minutes before her. They'd keep their visible interactions here to an absolute minimum.

At least, that was the theory. But Lea knew by now that Denis didn't always follow such details to the letter. Basically, because he saw himself as a bit of a maverick. The cool kid who could do what he wanted. At least, as long as none of their superiors were watching or listening.

Which probably explained why he was still hanging around in the lobby – waiting for her? – when the sensible and planned thing for him to do was to have gone straight to his room.

Soon she was done, keycard in hand, and she made her way across the lobby to the bank of lifts. She didn't make eye contact with Denis but noticed him scurrying adjacent to her. She hit the call button and two seconds later the doors on the right-hand lift opened and she moved inside and pressed for the sixth floor. Denis strolled in behind her.

'Fancy seeing you here,' he said, a playful smile on his face. Despite herself, she very nearly smiled back as she caught his eye but then, as the doors rolled closed, a man came darting up. Denis saw him in the mirror, whipped around, one hand reaching inside his jacket. Lea tensed and readied herself too.

The man threw his hand in between the closing doors, and they banged against him before reopening.

'*Excusez-moi*,' he said as he stepped inside, a half empty beer glass in his hand, the liquid sloshing. Definitely not his first drink. And he definitely wasn't French, given his poor accent.

'Fifth floor, please,' he said to Denis. '*Cinq, s'il vous plaît*,' he added, as if an afterthought.

Denis looked a little put out, not just by the request, but the entire intrusion, although he was standing closest to the control panel, so the request wasn't that unreasonable.

He pressed the button and the lift got on its way.

Silence. Uncomfortable on Denis's part, Lea could tell, his jaw clenched, hands at the ready by his side. At least not in his jacket now, where Lea knew he had a knife. No firearms on this trip. Hopefully the knife wouldn't be needed either, but it at least remained simple, basic security. Carrying *something* was simply habit.

She caught the stranger's eye, and he smiled and shook his hand as if in pain from the doors hitting it.

'At least I didn't use the other hand. Would have wasted my beer.'

He raised the glass in toast to Lea and Denis a moment before the lift dinged and came to a stop on the fifth floor.

'You two have a great evening.'

He headed on out and the lift was soon moving again. Denis finally relaxed.

'If you ever wondered why English tourists get a bad rep...'

Lea just shrugged before the doors opened on the sixth floor.

'Shall we do a brain dump before—'

'I think we're on the same page already,' Lea said, doors already closing. 'See you downstairs later, yeah?'

Denis didn't get another word in before the doors clanked shut.

* * *

An hour later, Lea had taken a stool at the bar. She sat side on so she had an unobstructed view, the bar area to the left, the mirrors behind the bottles of spirits on her right, in which she could see the lobby, the restaurant directly ahead of her.

The restaurant was quiet. The lobby too, really, although Denis sat there in an armchair with his iPad and a cafetière.

The bar was busier, but mostly because of a group of twenty- and thirty-something men. English. Not rowdy, but definitely the start of a long and probably increasingly boisterous night for them given it was only 7 p.m. and they already had stashes of empty beer glasses around them.

The man from the lift earlier was among the group and more than once he caught Lea's eye as she sat there taking her time with her second cocktail. The first had had alcohol. Why not? This second one didn't.

'He's been up in his room too long,' Denis's voice came in her ear. She glanced over in his direction. He had his eyes on his iPad as he spoke. 'You don't think he went out another way?'

'The only other way out is the service entrance,' she said, head down, trying to be as discreet as possible. 'Can't see why he'd do that unless he's been spooked already.'

'Which is a possibility.'

'Possible, but very unlikely unless he was tipped off about us being here.'

Movement to her left. Three of the English group were coming over to the bar, arms around one another, cackling at something or other. One of them caught Lea's eye and nodded to her but she quickly looked away, hoping he wouldn't engage her. He didn't. The trio ordered their round which included beers and chasers galore.

'I see him,' Denis said.

Lea couldn't. Not at first, but as the Englishmen moved back to their corner, her view opened up and Abdul Hadjam walked towards her from the lobby. Towards her back, anyway. She looked down at her drink, eyes focused there, but her brain focused on her peripheral vision of Hadjam in the mirror as he moved right past her and into the restaurant.

'You see him still?' Denis asked a few seconds later when Hadjam was seated in a booth that had five place settings laid out.

'Yeah.'

'Good. Don't move. Once he's got company, I'll go find a table myself. Why don't you get some food ordered at the bar, so you look more settled?'

And it did look like Hadjam was staying. Which they'd expected. Hoped. They knew Hadjam had checked into the hotel that afternoon, like them, and their intel was that the French-Algerian businessman was due to be meeting with a cohort from the Middle East at some point during his stay in the city.

The purpose of that meeting?

Dirty deeds, as Victor Reynolds – one of their pen-pushing superiors – had put it when he'd explained the assignment several days ago in central London, even if the deeds in question were as yet unspecified.

Hadjam was French born, the son of Algerian immigrants, although it was widely believed that his mother's brother had been a leader within the now defunct Groupe Islamique Armé, one of the two main Islamist insurgent groups that fought the Algerian government and army in the Algerian Civil War around the turn of the twenty-first century. Although the Islamists had ultimately lost the years-long war, and the GIA had been torn apart in the process, a number of rebel Islamist factions had lived on both in Algeria and in France, where millions of migrants had headed to both during and after the war.

Despite his family history, Hadjam himself wasn't believed to be directly involved in any previous terrorist acts, or with any active groups. He was a multi-millionaire who enjoyed all the things a comfortable Western lifestyle brought him. The biggest problem – the possible threat the UK security services were most nervy about – was that Hadjam's daughter had married a man of Iranian descent who was recently elected as a Member of Parliament in the UK. Again, no direct links between the MP and any terrorist group, but such links, even if innocent, needed to be monitored carefully in the modern world. Hadjam was a man with a questionable history, who'd become rich through his hard work but also the hand of outside forces, who now potentially had access to contacts and information that foreign governments, foreign adversaries, would be very interested in.

So the plan here was simple. MI6 knew Hadjam was in town to meet with a cohort from the Middle East, which included at least one businessman from Iran. Denis and Lea had to figure out who these people were, and, if possible, determine what Hadjam had to offer.

Could everything here be above board? Yes, it was possible. But the intelligence that SIS already had on Hadjam suggested the suspicion was warranted given some of Hadjam's business dealings were only two clear steps removed from people who were directly involved with known Islamist groups.

'This looks like his company,' Denis said a few minutes later when the two men walked into the lobby. Lea had spotted them too. Actually, she'd first spotted the man who preceded them through the entrance. A man who, with his dark suit and sunglasses, was obviously a security detail for one or other of the men who followed. A fourth man – another security type – entered soon after, propping up the rear, so to speak.

Lea again kept her eyes on her glass as the hefty security man walked right past her and propped himself on a stool at the bar – the very last one at the end far end, closest to the restaurant. He was a lot less bothered about being visible than Lea and Denis, sitting on the stool with his chest puffed out, sunglasses now off as he scanned the space all around him.

'Know them?' Denis asked as the two men moved along behind Lea.

She thought she recognised the oldest of the two, on the left, although she couldn't recall from where. So she gave a slight shake of her head before she looked up and the security guy caught her eye. Glared for a second before she looked away again.

The next twenty minutes played out slowly, calmly. The other security guy remained standing guard in the lobby. Hadjam and his new friends enjoyed a drink and awaited their food. Lea's club sandwich arrived too, and she slowly munched through it as she played on her phone, snapping a few pics of all five of the men as carefully as she could. Denis was the only one of them who'd moved position in the intervening period, taking up a table on his own in the restaurant, with a better view of the meeting than she had. Possibly within earshot. She'd find out later, because they hadn't exchanged a word in that time. Too much going on now, too many eyes potentially on them.

As Lea ducked down to take another bite from her sandwich she spotted two of the men from the English group approaching the bar and for a moment there was a traffic jam with a waiter headed from the lobby to the restaurant, and a waitress headed past from the restaurant towards the lobby area, one of them brushing Lea's back in the process.

Lea bolted upright, looked across the bar, trying to get a good look at who'd made contact with her...

But instead found herself staring into the eyes of the guy from the lift. A toothy smile on his face, his pupils wide – perhaps because of the beer – and drowning out his green irises.

He gave her a salute.

'Evening. That looks nice. What is it?' he said to her, nodding to the bar top.

She heard Denis's grumbling voice, but it was only in her head.

'Club sandwich.'

The man laughed. 'I meant the cocktail.'

'Old fashioned.'

'You look anything but to me,' he said with a wink.

The laugh slipped out of her mouth before she could catch it. Laughing *at* him.

'Yeah, I know. That was poor,' he said, but apparently remained undeterred. 'You want another?'

'I'm good, thank you.'

'Shit, is this yours?'

She squirmed back a little as he stepped over and reached down to the floor right by her, his head nearly in her lap. His cologne tickled her nostrils before he stretched up and handed the credit card out to her, her head spinning with thoughts.

The card was hers. She glanced at her purse, open and hanging on its side.

'Think maybe that waitress knocked it. Or the guy. Not sure.'

Not good. Not good at all.

'What the fuck are you doing?' came Denis's voice. His actual voice, hissing in her ear. Not her imagining his complaints this time.

She didn't answer.

'Thanks,' she said to the man, taking the card from him and putting it back in her purse which she pulled off the back of the stool and placed on her lap.

'I'm Callum,' the man said.

'Lea,' she responded.

'Lea Torrence. Yeah, saw it on the card.'

The guys' drinks had arrived, and Callum's friend had gone back over to the group with the bulk of the order. But he remained hovering.

'You in town for business?' he asked.

'Yes. A conference. Look, sorry, Callum? I don't mean to be rude, but—'

'Sorry if we're getting a bit noisy,' he said, all jovial and eager still. 'We're on tour.'

'*Lea, get this dickhead to go away. You've got eyes on you.*'

Denis again, obviously. She glanced across and noted the security guard looking at her. But wouldn't he just see this for what it was?

Actually, it was good cover, if anything.

'Tour?' she asked. 'Ah, let me guess. You're a football team?'

His smile faltered. Of course she knew it wasn't football. This guy was easily over six feet and probably sixteen, seventeen stone, a lot of it muscle judging by his shirt, which was pushed to bursting in all the right places.

Same for the rest of the group too. But she also figured such a man was probably hugely proud of his sport and decided to tease him on it instead.

'Rugby, actually, we—'

'Rugby team? You came for a boozy lad's weekend to France and you're staying in a five-star hotel next to the opera? Talk about clash of cultures.'

He laughed. 'Hey, we're plenty cultured enough. But actually, the dad of one of the guys owns a travel company. Got us a good deal. Perkins? You may have heard of it. You're west country too, right? I can hear it.'

A slight shiver ran through her at his deduction. She suddenly felt more vulnerable. An odd feeling for her.

'I'm from Bristol,' he said. 'You?'

'Near there,' she said, quickly calculating how much of the truth to give.

None was her preference.

OK, she needed this guy to go away now.

'What school did you go to?' he asked.

'It's a... small one. Small village. You probably wouldn't know it.'

'I'm not sure. You actually look kind of familiar. Maybe I've seen you around somewhere.'

'Oh yeah, I've never heard that one before,' she said with an eye-roll.

He held his hands up, a little of his nearly full beer spilling over onto his shirt as he did so, although he didn't look in the least bothered. Perhaps hadn't noticed. 'I mean it. Seriously. I think I've met you before.'

'Riverdale RFC,' she said, ignoring his claim, instead reading the emblem on his shirt.

'That's the one.'

He pounded the badge with pride, and on cue there was a roar from the rest of his group at hearing their name and a vociferous chant started up.

She knew a few of them had been looking over. Hadn't realised they'd been hanging on their every word.

She glanced around the bar and restaurant. Everyone looked, Hadjam and co included.

She blushed.

Good cover? Shit, now everyone here would remember her face...

'Not Bristol or Bath, though,' she said to him. 'I've heard of them. Maybe less touring and more playing and you'd be on one of those teams instead.'

For just a moment, he looked a little offended but quickly composed himself again. 'Ouch,' he said, but was smiling. 'You in town for long?'

'Not long.'

'Just you here?'

'From my company, yeah.'

'Well, if you *want* some company.'

'Probably not—'

She stopped speaking when she realised the security guys were on the move. Assembling themselves ready for their clients – bosses? – to move out.

'*Lea, for fuck's sake, get your head back in this*,' Denis said.

'I can give you my number—'

'Thanks, Callum. But... I'm going to be really busy while I'm here. And...'

He looked genuinely disappointed now, even if he tried to hold on to his smile.

'Maybe I'll see you around Bristol some time then,' he said. 'Riverdale... We're not *that* bad. Come watch us some time and see.'

And with that he turned and walked back to his group, receiving a rapturous welcome as though he'd just conquered his foe in the Coliseum.

'*Lea, move. Now*,' Denis said to her.

So she did.

5

Darkness had arrived as Lea exited the hotel, alone. Denis would stay. They hadn't had time to set up any unmanned surveillance in the hotel itself to keep tabs on Hadjam's movements, so at least one of them needed to remain to watch for him leaving, or for anyone else arriving to meet him. Far from a flawless plan, but it was the cards they'd been dealt so far, at least until they found anything juicier on Hadjam and his associates that'd get them over the threshold with Reynolds to up their budget and their remit.

Lea left the hotel on foot but assumed that the foursome who'd come from dinner would have a vehicle. Which turned out to be correct when the men made their way across the road to a parked black car. A luxury Mercedes. The two dinner guests got into the back, the two security up front, still scanning the streets as they moved and Lea slunk off in the other direction, both to be discreet and to also reach the motorbike she'd earlier parked around the corner.

When the Mercedes pulled away, she moved a little more quickly, hopped onto the bike and unlocked the helmet from the handlebars – she hadn't brought that into the hotel as she'd not wanted to sit in the bar with the bulky object so obvious. She fired the engine and spun out onto the street.

'They're in a car,' she said to Denis, the two of them still connected. She read off the number plate though most likely it was simply an expensive rental. 'I'll follow.'

'Got it. Nothing happening here. Hadjam's up in his room.'

The Mercedes was already a hundred yards ahead on the road but on the narrow streets of the old town, with slow traffic and junction after junction, she soon caught up and managed to keep a safe distance with other vehicles between her and them. And the Mercedes didn't travel far. Not even a couple of miles before the car pulled into the drop-off for the Metropolitan, another grand old hotel.

'OK, we've stopped,' Lea said. 'Metropolitan Hotel. I'll try and follow inside.'

'Be careful. You—'

'Anything happening there?'

'Nothing. Your new admirer and his friends have finally left though, so it's a lot more peaceful here now, thank fuck.'

A snotty tone. She didn't respond.

The driver remained in the car but the other three stepped out and into the hotel lobby. Lea parked her bike on a side street, replaced her helmet with a cap and kept her head down as she moved quickly for the entrance. The Mercedes remained; she faced away as she passed it. She pushed through the revolving doors and into the plush lobby.

Lifts. The men were already there.

She headed across the marble tiles, towards the door for the stairs. From the outside she'd already seen the hotel only had six floors, and she'd bet her worth on the men being in a suite on the top floor. Once they were inside the lift she picked up her pace, pushed open the door, then sprinted for the stairs as quickly as she could.

She bounded up, grasping the handrail as she went, helping her to swing around the corners, taking two steps at a time. By the time she approached the door for the fourth floor her chest heaved, lungs burned, heart thudded, the muscles in her calves and thighs on fire from lactate build-up.

'Are you OK?' Denis asked.

'Taking... the stairs. Sixth floor.'

He laughed but didn't say anything more.

She pushed through, made it to the top and took only a couple of beats to compose herself before she ever so quietly opened the door and peeped into the corridor.

Just a little too late – not a surprise, given her route – but literally only by a second or two as she heard the soft clunk of a door closing further ahead.

She homed in on where the sound had come from as she moved steadily, a little warily along the carpet. Not many rooms up here anyway given the size of the suites, but she was sure the door that had just closed was room 604 – a shiny little placard on the wall beside the door gave the suite's name as Raymond IV.

She didn't quite go as far as the door itself, in case the security guard was standing sentry on the other side, looking out. Unlikely, but in any case, she turned and moved back for the stairs.

'Room 604. Raymond IV suite. I'll see if I can figure out the name on the record.'

'You don't need to. Regroup. With the pictures we have we've got enough to start digging.'

'I'm here. May as well try.'

A much more casual trip down the stairs, getting her heart rate and breathing back under control, wiping sweat droplets from her brow as she went. By the time she reached the lobby she was still a little overheated and clammy but moved out into the open regardless.

A single worker stood behind the reception desk that was big enough for three or four, but at this time on a weekday night there wasn't much need for anyone else. Lea hovered a few moments then took up a seat on a bench, watching for a few minutes as she tried to figure things out. Behind the reception desk a door led to an office. She'd seen it open and close a couple of times. Initially there'd been two other workers in there but one had left.

She opened a website on her phone and found the hotel's number and called. The guy on reception picked up and she killed the call. He looked bemusedly at the receiver before slotting it back in place. She waited thirty seconds and did it again. The guy again picked up. She sighed and ended the call without a word.

'*What are you doing?*'

'Just... give me a minute.'

Two ladies walked in through the outer doors, a suitcase each, and headed to the desk, occupying the guy there. Lea called again. Answered, but not by the man she could see this time. A woman.

'Do you speak English?'

'Yes.'

'There're men fighting. Outside the rooms on the fifth floor. It's... bad. Someone needs to stop them.'

She ended the call.

Not a second later and the woman rushed out of the office, rattled off something to her colleague before she sped off out of sight.

He looked put out but carried on tending to the two ladies, so Lea got up and headed across the floor, to the edge of the reception desk, just a little behind the guy. She waited for her moment...

Two security guards rushed out of a door across the way. Reception guy saw them and shouted over, and the moment the guards turned away again, with reception guy still torn between the ruckus upstairs and the guests in front of him, Lea slipped behind and into the office.

She rushed to the computer terminal and sat down on the chair. The machine was still awake. Still logged in. Lea worked as quickly as she could, navigating through the unfamiliar system.

Didn't take too long though. Room 604. A three-night stay registered to Mohammed Jalali. She didn't recognise the name but took a picture of the contact details – phone number and address – and his passport. Iran? Jalali wasn't one of Hadjam's dinner guests but the one who'd sat near her in the bar. Interesting.

She was done. She closed the screen and moved to the door. Peered out. Reception guy was still busy. Across the floor though she spotted the woman from the office moving back over.

No other choice. Lea stepped out and, head down once again, scurried towards the exit.

The woman called over. Lea took no notice. She was already at the door. A porter stood there but he didn't try to stop her.

She was outside.

The Mercedes had gone but...

As she lifted her head to scope out threats she spotted the suited security guard, puffing on a cigarette a few yards away. Mohammed Jalali, apparently.

He turned his head towards her...

She whipped her face back the other way and carried on.

Didn't look back at all.

Not even after she'd reached her bike.

Helmet on, she gunned away down the street.

* * *

Lea and Denis congregated in his room for breakfast, given it was nicer, more spacious than hers with a seating area with sofa, coffee table with four chairs. She wasn't sure how he'd wrangled that.

They sat at the table, both engrossed in their screens as they filtered through information, barely touching the tray of pastries, although both had had plenty of the coffee to perk them up.

'Raymond IV,' Denis said. 'That was the name of the suite, right?'

'Yeah.'

He chuckled. 'Wonder if those guys know the significance?'

'Because?'

'Raymond IV was Count of Toulouse. I guess that's why his name was on a hotel suite here, but the guy was famous as one of the leaders of the First Crusade. That guy literally went to the Middle East to slaughter non-Christians. Helped set up the Crusader state of Tripoli, the last of the Crusader states.'

'You think them staying in that room has significance?' she asked.

'I think they probably have no clue. Just a bit of irony. Maybe a joke at their expense.'

Lea chewed on that a few moments before yawning and taking another sip of coffee.

'Tired?' Denis asked.

'Yeah. Didn't get much sleep. Head all over the place.'

He stared at her as though not believing something or other she'd said.

'Some of those rugby cretins are on my floor,' he told her.

'OK?'

'Staggered past my door blathering and singing after 3 a.m.'

Lea smiled but said nothing.

'What?' he said.

'It really got you all twisted, didn't it? Seeing that guy trying to hit on me?'

Denis scoffed. 'So you admit, you two were flirting.'

'Did I?'

'I did wonder if you two would *bump* into each other again.'

'Oh yeah? Is that what you're asking me? Am I tired because I met up with a hunk last night when you were tucked up in bed?'

He rolled his eyes. 'No, just... keep it focused, Lea. We're in the middle of something here.'

'I did keep it focused. That's why I shot out of the bar and after those men the moment I needed to.'

'You know what I mean.'

'Do I?'

He didn't respond, though she could tell he really wanted to say more.

'He actually seemed like a nice guy,' she said. 'Another time and place and—'

'He was a loudmouth drunkard. If you really want to hook up out here, you could do a lot better.'

'So it's not the idea of me *hooking up* with someone that's got you all antsy, but the choice of man?'

At first, he didn't say anything. But then, 'Like I said, you need to stay focused.'

But she knew that wasn't where it was coming from at all.

'Your misogyny is a real turn off, you know.'

'Misog... Where the hell has that come from?'

'From working with you for long enough. It's not like you're celibate,

Denis, waiting for the right woman to come along. You do what you want, when you want. So why can't I?'

'You're barking up the wrong tree—'

'Actually, I don't think I am. You think it's unladylike of me to chat to a random guy in a bar and flirt with him a little. What if I'd chosen to sleep with him last night? You'd have a problem with that?'

No response.

'Do I need to have had a certain number of dates first? A certain passage of time? Move around the bases before I let him right on in to screw me senseless whichever way he wants?'

He cringed. 'That's not what I'm saying—'

'But it's what you're thinking. I'm a single woman in my late twenties. You might not like it, but I have the same rights and the same urges you do—'

'Fuck me, *urges*...' he said, cringing even more now.

Lea laughed. 'Yeah. See what I mean? Bet you wouldn't think that was so bad if I was a male colleague and had been chatting up the hot blonde at the bar. Took her back to my room for the night. Right? You'd probably be high fiving me this morning, slapping my back and asking for the juicy details about what she did for me.'

He shook his head.

'James Bond fan, by any chance?' she asked.

'What, 'cause we work for MI6?'

'No, because it's a popular series.'

'Yeah, I've seen a few.'

'And I bet you didn't bat an eyelid at all the times he ended up in bed with a gorgeous woman he just met.'

He looked sullen now, but she knew he wouldn't concede the point.

'So you're saying... what?' he started. 'You and this guy...'

'Me and that guy nothing. I'm just trying to point out your hypocrisy. And basically... I'm telling you that who I choose to speak to, flirt with, have casual sex with if I want, has absolutely nothing to do with you.'

He sniffed. Sipped his coffee. 'Whatever.'

'And, of course, I know it's because you're jealous because you think I'm hot,' she said with a wink, and he struggled to hold on to his scowl at that.

His phone chirped. He answered and spent a couple of minutes mostly in silence before he was done.

'Karim?' Lea asked.

Karim being one of the tech whizzes back on English soil.

'Yeah. He's ID'd them.'

'All of them?'

'All of them. Jalali from what you sent. One of the two dinner guests from our pictures, but he had to do some digging on travel records for the other.' He had his iPad in hand, likely going through whatever profiles Karim had just sent over. 'Like you said, Jalali is one of the security guys. Believed to be a member of the Iranian Revolutionary Guard…' Which even without saying anything else most likely meant that one if not both of the men who'd met Hadjam were involved with the Iranian government in some capacity. 'The two bigwigs? Ali Azmoun and Hossein Taremi.'

'And?' Lea said when Denis went silent, staring at his screen.

'Azmoun… Not much known about him. Government employee, but not on any watchlist. Taremi… He's an engineer at Integrated Electronics Industries.'

And he didn't have to explain more than that for Lea to get the significance. IEI was one of several state-owned operations in Iran responsible for equipping the country's Ministry of Defence.

'What the hell would they want with Hadjam?'

'Exactly. That's what we need to find out. We've got approval. Level three surveillance.'

Now things were getting interesting.

'Then let's get to it,' Lea said.

6

LONDON

Present day

'You played rugby, huh?' Jasper said, as though that was the important part of the story he'd just told about the night he first met Lea. She stared at Callum over the desk in the basic room – this one even more plain and functional, more unassuming than the meeting room in the police station in Bristol from earlier.

Was that really the same day? It felt so long ago already.

'A ruffian's game, played by gentlemen,' Jasper added.

'As opposed to a gentlemen's game played by ruffians?' Callum suggested, referring to the more popular football. He'd heard the saying before, even if he couldn't remember where it came from. He kind of agreed with it and knew that – at least in England – it rang true to a degree given the amount of rugby historically played in private schools versus state schools, though he knew plenty of people in his game who were far from gentlemanly.

'I *did* play rugby,' Callum said. 'Now, I'm... more of a spectator.'

Rugby was one thing he'd been genuinely good at in life, where his dyslexia didn't limit him at all, but his body simply hadn't been able to cope with the abuse.

'That's really how you two met?' Jasper asked. 'A bar in Toulouse while you were on a rugby tour?'

'Why would I make that up?' Callum said.

He got no answer to the question. They'd been in the room together for twenty minutes now, the conversation a bit all over the place, which kind of matched the state of Callum's mind.

The drive to London had taken a little under two hours. The two officers who'd escorted him hadn't spoken a word on the journey – at least not to him. They'd also taken his phone away from him. *Demanded* his phone from him, at least. Just one of many oddities in the oddest day and night of his life, but he'd done everything they'd asked.

The phone was now on the desk in front of him, and he had no idea why they'd taken it from him before. He hadn't touched it yet, his mind too preoccupied.

Callum didn't know London that well – had only been a few times as a tourist – though he had a vague sense of where they'd ended up, on the banks of the Thames, given the nearby skyscrapers at Canary Wharf.

Another unexpected turn, really. That they'd not taken him to New Scotland Yard, the Met's headquarters, nor even to MI6 headquarters – that iconic building, made famous in films, directly on the river.

Odd for a building housing spies to be so conspicuous, wasn't it?

He didn't know, really.

What he did know was that he'd kind of expected to end up at one of those places. Not here.

What *was* this place?

Just a standard looking stone-fronted office building, from what he'd seen, all pretty quiet at this time of night. Jasper had been in tow in a car directly behind Callum's and they'd all entered through a side entrance and up to the fourth floor. Callum hadn't seen anyone else around the place as they'd taken him to this room. Just him and Jasper inside, though not for the first time his eyes flitted to the little camera up above, staring down at them both.

'Who's watching us?' he asked.

Jasper didn't answer.

'MI6?'

'I can't tell you what I can't tell you.'

'You know, if you tried a bit harder to win me over—'

'I'm sorry, Mr Murphy. I'm not trying to win you over. I'm not trying to rile you up either. I'm just trying to talk to you about your wife. Why don't you carry on the story.'

'Because I don't understand why any of this is necessary.'

Jasper sighed and tapped the desk with the tip of her nails a few times, as though contemplating, or just trying to channel agitation or something.

'Why don't I back things up a bit for you,' she said. 'It feels like perhaps we got off on the wrong foot, so to speak. I work for SO15, Counter Terrorism Command. The name's pretty self-explanatory, right?'

'I guess.' Although it sent a whole wave of further questions and concerns spinning in his mind.

'We regularly work with other agencies. MI5, the National Crime Agency. Again, you're probably familiar with their names, existence, whatever. Yeah?'

'Again, I guess so.'

'Honestly? What we don't deal with very often... as in, never personally in my seventeen years in SO15, is MI6. Why?'

'Because... it's... secret?' Callum suggested. Felt a bit stupid about it, really, only confirmed by Jasper's slight chuckle.

'Yeah. They certainly like their damn secrets. But I meant more from a jurisdictional point of view. MI6 is an external agency. We're internal. Hence even though intel crosses paths, necessarily, operations generally don't.'

'So why are you involved here?'

'Now that is a good question.'

'Are you saying you don't know the answer?'

'I'm saying you might be surprised at how little I do know. About your wife. Her role. Her death.'

'Then why are you speaking to me at all? Not someone else?'

'Because... as I understand it, your wife's death could have a direct impact on national security. And quite simply I've been asked to do this.'

'What are you... This just...' Callum put his head into his hands, and not for the first time. He couldn't find the words or the thoughts to make sense of anything.

'Mr Murphy, I'll ask this really simply. Did you really not know anything about your wife's... *real* life?'

'No!'

'From the profile I've been given she worked for MI6 for nine years. So for a long time before she met you... three years ago?'

'And?'

'And... I just don't get how you *couldn't* know. *Something*.'

'Because I'm stupid,' he said. 'Plenty of people think so, always have. Now I really can't suggest otherwise.'

'Because you're dyslexic?'

He didn't say anything, but clenched his fists under the table, his mind humming with thoughts of what else she – the people watching – knew about him and his life.

'It's not that uncommon,' she said with a shrug. 'Certainly nothing to be embarrassed about. Plenty of people with dyslexia live perfectly... normally.'

She cringed a little at the last word as though it wasn't the one she'd intended.

'Yeah? Well, I'm not plenty of people. It's fucked around with my life plenty.'

'I'm sorry to hear that. But getting back on track, I didn't say you were stupid.'

'Lea never told me, so how could I have known?'

She nodded. He had no idea what that meant. 'Back to what I was saying. I got a call earlier from a senior guy at MI5, giving me the basics. He told me to take a team to Bristol to pick you up and bring you here. He told me you were the husband of an agent killed overseas. It was that simple. We weren't expecting the company you had, and that's caused quite a bit of noise around the whole thing. But the basic remit? What I understand is that your wife's death is believed to revolve around a cache of data. Data that's gone missing. Data that if it gets into the wrong hands—'

'Creates a national security risk?'

'Something like that. But—'

'But I don't know anything! There *is* no data that I have or have ever had or have been told exists or been asked to keep safe or anything like that! If what you're saying is true, about her double life, she fucking duped me! Lied to me! Right now, I don't know if *anything* about our life together was real!'

The angry tirade caused Jasper to sit back in her seat. Callum was pretty shocked by it too, in truth. It'd sprung from nowhere and he immediately felt bad for it. Bad that he was thinking ill of his dead wife.

'Nothing was found in your home,' Jasper started, and the connotations caused Callum to squeeze his fists closed even harder. *They'd searched through his and Lea's things while he wasn't there?* 'Nothing at all that relates to her work—'

'You're telling me she was an MI6 spy. You're actually suggesting you thought she would leave papers and electronic data about top-secret missions all over our home?'

Jasper had no answer to that and the room fell silent for a few moments. Callum glanced up at the camera again.

'Say I believe you,' Jasper said. 'That this is mostly all news to you. But... you must still *know* your wife. Even if it's just her concocted identity.'

'And?' he said angrily, Jasper's choice of words doing little to win him over.

'If there was somewhere safe, she'd hide what we're looking for... Can you think of anywhere at all? At home? Elsewhere?'

He stayed silent. Not because he was hiding an answer but because he was genuinely trying to think the question over properly.

An ill-formed thought struggled to take hold.

'Callum?'

'No,' he said. 'She lied to me. I just don't know... *anything* right now. Who was she? Really?'

'Her real name?'

'Yes.'

'Claire Simmonds. Born and raised in Clemens. It's a village south-east of Bristol. Not that far from where you grew up, I believe?'

His heart pounded in his chest. He tried to show no reaction. Thought he did a pretty good job of it, even if Jasper's eyes narrowed a little as she continued to stare at him.

'Does that mean anything to you? The name? The place?'

He scoffed. 'Why would it? To me she was Lea Torrence. And Clemens? Heard of it. Never been.'

She looked like she didn't fully believe him.

'Look, it's been a shitty day,' he said. 'A shitty night too. I just want to go to bed and sleep. I mean... can I do that? There's nothing more I can give you right now. I don't know why you drove me all the way out here.'

She didn't respond but glanced – a little slyly – towards the camera.

'I'm not under arrest, am I?' he asked.

'Of course not.'

'So you can't *keep* me here.' Although even as the words left his lips, he doubted that statement. Nothing about this situation was at all 'normal'. Lawful? He had no clue. The only experience he had of MI6 and the like was from watching films. And in those films the agency could quite literally do what they wanted. Get away with anything they wanted.

Keep a man held in a room against his will? Hell, perhaps they'd pull his fingernails out, one by one, before slitting his throat and burying his body somewhere it'd never be found.

Except why would they do any of that?

He gulped at the grim thoughts, nonetheless. And Jasper didn't even attempt to respond to him before a light knock on the closed door broke the silence.

The door opened. *Unlocked*, he realised. Interesting. Because earlier in the day, at Bristol police station, *that* room had been locked. Did that mean anything or was it simply facets of the rooms themselves?

He hadn't decided on an answer before a casually dressed man walked in. Tall, perhaps six-foot one or two, and lean with a clean-cut face. Mid-thirties, a wide jaw and dark brown eyes sunken under a prominent brow. Those features weren't so extreme as to give him a stereotypical thuggish look, just someone who looked like he meant business and was obviously more than confident in himself. Callum quickly glanced into the corridor outside before the man closed the door. He noted the shoulder of one of the uniformed police officers standing guard there. Still armed? Callum couldn't tell.

Before the man had said a word, Jasper, a wary look on her face, got out of her chair and moved to the side of the room where she stood, arms folded, as the man took her seat. He leaned across the table and offered his hand to Callum.

'I thought it easier if I just came in and took charge of things for a few minutes,' he said, before sitting back in his chair. 'It's not DCI Jasper's fault that she's not privy to every detail, and it feels like the conversation's starting to get a bit stuck.'

'And you are? Privy to every detail?' Callum asked. A nod in response.

'And in answer to your questions to DCI Jasper... No, of course you're not under arrest. And yes, you can leave this room at any time. If you want to. But... why would you want to leave our care, Callum, when you've already seen tonight that there are people out there who are looking for the same thing we are, and who might not be quite so friendly and law-abiding? And when you likely still have so many unanswered questions.'

'*So* many,' Callum said.

The man smiled a little. 'Let me start by saying... I knew Lea. Personally. We worked together multiple times. She was a great agent and a really good, honest person. And I'm very sorry for your loss.'

Sorrow flashed through Callum, his heart thudding a little erratically as those words brought the reality, the gravity of the situation back to the fore. But it didn't last long. Partly because he forced it away, still not yet ready to fully face it, and partly because of one of the words that the man had used to describe Lea.

Honest.

'You're with MI6?' Callum asked.

A nod.

'You haven't told me your name.'

A pause before the answer. 'Andrew White.'

The truth? How the hell was Callum supposed to know?

'You have an ID card, business card or anything?' Callum asked with a chuckle. The quip got no response from either of the other two. 'So what are you suggesting?' he asked. 'Am I staying here, in this building? Tonight? For how long?'

'We can move you to a safe house when we're done here. We have one not far. It's just... an apartment, to you. But it'll be secure. We'd rather keep you close while this plays out.'

'While *what* plays out? Tell me what's happening,' Callum said. 'Were you... were you with her?'

'No. But I know about the operation.'

'And are you going to tell me about that operation? It seems the whole purpose of everyone being after me, you included, isn't really about my protection, because why the hell would you care? It's because you think I know something. Either directly or indirectly.'

No response to that. Just a confident stare Callum's way.

'But I know nothing! I didn't even know she was in Bucharest.'

'I'm sure you're sick and tired of saying that by now.'

Damn right he was.

'The problem is, Callum, I'm not so sure I believe you.'

Callum grunted, 'Why? I don't know what you want from me!'

'Can I tell you a little something about the people I work with? People like your wife?'

Callum didn't answer. An invitation for White to carry on.

'It may or may not surprise you that we're really much more analytical, intellectual perhaps, than brawn. I can count on one hand the number of violent scrapes I've been involved in, although I'd also say that in all those scrapes, I came out on top.' A self-satisfied grin at that. 'But mostly we're savvy, thinkers. Planners. Tricksters? Yes. And... take a guess. What percentage of MI6 field agents do you think have spouses?'

'I have no idea.'

White pursed his lips and glanced momentarily at the ceiling, as though thinking. 'You know what? Neither do I. It's not like it's a statistic that's widely available. But I do know this. Other than Lea, I never met a single other married field agent. It's pretty fucking obvious why. Our job is dangerous. Leading a double life only adds to the danger. For the agent, their spouse, the entire damn agency.'

Callum stayed silent. He didn't really know if he was expected to respond or not.

'Except Lea had you. And I don't know the full details of how that came about. But I do know it would have to have been sanctioned, one way or another.'

Callum's anger was rising again, his fists clenched.

'That's right, Callum. Your marriage, most likely, was given the green light by my superiors. There's no way it could have happened otherwise and for Lea to have continued working in the field.'

Callum held his tongue. He knew exactly what White was insinuating. That the whole marriage was a sham. But it certainly had *never* been a sham on his part. What about for Lea?

'So this is the question I ask myself. Why? Why did she marry you? Love?' He let that suggestion hang, but it went unanswered. 'It's possible. The most romantic notion. In my eyes, the most unlikely too. Another option? She just wanted a regular, easy fuck. We all have needs, don't we?'

Callum had to really hold himself back this time, pushing his weight down in his seat so he didn't spring up and launch himself across the table.

'Callum, I'm not trying to offend you,' White said, looking smug at his obvious lie. 'But it's important to look at this logically, unemotionally. Perhaps she chose you as a partner for the very reason that she thought she could easily dupe you.'

'You mean she thought I was an idiot?'

How many times was that today that his intelligence had been questioned?

'I'm posing scenarios, although personally I'm not sure that's the right one either. Mainly because, like I said, I don't know any other agent in that position. And I'm pretty sure plenty of others would go for it, were it so easy. Find a good-looking person of below-average intelligence and con them into a marriage for the sake of convenience.'

'You sound like such a gentleman.'

'I didn't say this was *my* approach, did I? But there is another option, and to me it makes the most sense.'

He paused there. And Callum, despite himself, grabbed for the carrot. 'And what's that?'

'There was a reason, other than love, other than sex, why she was with you. Why she wanted to be close to you. *Protect* you.'

Callum shook his head, showing he wasn't on the same page.

'You were her asset. In an intelligence sense, I mean. What better way to protect an asset than by keeping them *really* close.'

'Are you suggesting...' But Callum couldn't quite finish the sentence, or the thought.

'In my field we *all* have assets,' White said. 'Some are sources of information, some are mercenaries that we use like weapons. Some are disclosed to our superiors, many aren't. And that's fine. It's almost expected of us to have assets that no one else knows about. Like a journalist has sources. I said to you before, we're savvy people, thinkers, game players, often.'

'This is ridiculous, I—'

'What's ridiculous? It's an answer that makes a lot of sense to me. And even if I can't figure what use she saw in you as an asset, what you could know that would be of use to an MI6 field agent, I start to think to myself that if that was the case, then *you damn well know it*. You know exactly what it is that you hold that was important to her. And she damn well would have confided in you when things were looking bad for her. When there was heat on her. When she got scared for her life knowing the grand nature of the information she had.'

'But none of that is true! I have no idea what she was working on!'

'So you say.'

White reached into the envelope he'd brought into the room and took out a small bundle of papers. Pictures?

'Tell me, do you recognise any of these people?'

He pushed the first photograph over the table to Callum. A man. Middle Eastern origins, perhaps, or North African, something like that. Thirties or forties.

'No,' Callum said.

'And this one?' Another man Callum didn't recognise.

'No.'

'What about him? Him? Him?'

'No. No. N... No.'

'You're sure about that last one?'

'I don't know these people!'

The cascade of photographs was in place as White studied Callum. Did this guy really not believe what Callum was saying? Or were these tactics designed to wear him down, make him question everything even more than he already was?

'You came into this room telling me I'm here under your protection,' Callum said. 'But it feels like this is an interrogation. Like you don't trust me at all.'

White had the audacity to laugh at that. 'Believe me, this is *not* an interrogation.' He let that comment sit a while, as though it'd add to Callum's discomfort. It did. 'The matter Lea was working on was highly sensitive, to say the least. The information she had in her possession, information which is now missing... It could cause chaos if it fell into the wrong hands.'

'DCI Jasper already told me this. National security, et cetera, et cetera.'

'This is no joke, Callum.'

'I never said it was. And my wife is dead. And you have still told me next to nothing about that. Do you even care about how she died or who did it? Is anyone even out there looking for the culprits? Because, more and more, based on what you've told me about her assignment, I'm thinking there was no accident.'

No answer.

'I'm right, aren't I?'

Still no response.

'Do you *know* who killed her? Do you *want* to know? Or do you only care about getting your hands on that missing information?'

'We're trained to see the bigger picture, Callum. That data could protect, or cost, a lot of lives. But of course I care about how she died too. She was a close colleague of mine.'

'Was it one of these men?' Callum said, jabbing at the nearest picture to him.

No answer to that.

'I'll say it one more time,' Callum added. 'I had no idea my wife worked for MI6. She tricked me. Not just once but repeatedly, for three years. I never once suspected she wasn't who she said she was, more the fool me.

And I have *zero* information relevant to you, about her life or her death or whatever it is you're after.'

White and Jasper still said nothing.

'I'd really like to go now. To the safe house, if we have to. But I just want to go and be alone and try and sleep if that's even possible right now and at least *start* to grieve for my wife in some sort of peace.'

White again took pause before answering. 'OK. We can call it a night.'

He gathered up the photos and put them back in the envelope, stood up, and pulled open the door.

'One thing, though,' Callum said, getting up too.

'Yeah?' White answered, glancing back over.

'You never once asked me about the people who were at my house.'

A perplexed look.

'Before DCI Jasper and the others arrived, they told me their names. But you never even asked me anything about them, if I knew them, their names, what they said to me. Nothing. Seems to me... the only reason not to is because you already know who they are.'

White still gave nothing away. No confirmation or denial. No reaction at all on his face.

'You're asking me to trust you, to be truthful with you, but... what's in it for me really, when it's so clear that I mean nothing to you, and when you're giving me so little back in return?'

'Get some rest, Callum. It's been a hell of a day for you,' White said, before turning back for the door.

But he didn't make it out of the room before Callum launched himself forward. He'd been contemplating the reckless move for some time. Wasn't quite sure he had it in him. Still wasn't even as he dashed forward.

I can count on one hand the number of violent scrapes I've been in.

Callum certainly couldn't. And yet he really, really hoped that statement from White was one of truth.

He grabbed his phone from the desk then straight-armed Jasper to push her up against the wall. He spun and smacked his elbow into the side of White's face. His head flopped and he dropped to his knee as Callum peeled the envelope from his weakened grasp.

'Hey!' shouted the police officer in the corridor who burst into view.

Callum launched his foot into the guy's groin and he doubled over and stumbled back.

Callum darted into the corridor. Looked left, right. They'd come in from the left...

That door burst open and two other officers barrelled through. Armed. Although the weapons were pointed at the floor.

'Stop!' one of them yelled. 'Stop or we'll shoot!'

And even if Callum partly believed the warning, he still turned on his heel and ran in the opposite direction.

'Stop!' came the shout again.

'Let him go!' came another shout. White. 'Just... let him go.'

Even if the comment only further confused Callum, he didn't dwell. Didn't look back. Just sprinted. Sprinted.

He crashed through the door at the end of the corridor.

Then carried on running for his life.

7

TOULOUSE

Three years ago

The twenty-four hours since Lea and Denis's assignment had been upgraded to level three surveillance had been a whirlwind of activity, putting their clandestine skills to the fullest test. Before the identification of the Iranians, they'd only been at level one, which encapsulated basic surveillance, out in public, following marks, taking pictures, that sort of thing. But level three brought a whole lot more of a hands-on – and risky – approach to surveillance and intel gathering, surpassed only by the highest level four which could, in extreme cases, lead to capture and interrogation and even elimination of targets.

None of the latter was yet required here, but still, since the upgrade they'd already broken into Hadjam's hotel room, planted surveillance devices, copied data from his iPad which had been sent to the lab in London. Not his phone, though. They hadn't yet managed to get that from him but were actively looking for a way to do so. Over at the Metropolitan Hotel they'd had less success getting into room 604. Lea had earlier set up a camera on the sixth floor corridor, and in the hotel lobby too, but in the time they'd been observing there'd always been at least one person left in the suite, giving no means of access without direct confrontation.

'*What do you think they're doing here, really?*' Denis asked as Lea stood on the street over from a jewellery store that Taremi had entered nearly thirty minutes ago.

'Buying something nice for his wife.'

Denis chuckled. '*You know what I mean.*'

'Anything happening where you are?' she asked.

He was still in their hotel, Hadjam too. Denis was keeping an eye on all their camera feeds as he searched through the data they'd stolen from the French businessman. The team in London were doing that in a more precise, methodical way but Lea and Denis were good at hacking and cherry-picking too, allowing them to quickly identify areas of interest.

'*Nothing,*' he said. '*I've seen nothing. And you didn't answer my question.*'

'I kind of did.'

'*You're saying you think there's nothing to any of this?*'

'Wouldn't it be good if that was the answer? Because worst case is these guys are planning to blow up a city or something and we never figure it out in time.'

Another chuckle. '*Blowing up a city? Lea—*'

'OK, looks like we're about to get on the move again,' she said when the door to the jeweller's opened. She remained where she was, at the head of an alley, waiting for Taremi and his minder – Jalali – to walk out. 'Wait... OK, Jalali has a briefcase now.'

'*What?*'

'He's carrying a briefcase. Black leather. Didn't have it when he went inside.'

'*Did we just land in the eighties?*'

'I think you're missing the point. Something happened in there. An exchange. They're going west now.'

'*Further away from the Metropolitan. So they're not done... shopping yet.*'

She moved out onto the street. Busy enough here in a popular shopping area that she should be able to walk along closely without drawing attention.

'*I'll do some digging into who owns that place, who works there,*' Denis said. '*Did you get any snaps?*'

'No. They were mostly out of sight.'

'Shit. So you've literally no clue who they were meeting in there?'

'No. I could go and find out—'

'Stay on Taremi. Whatever's in that briefcase... If he's not heading right back to the hotel perhaps it means there's another meeting or exchange to come.'

She didn't answer, already understood the situation. Even if she was angry at herself for not suspecting something untoward in the jeweller's sooner.

Nothing she could do about that now.

'They've stopped at the window of a clothes store,' she said. 'Just a... regular-looking store.'

Jalali was on his phone, looking left and right along the street. Lea was at least still on the other side and she pulled up outside a bookstore and pretended to peruse the display, a reflection of Jalali and Taremi clear to her in the window.

'Taremi's going in. Jalali isn't.'

'OK. I'm coming down there. I don't like how this is playing out.'

'It could be nothing. It could—'

'I'm coming. Be there in a few minutes.'

She didn't say anything more. She waited several seconds longer but she couldn't just stand there at the window all day.

So she moved along, slowly, to the next store.

A smartly dressed man she didn't recognise walked along towards Jalali. The two of them didn't indicate any awareness but the next moment, Jalali's phone call ended and he stepped aside as the man walked past him and into the store.

'Looks like Taremi's company just arrived.'

Lea moved again, once more aiming for the next store along, but momentarily glanced across the road...

Right at the same moment that Jalali looked over in her direction.

A pause in his movement. She was sure of it. But the next beat and he'd spun around and moved into the clothes store.

'Shit,' she said, admonishing herself, rather than trying to engage Denis.

'*What?*' he replied nonetheless.

She replayed that split second moment several times in her head as she moved away.

'I think... I've been made.'

Would Jalali remember seeing her at the bar the other night? Possibly at the Metropolitan too.

'He headed into the store, but I think he saw me.'

'*You think?*'

She glanced over her shoulder. No one outside the clothes store still.

'He's not following me, but—'

'*Move away but keep an eye out. I'm only two streets from you.*'

She did exactly that. For fifty yards at least. But she couldn't just leave the store unwatched. Not even for a few seconds. So she stopped and pulled up against the boarded entrance to a soon-to-open store and looked back down the street. All quiet. At least as far as there was any imminent threat to her.

'Where are you?' she asked.

'*Almost on your street. Less than two minutes from you.*'

She glanced further along the road, in the direction that Denis would be coming from. Couldn't yet see him. She moved again, in that direction, head spinning.

'They may have had an escape route,' she said, thinking out loud. 'Out the back of the store.'

'*Just... hold on. We'll figure this out.*'

'But...'

She never finished the thought, because in front of her she spotted the dark-clothed man striding in her direction, only ten yards away. A man she didn't know, but it certainly looked like he knew her, holding her eye as he moved, reaching into his jacket...

She did too. For the knife she had there. The only weapon she had. She really wished she had something more now...

Noise behind her. A motorbike. The sound stuck out above the otherwise calm street, the engine highly revved and closing in fast.

She whipped around, pulled the knife out, but not before the bike was nearly on her already. Two riders. Dark clothes, helmets.

She ducked down and dashed right across the front of the bike, flummoxing the driver and the tyres screeched as the driver tried to adjust and slam the brakes and twist the handlebars to follow her move.

The man on the street, though... Perhaps he'd seen the move coming, or perhaps just had rushed forward regardless and as Lea went to slash the driver the man thumped into her from behind and she felt pressure in her side...

A knife.

She swung her elbow out, catching... something. Shouting erupted. Fists flew. Hands grappled. Hers, others.

Shouting.

Her name.

'Lea!'

Not Denis.

Not at first, anyway.

'*What's happening?*'

That was Denis, in her ear. But the other man? He was closer by.

She spun around, but the man who'd shouted her name grabbed her arm and dragged her towards him. He slingshotted her past him before he bounced forward on his feet and delivered a brutal uppercut that sent the passenger off the back of the bike. A knife clattered away down the street. Then he pounced on the man who'd been on foot, shoved him to the ground before he launched his foot into the guy's face and—

'Callum!' Lea shouted. Warning him of the driver who was reaching into his jacket.

Undeterred, Callum bobbed forward as though about to attack but sirens cut through the air, bringing everyone to a halt. Lea grabbed Callum's shirt to hold him back and the rider scooped the walker up from the floor and the bike blasted off down the street.

The original passenger lay in a heap on the floor, unconscious.

'You OK?' Callum asked, holding her by the shoulders, gently shaking her as though to bring her to reality.

'*Lea, what the hell is happening?*' Denis asked. She didn't answer, though as she turned, she spotted him jogging towards them, twenty yards away.

Hand out flat, by her side, she signalled to him to not intervene. He got the message. The police car slammed to a stop.

'Lea? Are you OK?' Callum asked again before looking down at her side. 'Shit. You're bleeding.'

And the next moment her legs were like jelly and had he not been there she likely would have fallen flat on her face. Instead, she ended up on her knees.

'He stabbed you,' Callum said, crouching down to her level. 'Shit, Lea.'

She didn't say anything. Just watched as Denis casually strode past her towards the clothes store. He went inside.

The police wrestled the helmet off the injured passenger. A young man she didn't know. Probably only a teenager.

'Fucking petty thieves,' Callum said. 'Lea, say something.'

Denis had already come back out of the bookstore. He glanced over in her direction. Shook his head. She knew what that meant. Taremi and Jalali had already moved on. Probably out the back and on to wherever they needed to be. Head down, Denis walked away.

A police officer was barking something. At the boy on the ground? Or at her and Callum? She couldn't be sure, her awareness fading.

'Lea? Shit. She's hurt!' Callum shouted. 'She's hurt bad. We need help. Lea... say something.'

She dropped into his lap. Was only vaguely aware of him above her, gazing down.

'You... *really* wanted my number, huh?' she said before her head lolled, eyes rolling back as she drifted into unconsciousness.

8

Lea hadn't been unconscious for long, out on the street in the old town. Not fully unconscious, at least. She could vaguely remember the paramedics tending to her, the agony as they lifted her onto a stretcher and clattered it – and her – into the back of an ambulance. Probably they'd been a lot more careful than it felt to her. She also could remember snippets of the journey, the hospital corridors, but it really was just snippets, as were the more than twenty-four hours that followed. Mostly she drifted in and out of sleep, much preferring the sleep because the pain was less intense, her mind disconnected from reality even if she wouldn't say there was anything restful about the experience.

Denis had been to visit her more than once in the days that followed, but really, she didn't want to have to make the effort to speak to him, and really, really didn't want to have to think about what had happened. Not because she was necessarily traumatised by the experience – although she knew that she definitely was – but because she was hugely embarrassed by it.

How the hell had she got herself into that position in the first place?

Of all the stupid things...

A knock on the door and it opened before she could say anything and Denis walked in. She noted the uniformed police officer on the outside still. Not usual for a victim of a mugging gone wrong to have around the clock police protection, and the officer likely wouldn't know *why* this victim was being treated differently, but the order had come through at least.

'How you feeling?' Denis asked, face full of concern.

She hated people talking to her like that. It only confirmed all her worst thoughts about how damn useless she was right now.

'Like shit.'

He took a seat without being invited.

'Give me the latest,' she said, battling through the fog in her mind and the pain in her side to try and sound and feel like her normal self.

'You seem more with it,' he said, brightening a little. 'Last time I was here you could barely keep your eyes open. Couldn't string a sentence together.'

'I snuck out in the night. Found the medicine storage. Got myself a nice stash of extra morphine.'

He sniggered. She would have too but knew it'd only send pain shooting through her if she contracted the muscles in her abdomen like that.

'So?' she prompted.

He sighed. 'You won't like this.'

She pulled herself up a little in the bed but immediately regretted it and had to fight through the pain for a few seconds. 'Go on.'

'The kid they arrested—'

'Jamal Kone?' That was the name Denis had given her last time he was here. An eighteen-year-old local.

'There was an... incident last night. He was found dead this morning in his prison cell. Hanged.'

'Fucking bullshit.'

'Yeah. I know. Reynolds is pushing to try and get as much detail as we can from the police, but it's already been a huge headache getting anything at all, even the security for you, given we were here without the knowledge of the DGSI.'

The DGSI being France's internal security service. Likely they'd be seriously pissed off at the fact MI6 agents were on their soil on an operation they had zero knowledge of, but that was, unfortunately, the way espionage worked.

'The kid was murdered, clearly,' Lea said. 'I was a target too. Isn't that enough to get the DGSI to wake up and—'

'Take it easy,' he said, putting his hand onto her shoulder. Panting heavily from the exertion, the pain stabbing away all the time, she slowly got her surging adrenaline back under control. 'We *will* figure this out.'

'I'm not sure I have the strength to.'

'In a few days—'

'Seriously, Denis. This... I don't know. Maybe I need a break.'

He held her eye several beats, neither of them really knowing what to say.

'The other two kids... no one knows,' he said. 'The bike was found burned out. It was stolen. With Kone dead and no fingerprints and nothing else to help identify the others, maybe we'll never know who they are. Were.'

'But we know *why* they were there. Most likely the hit came from the Iranians.'

'Yes. Jalali, we're guessing, given who he is. But all four of them left the country—'

'How the hell—'

He put more pressure on her shoulder, pushing her back into the bed, a more forceful way of telling her to calm down.

'You know how this is,' he said. 'By the time we convinced anyone that they needed to stop these guys, they were already on a plane out of here. Jordan first, but I'll bet they've moved on already, most likely simply back to where they came from.'

'Probably not because of me, though. Probably because they already did what they came here for. And right under our noses.'

Denis said nothing.

'And Hadjam?' she asked.

'We'll keep tabs. The French police, DGSI have nothing on him. At least nothing that they're willing to disclose to us. So right now, he's a free man. No one's even brought him in for questioning.'

'Because he wasn't there and probably had nothing directly to do with what happened to me. And we still have no bloody idea what he and the Iranians were up to together.'

'Yeah. Maybe. But we'll keep on him anyway, I can assure you that, Lea. We'll figure this out. Find out what they're up to. And we'll make them pay. I promise you.'

He reached down and squeezed her hand.

'A lot of *we* in that statement,' she said.

'Because you'll be by my side for it, right?'

She didn't answer.

Both of them went silent, Lea's mind conflicted between chasing to the corners of the earth to find the Iranians and figure out what they'd been plotting here – and to get even with them, obviously – versus wanting to bury herself away somewhere quiet, warm and cosy. Safe.

'I fucked up,' she said.

His face creased over. 'What are you talking about?'

'I tipped them off. Somehow. In the bar that first night. In the Metropolitan. Or when I was following them around the streets. *Somewhere* I dropped the ball. But do you know the worst thing?'

'What?'

'I genuinely don't know at what point it was. And that's what scares me the most. Because I *should* know. And if I don't, how could I ever trust myself to be out there in the field again? How could any other agent, you included, trust to work alongside me when my next slip-up could cost *them* their life?'

She really wanted him to fight that statement. To tell her she was wrong. That she hadn't made a mistake. That what happened was simply the consequence of the high-stakes jobs that they held.

But he didn't say anything because both had heard the heightened voices outside the room. Not a threat, Lea soon realised. She recognised one of the voices.

Callum Murphy.

Denis glared at her and took his hand back.

'Please?' she said to him and hoped he'd understand what that meant.

He got to his feet and moved to the door and opened up.

Callum, remonstrating with the police officer, glanced into the room. First at Denis – with confusion – but then at Lea.

'Lea, it's me. I don't know what's going on, but—'

Denis rattled off something in French to the police officer. A simple explanation telling him to back down. She could tell Callum didn't understand.

'I'll see you soon,' Denis said to Lea before heading on out.

Callum sheepishly came in and shut the door.

'You… don't mind me being here, do you?' he asked.

'No. No, I don't.'

The confused look came back. 'That… guy…'

'His name's Denis, I—'

'He's staying at the hotel too, isn't he?'

Very observant. Very suspicious, too.

'He's at the same conference.'

'I thought you didn't know anyone else.'

'I didn't. At first. But he saw what happened too. The police spoke to him, and… you just saw, he's fluent in French so he's helped me out, you know?'

He looked like he didn't really, but he didn't question it any more.

'How are you feeling?' he asked.

'Like crap.'

'I mean… what's the damage?'

He blushed at his own question, perhaps at the lack of eloquence, and she tried really hard not to laugh.

'Lacerated kidney, liver. Apparently, I'm lucky not to have bled out on the street. Blood poisoning is still a risk but… the risk reduces every hour I make it through. Still… it could have been worse. If you hadn't been there.'

'I just… I reacted. I didn't even think about what I was doing.' He sighed and huffed and looked like he was struggling with something. 'Maybe I made it worse. They probably only wanted your handbag or something. So… I'm sorry.'

'Callum, that's ridiculous. Come on.'

'But I'm glad you're OK.'

'I will be.'

'Did they catch the other guys?'

'I don't think so.'

'Maybe the one they arrested will talk.'

'Maybe,' she said, instead of going into the real details. Too complicated. Too many lies to fabricate that way.

He looked at his watch. 'The police said they're done with me, so...'

'You're going home?'

'That was the plan. Everyone else is at the station already, but...'

'But what?'

'If you needed me to stay for anything—'

'You've helped me more than enough already. Callum, you saved my life.'

'Yeah... I...'

'I'll be going home soon enough.'

'You never did give me your number,' he said, rubbing the back of his neck, all sheepish and nervous. Kind of cute.

'Then get your phone out,' she said.

It was in his hand as quick as a gunslinger in the Wild West.

She read off the numbers. He called. Her phone vibrated on the nightstand.

'And now you've got mine,' he said, wide smile spreading up his face, perhaps relief too that she hadn't just given him a bogus number. He checked his watch again.

'I really have to—'

'It's OK. Don't miss your train.'

'I'll see you soon?'

They both held eye contact, and she'd be lying if she said she didn't feel something in her chest, even above the pain in her side.

'Yeah. I'll see you soon.'

* * *

Four months later

The bang woke her with a start, body primed and at the ready...

No need.

The bedroom door remained closed, and she was alone in the room.

A sliver of light spilled in from the gap in the curtains. A light on in the bathroom too, that door partly ajar, the shower running.

The door opened a few inches further and Callum poked his head out of the gap. Cringed when he saw she was awake.

'Sorry. Didn't mean to disturb you. I dropped the mouthwash.'

'Ever wondered what an elephant sounds like trying to tap-dance?'

He looked really confused.

'Sorry,' he said again before retreating.

Nothing she could do now her sleep was broken, particularly not with that shot of adrenaline coursing through her, readying her for action. Still, she sighed and closed her eyes and remained there a few minutes longer, even as Callum came out into the room. Actually, no, she opened her eyes at that point and watched him roam, skin glistening. He dropped the towel, giving her an eyeful, and he glanced over his shoulder to check if she was looking.

'Yeah, yeah, I know what you're thinking,' he said with a wink.

'Then think again, babe,' she said, grabbing his pillow and tossing it at him.

Moments later he was dressed. Work gear. Back on the construction site again. It was exhausting him. Out of the flat by seven every morning, rarely back by seven at night when it was already dark, and the last two nights he'd been asleep by nine.

You don't get to look like this sitting at a computer all day, he delighted in telling her.

Fair enough. Although walking around a construction site all day telling others what to do didn't build a body like that either. Very kind genetics was the only real answer.

'Any plans today?' he asked her.

'Physio later. Not much else.'

'You coming back here?'

'What time are you finishing?'

'Probably a bit earlier tonight. It's Harrison's birthday. We'll be out for a few drinks.'

She vaguely knew that name, though had never met the guy. Another of the rugby crowd, she thought, although she tried to steer clear of big gatherings with Callum.

'Not much point in me being here then, is there?' she answered, a little more edgily than she'd intended.

But Callum only beamed a smile at her, as though enjoying her jealousy. And she *was* jealous, even though she knew that was ridiculous. The truth was they spent more and more time together, more and more nights, mostly at his. Not because he had a nicer place than hers, but because that way it was just so much easier to keep all the lies on an even keel.

She *hated* having to lie about her past. About the present.

But what other choice did she have?

'Let me know what the physio says,' he said before coming over and giving her a lingering kiss on the lips. 'You ask me, you're doing great.'

She said nothing and soon he was out of the room, and she waited for the front door to open and close before she got out of bed.

Ten minutes later and she was out of the door herself.

And she hadn't actually lied about today. She really was going to see the physio, although she was way further ahead physically than she'd made out to Callum the last few weeks. Officially she'd been signed off from work for six months for rehabilitation. And to start with she'd actually felt that wouldn't be enough. The stab wound had been so deep it'd played havoc not just with her organs but with her nervous system, rendering her right leg more or less numb. She'd been assured that with careful rehab it'd heal but it really had been strenuous, gruelling work.

But she'd made it through with few side effects. Now the mental toll remained the main barrier to her wanting to be back on the job.

And, of course, this new life. A whirlwind romance.

She cringed at her own thinking. She hated that phrase, it made her – and it – sound so simplistic and almost childish. But there was no doubt she'd fallen for Callum Murphy, and he for her, and a few months ago she really didn't think she'd be saying that.

What she felt for him was real.

What wasn't real was the story she'd had to spin – and hold on to day after day – about who she really was.

First up she went back to her flat. She hadn't been there in three days, didn't really see the point in spending much time there as it was hardly a home, and hadn't ever been really, even if she'd owned the place for nearly five years. She simply spent so little time there, often preferring to stay in London in one of many government-owned apartments when she was back in the country between assignments.

She parked on the street outside and was moving across the road when she spotted the figure step from the car a few vehicles down.

Not the last face she expected to see here, but still a big surprise.

Erica Goldman. One of her superiors at SIS. Well, really her main superior, mentor. Handler? Something like that.

'Lea, how are you?' Goldman asked, indicating to the beefy man who'd half-stepped out of the driver's seat that he could stay there. 'Can we talk?'

Not really a question. A demand.

'Come in.'

* * *

Lea studied her boss while she fixed them both a coffee. Goldman mooched, intermittently sighed or smiled as she did so, although there wasn't really much to see in the sparse space.

Goldman had never been here before. Lea was sure Goldman hardly *ever* visited agents at their homes. Not that she wasn't a personable boss. In fact, she was more than personable, almost motherly to Lea – just in an often very overbearing, my-way-or-the-highway type way. From what Lea knew, Goldman had been tied to MI6 for more than four decades. Originally a field agent herself she'd taken up a desk job over thirty years ago. She was married, but had no kids, three dogs. Lea had never spoken to her much about her personal life, but she'd sensed the lack of kids was a hole in her life that would now never be filled. A choice she'd had to make for her career, not just because of the added complexities it'd entail with the clandestine – often dangerous – nature of the work, but because of the struggles of a female trying to make it in a male-dominated environment, particularly back in the day.

Those barriers were breaking down now. As far as Lea saw, field agents were almost fifty-fifty men and women. It made sense. Physicality aside, women were equally good at espionage, and in fact were a lot better in many situations. That mix of sexes was slowly filtering through to the jobs in higher office. Goldman's short hair, her suits, her often aggressive approach with people had probably seen her through a more misogynistic era, although Lea didn't know for sure how much of it was the real Erica and how much was her being what she'd needed to be.

'You like it here?' Goldman asked.

'It serves a purpose,' Lea said, coming over with the two coffees. Goldman was at the window and turned around just as Lea reached her.

'And what purpose is that?' she asked.

'Excuse me?'

'Is this what you call *getting away* from it all?'

Lea said nothing. She wasn't really sure what she was expected to say.

'Your man's not here this morning?'

'He's working.'

'Must be hard living a lie every day.'

Lea pushed the cup into Goldman's chest and a little coffee spilled out onto the floor. But Goldman only smiled as though pleased with the reaction.

'My whole adult life has been a lie, not just the last four months,' Lea said.

'I didn't mean to upset you.'

'Yes, you did.'

'I've just never seen an agent go cold turkey like this before.'

'Cold turkey?'

'Living this cute little civilian life, shacked up with your man.'

'Fuck you, Erica. You've no idea—'

'Then tell me, Lea, what?'

Lea held her tongue.

'Seriously, what's your plan? Now? In six months? In five years?'

Lea didn't. Couldn't. Because she knew as well as Goldman did that there was no plan.

'You're torn, I get it. You've had a taste of love or whatever, of normality, and it's brought you comfort that I and SIS couldn't offer you. *Safety*. That's what it is, Lea. It's brought you safety. But not satisfaction.'

'You don't know that.'

'I think I do. So, I'll ask again: what's your plan? Get a job at the nearest supermarket checkout for a few months before you're knocked up and start a family?'

Lea clenched her jaw rather than answer that.

'Tell me this... Does he know *anything* about you? The real you?'

'Are you asking me because you're concerned I've been talking? About my job?'

Goldman didn't answer.

'He knows nothing. I'm Lea Torrence, consultant at BTS. That's it. The same profile you invented for me. It's who he believes I am because it's the only me the world sees now.'

'So you haven't even taken him to meet your parents yet?'

A snide smirk accompanied the question. Of course Goldman knew the answer. No, Lea hadn't introduced Callum to her parents, because to her parents she wasn't Lea Torrence but Claire Simmonds. Yes, the whole thing was fucked up, but there was no way out of it now.

'Do you love him?' Goldman asked.

A pause. Damn it, she really wished she hadn't paused. 'Yes. I do.'

'I'll ask again. What's the plan?'

No answer.

'You're scared.'

Lea looked at her cup, the liquid trembling in her shaking hand. She put it on the side.

'It's normal, Lea. Believe me, I've seen this *so* many times. You had a bad experience. Your first. And I know you're scared, not just because of what happened to you but because you think you let others down. You're scared you made a mistake, that it might impinge on your reliability in the future. That others will see it as a weakness. That you—'

'Yes, yes, I get it! Why are you here?'

'Isn't it obvious? I've been receiving all the reports from the physiotherapist, the psychotherapist. It's time for you to come back.'

Lea said nothing. She went to pick up her drink but realised she was still too shaky so left it right there.

'The only way you'll truly get past what happened is to get back to what you're good at. And, quite frankly, don't tell me I wasted all that time, money, effort on training you only for you to bail at the first setback.'

Lea still said nothing.

Goldman sighed. 'Let me throw a little sweetener in for you. I want you back, Lea, but I want it long term. I want you to feel satisfied. So how about this? You get to keep this nice little life you've started, if that's what needs to happen. It can be done. Plenty others have managed it over the years. I've been married nearly a quarter of a century. You think my Paul knows the whole truth?'

Once again Lea didn't respond. Goldman sighed.

'I hoped I'd convince you more easily. But... I guess I need to twist your arm right to breaking?' Luckily Lea realised Goldman meant figuratively. 'We've had a development. On the Iranians.'

'You're dealing with it now?' Lea said. Because it hadn't initially been her op, but that of her peer Victor Reynolds.

'We all have to keep our superiors happy,' she said with a smile. 'Mine thought it best to bring in another head to oversee things given what happened in Toulouse.' Her smile faded. 'If you ask me, it was rash of Reynolds to have you and Denis out there on a scavenger hunt in the first place. You both should have been more prepared. But...'

'But?'

'I think you should plan on being out of town for a little while. Your boy will be here waiting when you get back.'

'Because?'

'Because I do need you, Lea. And so does Denis.'

'Denis?'

'Two days ago, he landed in Egypt. He'd been tracking Taremi and believed he was meeting with a new financier there.'

'Financier for what?'

'No, Lea, the bigger question right now is about Denis.'

'I don't get it.'

'Then I hope you will very soon. Denis landed in Egypt two days ago, but for the past thirty-six hours he's been completely dark.'

'Dark? You think he's been captured?'

'He was last seen a quarter of a mile from the US Embassy in Cairo. He'd been there to meet a CIA asset. After that... nothing.'

Lea was silent again, mind in turmoil.

'And he wasn't alone, Lea. Naomi was with him.'

Naomi Hjelde. She was the same age as Lea, only six months separated them and they'd joined MI6 at the exact same time, had completed so much of their training period together even if their field experience had seen them move further apart over recent times.

'Lea, I need your help to find them both. You'll do that for me, won't you?'

The words spilled out of Lea's mouth before she could stop them, before she could even think about the lies she'd have to tell Callum and what it might mean for a happy – normal – future that was so tantalisingly close but being held up by the thinnest of threads.

'Yes, Erica. You know I will.'

9

BERKSHIRE

Present day

Nearly 10 p.m. as the Uber rolled to a stop on the quiet tree-lined residential street. Callum thanked the driver and stepped out and walked off behind the car, an eye over his shoulder until the Uber had pulled away, taken the next right turn and moved out of sight.

He checked no one else was around then turned and carried on in the opposite direction, past where the car had just dropped him off. A little decoy he'd decided on.

Would it work? Would it make any difference at all? He had absolutely no clue. He'd never had to think like this before, watching his back, expecting eyes on him, police or others hunting him down, and knowing that every move he made would leave a trail of sorts.

The Uber trip would be recorded. Would show a drop-off at this location. It was possible – if not necessarily plausible – that the police and White had already tracked Callum's phone to here in real time. One of the reasons why he'd left the phone in the Uber, stuffed under the footwell. He felt a little naked, lost without it, but what else was he supposed to do?

Yeah, the Uber records would show – and the driver would remember

– dropping Callum on this street. Hence the added decoy as the location he really came here for was another half a mile ahead of him.

He kept his head down and strode on, his nerves steadily growing, if that was even possible.

The journey from London had taken less than an hour. Ultimately, getting out of that building hadn't been so hard.

Let him go. Just... let him go.

Why had White shouted that? Because he didn't want Callum shot? Because they really were on his side, protecting him?

Or something else?

Either way, Callum had made it clean out of that building, no one in sight giving chase. And he'd kept on going. Running at first. A quarter of a mile. Then he'd slowed, to make himself less obvious on the night-time streets of the city. Half a mile, eventually more than a mile on foot until he'd stopped to properly consider his options.

Not many.

He had no transport in London, and he wasn't about to hop on the Tube, where he'd have to go down into the confined stations. Nor a bus which would be stop-start to wherever he was headed. And he definitely didn't want to stay in the big city. He had to get out. He had to get *home.*

Or close to home, at least. He had a destination in mind, but chose to make this closer stop first because he just needed...

Because he needed help.

Or at least an ear to which he could download the day's crazy events. Someone who'd listen to him, calm and collected. Someone who could think clearly, logically, analytically, at a time when Callum certainly couldn't.

His older brother.

He cringed at that thought. He loved and despised Aaron in equal measure. Or, at least, he despised how people saw Aaron compared to him. Comparison was inescapable for any siblings, but for Callum at least it had never been a favourable process.

Aaron was the golden child. Callum was the runt of the litter.

Aaron had rarely been directly cruel to Callum about any of that, but he had taken all the kudos and the goodwill and basked in it for years.

Had he stuck up for Callum too? Yeah, at times. But not enough. Not in the right way, or at the right times.

But still... Right now, his older brother was who Callum felt he could turn to, even if a big part of that was purely geographical, given the proximity to London, because he also knew coming here was a potential risk. Wouldn't his close family be the first place whoever was looking for him would go?

He'd soon find out, and he really didn't have any other good choices.

And the fact was, he and his brother weren't that close anyway. Callum hadn't ever been to this house before. Hadn't seen his brother at all in two years, actually. They hadn't even spoken in a few months.

Aaron had moved from the West Country to London seven years ago, just after his wife, Deena, had given birth to their first child. He'd got a new job at a big accountancy firm in the city. For a while they'd lived in a cramped flat close to his work, until another promotion had given them enough financial clout to move to the suburbs and an actual house with outdoor space. The street Callum found himself on consisted of two mirror-image rows of semi-detached homes from the fifties or sixties. Nothing particularly grand or awe-inspiring about them, but he could bet in this area, within commuting distance of the city, they were worth an eye-watering amount. At least compared to what a similar home would cost back in the suburbs of Bristol. Or any other city in England, really.

He checked his watch as he neared the drive. After 10 p.m. now. Midweek, he expected the whole family would be home, though it was possible even the adults were in bed already, or at least would be planning on being so very soon.

So he was glad to see a couple of lights on downstairs.

He made his way up the drive and pressed the bell and waited. Waited. He pressed again and a couple of seconds later heard a rattle the other side before the door opened and caught on a chain. The hallway beyond was in darkness but there was no mistaking the angry face that poked out through the gap.

'What are *you* doing here?' Deena sneered.

'I... Is Aaron around?'

'I asked you a question. Do you know what time it is? And just turning up out of the blue like this?'

'Deena, I—'

'Honey, who is it?' came Aaron's voice from further inside and her sneer only grew, but only likely because she'd hoped to get rid of Callum before her husband realised what was going on.

'Aaron, it's me,' Callum called out, deciding it best to just get his brother's attention.

Silence for a few moments before Deena's face disappeared. The door closed and he could hear them talking the other side – a hissed conversation, trying to keep their voices low but failing.

Eventually the door opened, no chain now, and Aaron was standing there, his wife hovering over his shoulder and not doing a very good job of hiding her distaste for Callum. And he knew exactly where the distaste was coming from.

He *mostly* deserved it. Mostly, but not entirely.

'Can I come in?' Callum asked.

'It's been a while, brother,' Aaron said, offering a hand. 'This is... pretty unexpected.'

'But not without good reason. Please, can I come in and explain?'

'You're in trouble?' Aaron said, picking up on Callum's nervousness and glancing over his brother's shoulder to the street beyond.

'Yeah. I think so.'

'Jesus, Aaron,' Deena said, 'we don't *need* any trouble here.'

'Please?' Callum said. 'Just let me explain.'

'OK,' Aaron said. 'Come on.'

He moved aside and Callum headed on in. Aaron closed the door behind them.

'Lea's dead,' Callum blurted. He really didn't know how else to start the conversation.

Deena's face fell. Shock, horror. Aaron didn't react at all.

'Did you...?' Deena started and even if she didn't finish, Callum figured what she was trying to say.

'Of course I didn't hurt her!'

Though he knew exactly why she might suspect that, even if it was – largely – unwarranted.

Callum glanced around the hall. At the photos on the walls. None of him. None of Lea. None from one of the biggest days in Aaron and Deena's lives either.

But their relationship had been complex right from the start, and in truth they'd stuck it out for far longer than Callum had ever imagined possible. The big hurdle? Deena had originally been Callum's girlfriend. They were in love, in his eyes at least, and were together for more than two years until he found out she'd been sleeping with a co-worker for over six months. So he'd ended it, kicked her out of their flat. And that should have been that. Except a little over a year later she'd hooked up with his brother...

Not a total surprise, in a way, even if Callum had hated the idea of it. Not because he still held feelings for Deena – no positive ones, anyway – but because he couldn't stand the thought of her hurting Aaron like she'd hurt him. Yet the relationship made sense in some ways. The two of them weren't strangers. Callum and Aaron and Deena had all been part of the same friend group back in their schooldays. Even if the boys were very different to one another, the fact they were only separated by one school year meant they ended up hanging in the same circles for years.

Perhaps Aaron should have known better, could have *done* better. But who was Callum to get involved? Both parties were well aware of the past.

So even if he hadn't intervened – much – things had never been easy between Callum and Deena since the relationship had started with Aaron. But *her* infidelity didn't explain her animosity towards Callum. That was down to something else.

'Tell me what happened,' Aaron said.

'I don't even really know,' Callum said, shaking his head in despair, trying to hold himself together. 'The police came to my job site today. Told me she'd been killed in a motorbike accident in Bucharest.'

Aaron put his hand onto Callum's shoulder. 'Shit. I'm sorry. Come on, let's go sit down.'

Callum nodded. Deena looked really put out still.

'Babe, get us some water or something?' Aaron said before directing

Callum through to the table in a small dining room at the back of the house.

They took seats. Deena brought in two glasses of water and hovered, still suspicious as hell.

'But that... doesn't explain why you're here?' Aaron said, part question, part statement.

'She told me she was in Prague,' Callum said. 'And a motorbike accident? She's never ridden one in all the time I've known her.'

'So... what are you saying?'

'What I've explained so far is only the start. When I got home, there were two people already there, inside. A man and a woman. They claimed Lea wasn't who she said she was. Before I know it, the police turn up. They start shooting at each other!'

Callum laughed at the ridiculousness of it. He knew how outlandish it'd all sound to his brother. It certainly did to him. Aaron looked really confused now. Deena grunted like she was hearing the ramblings of a madman.

'I'm not fucking making this up!' Callum shouted.

'Shh, keep it down,' Aaron said. 'No one's saying that. But... Cal, what the hell is this?'

'*Exactly*. The police got me away from those intruders, took me back to London. This... office or something. I'm interviewed by a detective, then a guy from *MI6*. They're telling me Lea worked there. Was killed on an operation overseas. And they think *I* know something about it.'

'And do you?' Deena asked, still sneery.

'No!'

'And now... you're here? Are you on the run?' Aaron asked.

'I... think so.'

'Shit...' Deena said. 'So any minute we could have the police breaking down our door—'

'*Deena!* Why don't you... go and check the boys,' Aaron said. 'Give us a minute. And keep fucking calm, will you?'

She hesitated but then humphed and stormed out. Neither brother said a word for a while, both looking around each other.

'This is something,' Aaron said eventually.

'I don't know what to do,' Callum said. 'What to believe. Who to trust.'

'You can trust me,' Aaron said, putting his hand on top of Callum's.

An unexpected gesture, though it genuinely did provide comfort, if only fleetingly.

'MI6, you say?'

Callum nodded.

'Damn.'

Callum had no idea what that meant. 'She lied to me,' he said. 'About everything.'

'I'm sorry... Did the police say what they want from you? It doesn't make sense that you're a suspect in anything, based on what you said.'

'You're right. It doesn't. And I don't know exactly what they want, only that Lea was killed over some intelligence she had. Data that's now missing. And they think I might know about it, know where it is.'

'Do you?'

'No!'

'But, I mean... *do* you? As in, *could* you?'

He didn't get what the question meant at first, but then a thought swirled and swirled.

Claire Simmonds.

'No,' he said.

'Callum, think about it. If what you're saying is true... These kinds of people? Police, intelligence agencies... They're not just going to come after you for no reason. If they suspect you know something, there must be a good reason why. Maybe there *is* something. And you just missed it.'

'Because I'm an idiot?'

'I didn't say that.'

'But you've always thought it.'

Aaron scoffed but said nothing. But Callum knew it was the truth. He loved and despised his brother in equal measure.

They were like chalk and cheese. Physically, Aaron was as tall as Callum but lean and wiry. He had a handsome, almost boyish look about him which together with his wide smile and his natural charm made him popular with pretty much everyone, but particularly girls. And he was so damn clever too. Intellectually smart but also calm and considered and able to think things through rationally, logically. No wonder he'd aced every damn exam he'd ever taken, had gone off to UCL to study business management, and had since worked his way up the corporate ladder to partnership at a major accounting firm.

Growing up he'd been the shining jewel of the family at every stage. Callum was the unpolished turd. Of course, to start with, no one had known about his diagnosis. Up until he was fourteen, his parents and everyone else had flitted between assuming he was either simply bone idle and couldn't be bothered to try at school, or was just plain stupid – the latter the most usual. If he hadn't been so insistent about his struggles at school, he'd never have gotten the dyslexia diagnosis and he'd have headed into adulthood probably thinking the same about himself as everyone else.

Not that the diagnosis, at such a late age, had really helped much. The school he was at had no teachers experienced in dealing with it and he was still put through all the same classes and exams as everyone else without any special attention. Which explained why he'd failed so many.

At sixteen he'd left education and started an apprenticeship as a bricklayer. A practical job. And he'd been good at that and had worked hard, moved up to where he was now.

But he had never had so much as a well done or congratulations from his parents who still couldn't understand why he was so different – so much less successful – than their star son, Aaron.

Even Callum's sports prowess didn't impress them much. Aaron had never been into sports, even if he was athletic enough. Callum's natural bulky physique had seen him fight his way to a high level at rugby. Not quite high enough to make it as a pro – a further disappointment to his parents – but he'd come pretty damn close, although now even those days were mostly behind him, the toll of the brutal game on a man in his early thirties simply too much.

His brother had the looks, the intellect and the charm. Callum had the brawn. Yet even that had bitten him, in more ways than one.

He glanced around the room again. A few photo frames in here too. Lots of smiles, lots of good times between Aaron and Deena and their boys.

But, just like in the hallway, not a single picture of their wedding day.

That was Callum's fault, and the reason for Deena's continued hostility towards him.

He'd never been fully comfortable with his brother marrying his cheating ex and there'd been a few uneasy standoffs between the brothers when Aaron and Deena had started dating, and in the time that followed. But everything had come to a head the night before the wedding. The brothers were together with the rest of their family in a hotel near the venue. The evening had gone pretty well, really, until alcohol had got the better of them both. By midnight only the two of them were left drinking in the hotel bar and they carried on until after one, drink after drink, recalling good times and bad and... Honestly, Callum couldn't even remember the exact spark...

Aaron claimed Callum threw the first punch, angered by something he'd said. In Callum's blurred memory it was him who'd insulted his brother and Aaron who'd grabbed him by the scruff of his neck and angrily shoved him up against a wall before that first punch.

Whichever was the correct version of events, the unfortunate truth was that that first punch had been followed by a second and then a third which had caused Aaron to keel over and smack his head off the corner of the bar.

Perhaps the short-lived fight had been brewing for some time before that, but Callum was no aggressor, really. Other than that one time, he couldn't ever recall lashing out in anger. Yeah, he was big, strong, capable physically, and was certainly no stranger to physical confrontation, but in his whole life he'd never *started* a fight. Except perhaps that one. If Aaron was to be believed.

Whoever was right, the next morning, the day of the wedding, Aaron had one black eye, almost entirely swollen shut, four stitches in his other eye where he'd hit the bar, a bulbous nose, and a split bottom lip.

The wedding went ahead – although it'd been touch and go – and the wedding photographer was still there to do his job that day, but Callum had never seen a single picture from the event. Not even any of the many that had been taken without Aaron in them, as though Deena – and perhaps Aaron too – had just decided to forget about the whole thing.

Of course, Callum had been profusely sorry come the morning after the fight. And over time, Aaron had *said* he'd forgiven Callum. But Deena certainly never had, and the brothers had simply carried on, the years passing with that regretful moment separating them over an ever-growing distance.

'Come on, Cal, give me something,' Aaron said. 'You came here for my help. So *how* can I help?'

But Callum was too busy in his own mind.

'You need to think, *Cal*. The police think you have this information. And you either do or you don't—'

'I don't—'

'But even if you don't, perhaps they think you could have access to it. That you know something that could help them. Did... did Lea really never tell you anything at all?'

Claire Simmonds.

'I... don't think so. But... maybe.'

'Maybe what?'

'There's somewhere I need to go. To be sure.'

Aaron's eyes narrowed. He nodded as though understanding. Good for him, because Callum certainly didn't.

Deena came back into the doorway. She stood there with her arms folded, still sneery but also a little smug.

'You're on the news,' she said.

* * *

Ten minutes later and standing over the laptop in the dining room, the three of them had rewatched the clip on the BBC website five times.

Lea Torrence, a UK government employee, had been found dead in Bucharest. The authorities wanted to speak to two men in connection with the death. Callum Murphy. Denis Petit.

'They're saying death, not accidental death, not murder,' Aaron said ponderously, as though thinking out loud. 'And you're *wanted in connection* with the death. You're not a suspect.'

'Are you serious?' Deena said. 'We need to call the police, Aaron.'

'Please don't,' Callum said.

'Why not?' she said. 'What have you got to hide?'

'It's not that... simple. This goes further than the police. I don't know if they can be trusted.'

'Bullshit, you—'

'Who's the other guy?' Aaron said, cutting in.

A very good question.

'I've met him before. He came to our fucking wedding. Lea said he was a coworker—'

'So this guy's MI6 too?'

'I haven't got a clue. All I know is he's called Denis and he and Lea knew each other pretty well. And... when the police were talking to me... they said Lea was killed, but the data she had was missing. And so was another MI6 agent.'

'Aaron... we just need to call the police,' Deena said.

'No,' he said, holding his hand up and she looked as mad as she was shocked by his stony intervention. 'Not until we know what's happening. I'll call Jack. He can help.'

'Jack?' Callum asked.

'He's a lawyer. About the best damn lawyer. He'll know what to do.'

'No, I don't want anyone else involved.'

'You already involved us,' Deena said. 'Aaron, we could be in serious trouble here—'

'I didn't come here to cause trouble.'

'Then why did you?'

'Because it was... convenient.'

Deena threw her hands in the air in despair. 'Wow! I'm so glad this is convenient for you, Callum.'

'That's not what I meant. I mean...' He turned to his brother. 'I told you. There's somewhere I think I should go. Where there might be some answers. But I need your help to get there.'

'Aaron, you are not leaving this house tonight!' Deena shouted.

'Where?' Aaron asked his brother.

'Near Bristol. Clemens.'

Claire Simmonds.

'Clemens?' Aaron said confusedly.

'I can explain on the way.'

'He's not leaving this house!' Deena shouted again.

'OK,' Aaron said. 'I can take you there. But I'm calling Jack on the way. I want to know where we stand, if this all blows up in our faces.'

Callum thought about it for a few seconds.

'OK. Call the lawyer. I've got nothing to hide.'

'Then you should turn yourself in,' Deena said, though nowhere near as animated as before. More dejected now.

Aaron moved over to her and put his arms around her and kissed her forehead.

'Come on, let's go,' he said to Callum before heading on out.

10

The hotel was basic, functional, convenient. Callum and Aaron shared a twin room, not to save on money but because both were wracked with nerves. Callum had barely slept, his mind twisting through the night with a mishmash of thoughts: good times with Lea, bad times with her, the moment of her death – imagined in his mind, at least. He also thought about the previous day's many events: the police, the interview with the mysterious Andrew White, the people in his home, the news reports naming him as a person of interest...

Too much. He needed *something* to clear his head. But what? He finished his coffee but as he put his cup down on the small table in the corner of the bedroom his eyes rested on the brown envelope on the bed. He reached across, picked it up and took the pictures out and looked at them one after the other, over and over.

The door to the bathroom opened and Aaron came out.

'Still thinking it through?' he asked.

'What else am I supposed to do?'

'Those people...'

'Have to be connected somehow. Why else would that White guy have showed me these?'

'But we don't even know who they all are.'

'We know of them.'

Now they did, anyway. Abdul Hadjam. A French businessman, apparently. A simple Google search of his image had identified him, and Aaron and Callum had both scoured what they could online since then – Aaron finding it easier, given he could read a news article more quickly and easily than Callum.

Aaron came over and sat down at the table.

'You said Hadjam is Algerian?' Callum prompted.

'Through his family, yes.'

'And his daughter is married to a British MP?'

'Omar Yousefi. Whose parents were Iranian immigrants.'

A British MP? Callum wouldn't say he was completely ignorant of politics, but he'd never heard of the guy before. Didn't recognise his face either.

'So what does it mean?' Callum asked.

'Feels like it's something geopolitical, doesn't it? Perhaps even, at a stretch, it could be... terrorism-related or something like that?'

'You think a British MP is involved in plotting terror attacks?'

Aaron sighed. 'We have zero evidence of that. But terrorism doesn't only have to be overt bomb attacks. It could be something more subtle. There could still be foul play with these people, behind the scenes, that manifests in some other way.'

Callum had no idea what he meant by that.

'Whichever way you look at it, these people are linked to Lea's death,' Callum said.

'According to one guy who talked to you. Who claimed to be from MI6, but based on everything else you've told me... why would you believe a word he said?'

A good question. And one of many reasons why Callum's head continued to pound. He couldn't make sense of any of it.

'I told you last night... we could run all of this through Jack.' Jack Wilcox. Aaron's lawyer friend. Although it turned out he was a corporate lawyer, not a defence lawyer. 'Whatever we tell him is privileged and it wouldn't do any harm to get his perspective.'

'No,' Callum said with absolute assurance. 'Not yet.'

Although they had spoken to the guy briefly on the phone last night as Aaron drove them west. Jack wanted them both to go to his house. Do a full, lengthy debrief and come up with a game plan, tactics, before he contacted the police directly to offer them time with Callum. Probably far juicier for him than dealing with legal contracts or whatever his day job usually entailed.

Regardless, there was no chance Callum was putting himself in front of the authorities willingly. Not until he knew more. Not until he knew who to trust.

He checked his watch. Five past nine. They'd waited long enough.

'Let's hit the road,' Callum said.

* * *

Aaron pulled the car up outside the bungalow. Only seven properties on the short side street away from the main A-road that dissected the village of Clemens, which had probably less than 200 homes total. Callum was sure he'd driven through the place before but had never had cause to stop until now.

'That's the one,' Aaron said, ducking his head down a little to look out at the modest home. Modest, but the redbrick bungalow had a vibrant, immaculately tended front garden with all manner of colourful flowers in bloom. 'You're sure this is a good idea?'

'Not really,' Callum said.

'But Lea *told* you to come here?'

He'd already explained this, both on the drive west and in the hotel room last night. This morning too, actually.

'Not directly, Aaron. But she... she told me Claire Simmonds was an old friend. Someone she was really close to when she was younger.'

'And Claire Simmonds died?'

Callum huffed. 'Yeah. In a motorbike accident in Bucharest a couple of days ago.'

'Not what I meant.'

'I know. Apparently, Lea *is* Claire Simmonds. But she told me Claire died of cancer when they were in their teens. Claire was an only child and her parents' lives were destroyed by her death. She said she always got along with them really well. That she visited them every now and then.'

Aaron shook his head, looked almost aggrieved. At the lies Lea had told?

'She said if anything ever happened to her... she'd really like me to go and see them.'

'A pretty odd thing to say.'

'It didn't seem odd at the time. Not the way she said it. It just seemed... caring. Like she was.'

Aaron scoffed at that.

'*You didn't know her*,' Callum said through clenched teeth.

'I'm not sure you did either. No offence.'

Plenty taken.

'And she told you this when? Recently?'

'A long time ago, actually. But... yeah, she reminded me of it recently. A few weeks ago.'

'And you think there was a reason for that?'

'It's possible. Like she was warning me. Or giving me a clue.'

'But she never told you she was in trouble?'

'No. Never.'

'Even if it was a clue, have you any idea what you're looking for here? You think she told them something? Gave them a message for you?'

'I'm certain she didn't.'

'Then what?'

'I have no idea.'

Aaron sighed. 'Cal, I want to help, but this just all sounds so... loose. Vague.'

'It is what it is. Worst case? Maybe I'll be able to make two lonely people who've just lost their daughter feel a little bit brighter.'

'They probably don't even know their daughter is dead. And no, that's not the worst case. The worst case is an armed response team turns up here and fills you with bullets.'

'Then what else do you suggest?'

'You know what I suggested.'

'Go see your lawyer friend.'

'Jack explained the situation to us both pretty clearly last night. Running isn't the answer. *Interfering* isn't the answer. It'll only make things look worse for you.'

Except Callum had done *nothing* wrong.

'So you're really doing this?' Aaron asked after a few moments of silence.

'I have to.'

'Want me to come in too?'

'No. Wait here. If... anything doesn't look or feel right, blast the horn.'

Aaron gulped, as though he hadn't really felt there could be a threat to him being here until that point.

Callum got out and headed to the front door. The ring was answered within a few seconds by a woman he didn't know – certainly not the woman who'd attended his and Lea's wedding pretending to be the mother of the bride. She was short, probably no more than her late sixties given Lea's age but she looked frail, with wispy white hair and droopy features.

'Mrs Simmonds?'

'Yes?' she said, obviously suspicious.

'I'm a friend of Claire's.'

She said nothing but her eyes welled. A man appeared behind her. He was only a little taller and equally withered.

'Is it the police again?' he said, coming up behind her.

Again. They already knew.

'He says he's a friend.'

'Callum Murphy,' Callum said, holding his hand out. Both looked hesitant but then each of them gave a limp shake in turn.

'Why don't you come inside.'

***

They sat in the living room. Mrs Simmonds – Janet – had made a pot of tea and was propped on the edge of one end of the sofa, Callum at the other. Her husband, Fred, sat sunken in an armchair. The furniture – like much of the decor – was a little dated, but everything in the house was neat and tidy and well-kept. Photo frames adorned most surfaces. Plenty of them were of Lea. *Claire*. Even some pretty recent ones of her abroad – both trips she'd taken with Callum, and some 'business' trips.

Callum had spotted the photos the moment he'd stepped inside. The truth smacked him across the face.

It'd been years ago when Lea had first mentioned her old 'friend' Claire and her parents. When she'd said she'd like for Callum to visit them if anything happened to her. And he got it now. *This* would have been her reveal to him, because the second he walked in she knew he'd have seen all the pictures and the dots would have been connected in his mind within the first few moments of speaking to her mum and dad.

But she'd specifically mentioned Claire Simmonds to him more recently too. That had to mean something.

'What did the police say?' Callum asked.

'That there was an accident overseas,' Janet said. 'Prague, I think they said?'

Fred nodded. Callum inwardly cringed. Prague? Was that some sort of insult to him? Obviously, the Simmonds hadn't seen, or at least not properly understood the news articles referencing Lea Torrence's death in Bucharest, but then the pictures of her in the news had been pretty unclear really. Perhaps deliberately so.

Not the picture of him, though. His picture had been pretty damn clear, but still neither Fred nor Janet seemed particularly alerted by his presence here.

'When did the police come?' Callum asked.

'Last night. Just after 6 p.m. We were eating dinner.'

'Did they say much? Ask you much about Claire?'

Fred's eyes narrowed with suspicion, but he didn't answer.

'Hardly anything,' Janet said. 'They only wanted to know when we'd last seen her. If she'd left anything of hers here.'

'Had she?'

'Like what?' Fred challenged.

Callum didn't answer.

'You knew her well?' Janet asked.

Callum dwelled on the question a few seconds before diving in. He'd thought about how to approach this, his relationship with Claire. He didn't tell them they were together, but he did talk, and talk, them asking him questions, him asking them. It felt good. It made him feel better. They were talking about the same person, he realised. Claire Simmonds and Lea Torrence were the same person.

He cringed at his own thought. *Of course they were the same person*, but he'd kind of expected that maybe... she'd created two wholly different personas or something. But she really hadn't. The woman he'd fallen in love with and was married to was the Simmonds's daughter. And yet that tugged at his heart so much. They'd never heard of him, never met him, had no idea their daughter had even been married.

Another thought wrestled for control in his head, not for the first time. Who the hell was the woman who'd come to their wedding? The one Lea had said was her mother?

That question pushed away a great deal of his growing fond reminisce.

The phone was ringing. Janet picked it up.

'Rachel! I'm so glad you called. It's... Yes... Horrible... just horrible... No, we're doing OK... But... Yes... But... We've got company—'

'It's OK,' Callum said. 'You carry on. Fred, do you think I could use the bathroom?'

He nodded. 'Down the hall. You won't miss it.'

Callum got up and headed that way, Janet's voice carrying through the small space.

Fred was right. Callum couldn't miss the bathroom. It wasn't as though there were many options off the hallway. Although he didn't actually make it there. Hadn't necessarily intended to really, because his intention was to mooch a little, and he found himself in the doorway of the spare bedroom – one of only two in the small home.

He stared at the painting hanging on the wall above a drawer unit topped with a variety of photos of Lea, mostly as a child. The painting looked a little odd, out of place versus everything else. It wasn't particularly big but was finished in an almost overly elaborate gold-tinged frame. What had first caught his eye though were the symbols in the bottom corner: the same characters Lea had tattooed on her wrist.

Hope and light.

The rest of the painting was of spring blossom, purples and whites. Something like that, anyway.

He moved forward, right up to the frame and stared at the picture, looking over every detail, brain whirring. It looked like...

'So you *did* miss it?' came the voice from behind him.

Callum spun around to see Fred there in the doorway.

'I'm so sorry, I... didn't mean to snoop. But I saw the picture. The symbols. They're the same as Lea—same as Claire's tattoo?'

Fred's frown remained and he didn't answer straight away. Callum wondered whether he'd made a big mistake.

'We hated when she got that tattoo. But what do we know? Everyone has them these days, apparently.'

'Hope and light, she told me it meant.'

Fred nodded. 'Yeah. I guess it could have been worse.'

'When did you get the painting?'

'The first time or the second time?'

Callum raised an eyebrow to show he didn't understand. Fred waved the reaction away.

'She brought the picture home with her a few years ago. She'd been in Singapore or Shanghai or something like that. Kind of unique, I guess, that it had the same message as her tattoo. That's why she said she got it for us.'

'It's... pretty.'

'It's not our style but... it's grown on me, to be honest.'

'You said... something about the first and second time?'

Fred sniffed, shrugged. 'It's been sat there for years. Then a few weeks ago, she came over and took it down. Told us it had faded from the sun. She wanted it reframed, so it was better protected. She brought it back... not even a fortnight ago and it's got that damn awful gaudy gold thing all around it. Talk about culture clash.'

Janet appeared over his shoulder, no phone now. 'Honey, don't be so rude. She paid for that herself. Must have cost her a fortune.'

'It looks... really good,' Callum said. 'If you ask me. Definitely a top-quality finish.'

Fred humphed again as though not impressed with the statement.

'Do you mind if I take a closer look?' Callum asked.

Really suspicious now.

'A closer look for what?' Fred said.

'Of course you can, dear,' Janet added.

Before Fred protested, Callum reached out and pulled the frame off its hook and turned it over and scanned the back. The phone rang again.

'For God's sake, I'd do anything for some peace and quiet,' Fred said as Janet wandered off to answer it. He stayed put. At least until, 'Fred! It's for you.'

'Be careful,' he said, glaring at Callum a moment before he wandered off.

Callum returned his gaze to the painting. To the sticker at the bottom left hand corner on the back of the frame. He squinted, as though that'd help him make sense of the jumble of letters. It looked like it'd been put there by the art shop Lea had originally bought it from, or the framer.

No. The latter. He recognised 'Bristol' in the address.

And another word stuck out too.

Adele.

He was sure that said Adele in a pencilled scrawl.

A message for him?

Had to be.

Please.

But he had no clue what the message was.

He took out his phone – the simple prepaid one they'd picked up on the way over this morning to replace his original phone. He took a picture, front and back, then he placed the painting back on the wall. Adjusted it to make sure it was straight.

Then he headed on out, ready to give his excuses to leave.

11

CAIRO, EGYPT

Two and a half years ago

A thick grey smog hung over Cairo, reducing the sun to a dirty, dull yellow disc. The air felt heavy and hard to breathe. Traffic trudged by slowly, exhaust fumes only adding to the choking air, as people moved through the streets, coughing. Many – like Lea – had their faces hidden behind scarves.

Lea adjusted her scarf as she looked out across the Nile, the water gloomy and murky, tourist boats sloshing sullenly along, everything feeling down and depressed here today.

Or perhaps that was only Lea's mood.

Four days now she'd been in the capital. She'd initially travelled here alone but had spent a lot of the time in Egypt with Sara Kitsch from the CIA – the woman who Denis and Naomi had met at the US Embassy shortly before they'd gone missing on the streets of this gargantuan city.

And looking across the hazy horizon, the city seemingly endless from this vantage point, Lea felt more than a little weary at the idea that Denis and Naomi could now be *anywhere* in this vast space.

If they were even still alive.

So far, she'd had no evidence that they were.

No evidence that they *weren't* either, though, which had to be a good thing.

And she still held out hope that they remained close by to where they'd last been seen, right around the corner from this spot. The US Embassy was one street from her, away from the river, in this district of business hotels – frequented by both tourists and diplomats – and myriad government buildings.

Many embassies were dotted through the streets here too. And that was what worried Lea the most, even though it was the theory she'd pushed most since she'd arrived here.

With Kitsch's help, and that of an insider at the Egyptian National Security Agency, they'd now traced Denis's and Naomi's last movements through CCTV footage, showing them heading south on foot from the US Embassy, along tree-lined Tawfik Diab Street. Except no feeds showed either of them emerging anywhere else nearby. They'd vanished. Even though there were definitely some black spots where they could have slipped away – either deliberately or accidentally – Lea believed there might be another more nefarious explanation.

'Lea,' came the voice from behind her, and she turned to see Kitsch approaching on the pavement. Like Lea she was dressed casually, but with the headscarf covering much of her face – a necessity with the smog, plus it was a good way to hide their faces as well as the obvious need to blend in culturally. 'You were right.'

Lea's heart sank a little. Although just the slightest relief too that she had some answers now.

'How do you know?' she asked.

'Our friend was able to get the details from someone who works there. Security.' Kitsch fished out her phone and turned the screen to Lea. 'It's one of the service entrances.'

Lea watched the blurry footage. Certainly not clear enough to pass an identification test in a court of law or anything like that, but it was still obvious to Lea what she was looking at. Two people, a man and a woman, hands cuffed behind their backs, being corralled into the building by a group of three. The man and the woman were Denis and Naomi, she was certain.

'And after this?'

'This is all I have. It's the best I've been able to do so far.'

Kitsch put her phone away.

'I'll keep pushing to find out more, but this at least tells you where they went.'

Lea said nothing.

'I had to pass this up the chain on my end,' Kitsch said. 'You get that, right? If there's gonna be a move after this... make sure your superiors let mine in on it first. Best for everyone that way.'

Lea still said nothing, her mind was only thinking through what that move would be. She knew what she *wanted* it to be...

Kitsch looked about herself a little uncomfortably, as though wary of being watched. Probably had every right to be wary, given the circumstances.

'I'll be in touch,' Lea said, before turning and moving away, phone pressed to her ear.

Goldman answered on the second ring.

'They were taken into the Syrian embassy.'

Silence for a few seconds. 'So you were right.' On this occasion she really wished she hadn't been. 'Any indication of what happened after that?' Goldman asked.

'Not that I've been given.'

'So they could both still be inside?'

'Could be.'

'There's a few options for how we can find out.'

Yes, because Lea had already suggested several options to Goldman as they awaited the confirmation of her hunch. The most basic? A purely diplomatic route to getting their agents back. But it was Lea's least preferred route and could also take the longest time. On the other end of the scale was bringing an elite special forces squad into the mix to raid the Syrian Embassy, but that method had a high potential for collateral damage, and much wider political ramifications if it even resulted in them finding Denis and Naomi inside.

Somewhere in the middle was Lea's preferred option.

'I've identified someone if we decide to… even things up,' Lea said. 'The more leverage we have here, the better.'

Silence for a moment. Then a sigh.

'Do it,' Goldman said. 'And do it quickly.'

* * *

Lea had already made preliminary arrangements even before Goldman had given her the green light, knowing that time was of the essence to get Denis and Naomi back quickly and safely, and also knowing that in virtually any scenario, if there were any underhand tactics at play in Denis's and Naomi's disappearance, she'd likely need physical help. Physical help that was better coming from people at least a further step removed from the British Government than she was.

Hugo Butler and Ash Titus were brutes, plain and simple. Both had military backgrounds in their native South Africa but had found nowhere near as much glory or money as either of them wanted there, the life of a mercenary far more aligned to their talents and desires. Not that they didn't have smarts to go with the brawn. They were both wily as anything, would easily have been huge assets on any elite special forces unit if they'd taken that path.

Instead, they took whatever work paid, however dirty. Still, Lea had worked with both men in the past, and MI6 had a pretty detailed profile on each of them, with very few holes in their career timelines, and based on what she knew about their exploits, she trusted them. These men weren't about to help MI6 and the British one week, then be fighting against the West with the mujahideen in the Middle East the next. And the two men knew Egypt, knew Cairo, knew the whole of North Africa a lot better than Lea did.

They were the perfect duo for this.

'I liked Denis,' Butler said as the three of them sat in the back of the van in the plush suburb north of the city centre. 'We had some good times together.'

'Yeah,' was Titus's bland reply as he played with a devilish-looking hunting knife, twisting the blade on the side of the van. Titus's name was commensurate with a man who rose to six-foot-five and weighed probably over seventeen stone. The first time Lea had met him she thought perhaps he'd adopted the surname, but it was genuine. He was as strong and hard as the name suggested.

Butler's prowess was a little less conspicuous. Six-foot dead, perhaps thirteen stone, but wiry and athletic and trained – and more than capable – in about every form of combat known to man. And, like Titus, had absolutely no fear.

At least, that's how they portrayed themselves, how Lea saw them. And the image worked.

'OK, you two ready?' Lea said as she watched the feed on her phone, the camera on the outside of the van looking along the darkened street. 'I see the car.'

'We're ready,' Titus said, sheathing his knife and pulling himself up from the bench. Although he was nowhere near straight in the cramped space.

'You're sure you want the family too?' Butler asked Lea as he pulled a balaclava over his head.

'Yes,' Lea answered. 'All of them. But none of them needs to be hurt. If it can be avoided.'

'Yes, ma'am,' Butler said with a salute.

Titus opened the van door an inch and an arc of light from the approaching car's beams shot in. Lea hunkered in the dark corner, as though worried about being seen, but a moment later and the car was past them and the interior of the van was black once more.

'Go,' Butler said, quiet as anything, and Titus silently pushed the doors open and the two of them dropped down without a sound. Lea left the doors like that and hopped into the driver's seat. She watched the car pull in past the now opened security gates. Spotted the outlines of Butler and Titus moving through the darkness and in through the gates although she had to really concentrate to see them at all.

Murmuring. Muffled shouts. A couple of gentle thuds. The gates initially started to close but then whirred back open again and Lea fired up the engine and swung the van around and reversed in, leaving the front of the van poking out between the gates so that even if they tried to close, they wouldn't.

The bangs and thuds continued for a few seconds, then became more heightened, ramping up to ten in the space of a couple of seconds.

'Get in the fucking van!' Titus boomed before a thump and a man's moan was followed by a woman's screech of terror.

The van bounced on its suspension as a man was tossed inside, and he skidded and banged up against the back of Lea's seat.

'I said, get the fuck in!' Titus roared and the woman and child – a girl around twelve – cowered down, moaning and crying as they were shepherded into the back.

The husband – Al Aswad – pulled himself up a little until Butler bounced towards him and delivered a meaty hook to the side of his head.

'Better if you stay down, dickhead.'

'Go, go, go!' Titus shouted to Lea as he slammed the van doors shut.

Lea slammed her foot down and the van shot away into the night.

* * *

Two days of taut negotiation had culminated in this. Lea had been kept abreast of the discussions, but people higher up the ladder than her had led them. In the intervening period, her job was simple. Make sure the Al Aswads remained in her custody. They'd moved the family three times in the two days, making sure they stayed one step ahead of whoever would be looking for them.

Perhaps no-one was *officially* looking. The public quietness around the kidnapping spoke a lot. The Egyptian government were aware of the brewing crisis taking place on their land and had acted as mediator, taking neither side, but certainly there was no evidence they had a team of investigators scouring the country, and their strong words suggested they wouldn't have allowed Syria to do that without their approval either.

As for the Syrians themselves, their government spokespeople, in the midst of civil war back home, had initially played a basic hand of denial, claiming they had no idea what had happened to Denis and Naomi, that the two British agents had never been inside their embassy either of their own accord or under duress.

Perhaps at the start the people Goldman and others were negotiating with really did believe that, as it wasn't at all unusual for individuals and even groups within intelligence agencies to operate under the radar of their own masters. But there was only so long the Syrians could hold such a line given the stark truth and given the bargaining chip Lea had. Al Aswad. An actual Syrian government minister, who'd been living in exile in Egypt for more than a year.

The war raging in Syria was complex, nuanced, with no clear line to victory for any side, and Al Aswad was perhaps as important to the embattled regime as he was to the rebel groups who'd delight in having such a high-profile scalp in their hands.

That reality was hard to ignore, so the negotiations got moving.

The Syrians then initially admitted they'd taken both Denis and Naomi in for questioning, but that both had been let go within hours. No evidence of that. Next, they claimed that Naomi had been let go, but that they'd kept Denis. MI6 refuted that too. Finally, the Syrians were forced to the inevitable outcome, admitting that neither Denis nor Naomi had ever left the embassy, and – although refusing to say why they'd taken the MI6 agents or what they'd done to them since – concluding that the only way through the mess now was a direct swap. The two Brits for the Al Aswads.

The swap wouldn't end the growing tensions, but it was the only way forward from immediate escalation.

And so here they were, out in the desert, the millions of lights from the city resulting in a hazy orange glow hanging in the sky on the horizon. Through binoculars Lea could just make out the peaks of the pyramids in that direction. In the other direction, behind their van... nothing but sand.

MI6 had toyed with the idea of bringing a heftier team to this swap, but Lea had insisted otherwise. Simple was better. And she fully trusted that Butler and Titus could see this through with her, even if things didn't go fully to plan.

And the plan was pretty simple. Swap. If anything didn't look or feel right, then run.

Lea kept her gaze on the open space in front of them, searching for the approaching party. Butler kept his eyes on the three bound and gagged prisoners in the back. Titus was concentrating on the airwaves, on radar, making sure there wasn't an imminent all-out assault coming this way, either on the ground or in the air. Although Lea felt that unlikely as it'd need the support – or at least knowledge – of the Egyptian government one way or another, and she highly doubted they'd want to go so far in support of either side here. If anything, they wanted this over cleanly and quickly and for everyone involved to leave their country and take their problems and whatever new-found grudges had been formed with them.

'This is it,' Lea said, lowering the binoculars.

'How many?' Butler asked.

'Two vehicles.' As expected. 'Jeeps.'

Travelling with their lights off, which actually helped her, as with the lights on, dazzling, they could easily have snuck other vehicles along with them.

Soon she could hear the rumble of the vehicles moving across the sand, could feel it too not long after that. She watched the objects growing larger and larger in the faint moonlight before finally the two Jeeps parked side by side thirty yards in front. A second later and the lights flicked on and Lea held a hand up to her face to shield from the initially intrusive brightness.

'Let's go,' she said.

They moved out of the back, Titus first, then Lea, then the three prisoners, each moving gingerly with their eyes blindfolded, their senses all over the place. Finally, Butler jumped down. He and Titus had M4 carbines dangling from shoulder straps, along with a sidearm, a knife each too. Lea was armed with a simple handgun which she kept stashed for now. Hopefully would for the duration of the swap.

'Wait for the signal,' Lea said to Butler before Titus grabbed Al Aswad and stuck the barrel of the M4 in his back and pushed him towards the front of the van. Lea moved behind them, inspecting the scene in front, half in cover behind the two men ahead of her.

Two vehicles. Five men out in the open, including one who was on his knees, bound and gagged like Al Aswad, although not blindfolded. His gaze met Lea's.

Denis. Battered and bruised, face swollen, clothes dirty, torn and bloodied.

She pushed her hand onto the grip of the gun.

'Where's the other one?' Lea shouted over. 'Naomi Hjelde?'

'She's not with us. We're sorry,' came a shouted reply from the man closest to the Jeeps.

Lea and Titus glanced at each other.

'You were told to bring them both!' Lea shouted over.

'I'm sorry. It wasn't possible,' the same man shouted back.

'Let's get out of here,' Titus whispered to her. 'Come back when they're playing ball.'

But she wasn't walking away from Denis so quickly.

'Where's the woman and girl?' the man shouted.

'They're here,' Lea said. 'And I know Naomi is too. Because that's what we agreed. Bring her out, and let's get this finished.'

A momentary standoff, but then the man who'd spoken motioned to two others and they disappeared behind the back of the second vehicle. Moments later they reappeared, lugging a big holdall which they dumped onto the floor right by Denis.

'Like I said, she's not with us. Not any more.'

A snide grin accompanied the grim remark.

'Fuck this,' Titus said. 'We'll bury them all, Lea, if that's what you want?'

And the knot of pain in her stomach pushed her further and further to that outcome. She tried to keep calm, collected on the outside. But inside...

'Honestly, she was already dead before you even had Al Aswad,' the man shouted. 'There's nothing that could be done. So let's just finish the swap.'

'Lea?' Titus prompted.

'Show me,' she shouted over. 'Show me it's really her.'

One of the men who'd brought out the holdall kneeled and unzipped the top. He reached in and pulled an object several inches out...

Lea held the queasiness inside, still showed no outer reaction at all as she stared at the ghastly death face of her colleague, the head suspended beneath her long, curly black hair. Even though the man had only pulled the head out to mouth level, the movement in the bag and the way the man had drawn her head up showed that it was at least still attached, but it really was the tiniest of dignities for the dead woman.

The man stuffed the head back down and zipped the bag up again.

'Lea, what do you want to do?' Titus asked her.

'I want my people back,' she said to him.

'We'll send the woman and girl first!' Titus shouted over and the next moment Lea heard the moans behind them and Al Aswad writhed as his wife and daughter hobbled past into the open. They carried on a few yards before two men from the other side rushed forward and took them and guided them on and into one of the Jeeps.

'Back up now,' Lea shouted. 'All of you. Leave my friends there in the sand. We'll come forward with Al Aswad.'

Slowly, the men all retreated to the vehicles, although the leader hung by his open door rather than getting in. Fine by Lea. She, Butler and Titus all moved forward. Denis moaned and mumbled, becoming more animated as they neared but Lea's main focus was on the Jeeps, and making sure there was no attack coming from there.

No. There wasn't.

'We good?' Titus asked Lea when she was right in front of the holdall.

'No,' she said. 'Not even close. But let him go.'

So Titus did. He kicked Al Aswad forward and the guy stumbled and fell flat on his face before struggling to get back up with his hands tied behind him. Two of the men reemerged from the Jeep. Titus and Butler had their M4s trained on their targets, fingers ready on the triggers.

'Up to you, Lea,' Butler said. 'Whatever you want.'

The men were right there. Not even four yards from her. They reached down to pull Al Aswad up from the dirt. Her eyes met one of them. Her fingers found the grip of the gun once more.

'Lea?' Titus said.

She didn't respond, although she did pull the gun out, the barrel pointed to the floor.

The two men bundled Al Aswad into the Jeep with his wife and daughter. The leader remained hanging by his door.

'This is the last chance we'll get,' Titus said to her.

The man went to move back into the Jeep. Lea lifted the gun. In unison Titus and Butler readied themselves too. The man froze.

Her finger covered on the trigger. Brushed it. Pushed it ever so slightly...

'No,' she said. She lowered her weapon and Titus and Butler did too. The leader smiled at her before he finally stepped into the Jeep.

Moments later both vehicles had swung around and were heading away into darkness.

'You ask me?' Butler said. 'You made the right call.'

She wasn't so sure. She'd really wanted to kill every one of them. Only two things had stopped her. Firstly, knowing that any more blood spilled would only escalate an already bad situation. Secondly, she didn't even know for sure the men who'd come here were the same people who'd killed Naomi.

'You OK?' she said to Denis. He nodded but continued to moan and Titus moved over to untie him and remove the gag. Lea reached down to the holdall and pulled the zip back again. Two glassy eyes stared up at her. The knot in her stomach grew.

'Lea, for fuck's sake, it's a trap!' Denis screamed.

And even if she was still processing the warning, she'd seen enough inside the bag, and was already moving, dashing away before Butler barrelled into her, taking her off her feet and more or less tossing her forward. Titus had scooped Denis up from the ground too and as the explosive detonated all four of them were already midair in their attempt to get as far away as fast as they could...

The shock wave slammed into Lea and flung her further forward, and she banged and rolled across the hard sand before coming to an ungainly stop. As she lay there dazed, fragments plopped down from the sky and onto her and the ground around her.

Plop. Plop. Plop.

She winced with each strike. Pulled herself onto her side.

'Everyone OK?' Titus shouted out.

He got a yes from Denis. From Butler too.

Not from Lea.

Plop. Plop. Plop.

A piece landed right on her head and wedged in her tussled hair. She reached up and pulled the object off and stared at the charred morsel.

Charred morsel? Burned flesh. Naomi's pulverised, burned flesh.

Hands shaking, Lea tossed it away before Titus grabbed her under the arm to lift her up.

'You OK?' he asked her again.

'Yes,' she said. 'I'm fine.' Although the truth was, she abso-fucking-lutely wasn't.

12

LONDON

Butler and Titus remained somewhere on the African continent, their job done, money in their accounts. Not quite so simple for Lea and Denis to move on. Lea didn't *want* to move on. A colleague of theirs had been brutally, savagely killed. Lea wouldn't forget, and she wouldn't let it lie. Still, even if the mission – official or otherwise – felt far from over, both had left Cairo immediately after the exchange and they were back in continental Europe by the following morning, with little chance to properly think about – let alone discuss – what the actual hell had happened, both before, during and after Denis's and Naomi's time at the Syrian embassy.

All of that came in due course over a gruelling three-day debrief in London. Most of it was one on one – Denis with the hierarchy, Lea with the hierarchy – but the two field agents had still found time here and there to fill each other in before the final conclusive meeting was scheduled for 7.30 a.m. on a drab Friday morning.

Lea had barely slept. She hadn't properly since that first night after Cairo when she'd slept like a log, barely stirring, but she realised now that was due to mental exhaustion more than anything. Since then... impossible to rest, given everything that tumbled around in her head.

She'd spoken to Callum plenty during the last few days too, his voice a constant source of comfort, even if she hated the lies that rolled off her tongue. At the simplest level he thought she was still overseas. He had no clue what was really happening in her world, nor would he.

She hated the lies, but if anything, she needed that part of her life more than ever now. The life that didn't have violence and backstabbing and constant danger around every murky corner.

She'd be back with him soon enough, even if only for a little while.

'Good morning,' Lea said as she walked into the meeting room. Three others were already in there: Denis, Goldman, and the plump silver-haired Victor Reynolds. Technically Goldman and Reynolds were the same level, but he was more senior and probably a step up the ladder, through longevity as much as anything else. His official title these days was deputy chair of counterespionage, though Lea had always thought that a strange and contradictory title for anyone in MI6 to hold.

'Take a seat,' Reynolds said, indicating the chair opposite him and Goldman, and next to Denis. A proper little interview set-up as though the two agents were about to be grilled.

Lea smiled at Denis as she took her seat. The swelling in his face had gone down some over the last couple of days but she knew other injuries were a long way off healing.

Some would *never* heal.

From what she now knew, both he and Naomi had been forcibly interrogated. Beatings to start with. But things had turned ugly the second day of their captivity in the Syrian embassy when fingernails were torn off, digits broken. Finally toes removed. Denis had lost two on his right foot. Seven of Naomi's had been cleaved off before they shot her in the gut and let her bleed out an agonising death, Denis tied up by her side as he watched her fading, knowing he'd be dead too, or at the very least more pieces of him removed, if he didn't start talking.

Brutal. Sickening. Haunting.

And that was just for Lea, having to hear it all second-hand. Denis had lived it and would have to continue to live with it.

'We don't need to go through the gruesome details again,' Reynolds said. 'I'm sure you've had enough of that by now. So let's just make sure we all know exactly where we stand and then we can bring this dark matter to a close and move on.'

'Move on?' Lea said. 'You think—'

'Lea, I think you know what he means,' Goldman interjected.

Lea didn't answer that though everyone in the room knew she wanted blood.

But that would have to wait.

'The Syrians have confirmed that the people responsible for this atrocity were Iranian nationals who held special diplomatic privileges with the Syrians,' Reynolds said. 'They are believed to have links to the Revolutionary Guard. We've been assured they had no official authority from the Syrians to carry out this barbaric attack on their soil.'

'So the Syrians are going to hand over those responsible?' Lea asked.

'No,' Reynolds said. 'We haven't been able to convince them of that. But they have confirmed that the people in question have all had Syrian diplomatic status revoked, and Egypt will make sure they're sent back where they came from.'

'And their identities?' Lea asked.

Goldman and Reynolds glanced at each other.

'We still don't know,' Goldman said. 'I'll continue to use channels we have to try and find out.'

'But most likely this is linked to Jalali, right?' Lea said.

Kind of stating the obvious there, given Denis and Naomi were chasing that lead – that had started back in Toulouse – in Cairo in the first place. Except from what he'd said, they'd uncovered no concrete evidence of Jalali or the other Iranians on their list from Toulouse actually being in Cairo at any recent point before he and Naomi were captured.

'So what's the next move?' Lea asked.

'There is no move,' Reynolds said.

Denis shifted in his seat but said nothing.

'This has been discussed at the highest level,' Goldman said, 'and we need to let things cool before either of you even considers going back out chasing the tails of these people again. I don't deny that all of the parties you previously identified remain persons of interest, but for now—'

'Do you have anyone else looking into this?' Denis asked.

'Right now?' Goldman said. 'No. As of now there is no official ongoing investigation into these parties, because so far, we have no concrete evidence of wrongdoing. So until that evidence comes into play—'

'Are you fucking serious?' Lea blurted.

'Deadly,' Goldman said.

'You can't find the evidence if you're not looking for it.'

'And you two are definitely not looking for it,' Goldman said. 'Not until we say otherwise. Got it?'

'Got it,' Denis said.

'I guess,' Lea said.

'You two should recuperate on home soil. A few days, at least.'

Denis scoffed.

'If you need longer, you can have longer,' Goldman added, directing the comment at him. 'But I didn't think you'd want it.'

'That's fine,' Denis said. 'I don't need it.'

He looked over at Lea, and she couldn't be sure if that was a sly dig at her or not. Six months she'd taken after nearly being killed. He'd been tortured and disfigured and witnessed a brutal murder of a colleague and apparently remained raring to go.

'Are we done here?' Denis asked.

'We're done,' Reynolds confirmed.

Not long after, and Lea and Denis were outside on the busy street by the river, soggy tourists in raincoats and ponchos roaming, men and women in suits heading to and from offices with big umbrellas to shield from the thrumming rain. Like the one Lea held up for both her and Denis, him moving gingerly – ponderously, too – with his still-healing debilitations, their shoulders brushing every few steps as she tried to stay close enough to keep him dry.

'Looking forward to getting back to your man?' he asked.

'I've missed him.'

Denis humphed.

'What?' she prompted.

'*I* miss you,' he said. 'We were a team.'

'We still are.'

'Then where were you when I needed you?'

Lea didn't answer – too gobsmacked really to think of anything to say.

He sighed and shook his head. 'I'm sorry, it's just...'

He hung his head. Lea put her hand on his shoulder as though her touch would bring comfort, make his harrowing experience disappear or something.

'Naomi...' he started but didn't finish.

'We'll get justice for her,' Lea said. 'I don't care what Goldman said. No official investigation? Then I'll do it myself, in my own time. And you'll help me, right?'

He looked unsure.

'What?' she said.

'It was her fault.'

'Naomi?'

'She let her guard down. I think she gave us away and—'

'That's not what you told—'

'Of course I'm not going to bad mouth her to the bosses. She lost her life. I nearly lost mine. But she caused it, Lea. You ask me, she wasn't up to it. *You* should have been there.'

'I'm... sorry.'

'I wish it was just like it used to be. You know?'

She didn't seek clarity, but yeah, she thought she knew what he meant. They'd worked so closely, side by side, for the best part of six years, assignment after assignment, from that very first time in Singapore where they'd spent four months living – as far as the outside world could see – as a married couple. The mission then had been to infiltrate a banking conglomerate where two English nationals were suspected of passing confidential data to Chinese spies. As far as Lea and Denis, and MI6 were concerned, the mission, which had eventually seen the two Englishmen returned home and put on trial and sentenced to life imprisonment, had been an all-out success. And Lea and Denis had formed a bond in those months that had seen them through countless other missions, often much more deadly, taxing in body and mind and soul than that first escapade.

But the bond had always been on a professional level, nothing more, even if Lea had long suspected Denis *wanted* more.

'Now you go swanning back to Bristol again, a few days screwing and sleeping in every morning,' Denis added, 'while I'm left to pull the pieces of my life back together.'

She tried not to let her rising anger show at his words, his tone.

'Don't forget they tried to kill me too,' she said.

'Yeah. I know. And what did you do? You ran away to try and forget about it, try and pretend it never happened. Maybe... that's what I should do too.'

'What are you saying?'

'I'm saying... I don't ever want to be in that position again. And you can already see Reynolds and Goldman don't care about us getting revenge. Justice. Whatever you want to call it.'

'I don't think they said that exactly—'

'So you go take your time off to Netflix and chill or whatever. Maybe I'll do the same. Maybe we should both just fucking quit and be done with it before one of us gets hurt. Again.'

He brushed past her and stormed off.

* * *

The train journey west to Bristol was anything but calm, peaceful, the carriages bustling and busy and Lea's mind in overdrive. She'd called ahead to check on Callum, but it was 2 p.m. on a Friday and he'd already finished work and was drinking beers with a couple of the guys from the site. Not a problem. Even though she missed him like crazy and couldn't wait for the moment that he wrapped his arms around her and lifted her off her feet and helped her forget all about recent events, if only for a few moments, she needed a bit more time to sort her head out before she went 'home'. And there were two other people not far away who she really needed to go see. It'd been way too long.

Her parents lived in a little bungalow in a village about ten miles outside the city. Nothing much out there really except fields and forests. As a youngster she'd hated it. Hated how everything felt so disconnected and there was literally nothing fun for a teenager to do other than hang around in the woods and smoke and drink.

Back then she couldn't wait to get away from this place. Now she saw the appeal in all sorts of different ways, even if she was sure she'd still be bored senseless after a few weeks or months.

But right now, she craved the solitude and the comfort.

A quick glance over her shoulder as she walked up the path to the door. No one else around on the street. She rang the bell and waited. Her mum opened the door and not even a second later had grabbed her daughter and pulled her in for a big hug, her head fitting right under Lea's chin. She was only sixty-five but she seemed to shrink more every time Lea came.

'Claire!' her mother beamed, standing back to admire her. 'Fred, it's Claire!'

Inside, Lea kind of winced at the name, her real name, but the name of a different person, really.

Her dad appeared in the hall. Damn, he looked so old and frail these days. Sixty-eight, but with his recent health problems – from a heart attack to a mini stroke to a hip replacement to a cancer scare – he looked older. Moved as though he was older.

'So good to see you!' he said, hugging Lea even more tightly than her mum had. But then he looked over her shoulder as though checking if anyone else was there.

And she figured why. At least, she *thought* she knew why. He wanted to know if she had a man yet. A future husband. A future father to his grand-kids. Someone to look after her – or was it her as the carer, the housewife? – because she couldn't possibly be happy, complete, without a man. At least in his outdated way of thinking. But that was fine. It's who he was.

The strange thing this time was that she *did* now have someone. She just wouldn't ever be able to bring him here or even tell her parents about him.

The only time they'd ever meet was if she was dead.

That sad thought gripping her, she stepped inside.

* * *

There was a lot of talking over dinner. Lea's parents caught her up on all the usual village gossip, health issues, the ins and outs of their friendships.

Lea also talked a lot about her 'job' with BTS, her recent travels, tried to use truth as much as possible. And felt the weight of those truths as she spoke. Noted the concerned look on her parents' faces growing.

'Did something bad happen?' her mum asked, putting her hand over her daughter's on the tabletop.

'Yeah. A colleague of mine, Naomi. She's the same age as me. She... she died.'

Her mum cupped her mouth in shock. Her dad solemnly shook his head.

'That's awful,' her mum said. 'What happened?'

'An accident. Overseas.'

'You were there?'

'In... Cairo, yes, but I wasn't there when it actually happened.'

'You poor thing.'

'I told you before about that job,' her dad said. 'All that travelling to those places. Only a matter of time before something bad happened. If you wouldn't go there on holiday, you shouldn't want to go there for work.'

Lea didn't say anything to that. Just another of his strongly held views, which had so many holes in it, really – not least the fact the two of them travelled to Cairo to see the pyramids many years ago. But, in a way, she brought this spotlight on herself by originally telling them about her globetrotting 'consultancy' job.

Although she hadn't told them a thing about what had happened in Toulouse, about her nearly dying there. Instead, she'd just not seen them for a while after that escapade.

She hated herself for that.

'Are you staying the night?' her mum asked as she started to clear away the plates.

'Is that OK? I need to get away in the morning, but—'

'We'd love to have you.'

'I'll go make up the spare room,' her dad said before heading off.

* * *

By 8 p.m. they'd all settled in the living room, her dad in the armchair, Lea and her mum on the sofa, Lea nestled into her mum's side.

'Fred, for Pete's sake you're asleep already!' her mum shouted at him, tossing a folded chocolate wrapper in his direction which bounced off his nose. His eyes sprang open and he sniffed and murmured but moments later was dozing, mouth wide open again. 'Every blood night!'

'Aw, leave him, Mum. He's happy.'

No response, but Lea sensed something and shuffled up in her seat a little.

'What?'

'It's nothing.'

'No, it is.'

'We *are* happy,' her mum said, looking seriously pensive. 'You know we are. But... he doesn't smile the same when you're not around.' Like a punch to the gut. Lea couldn't find the words to respond. 'He misses you so much. We both do.'

'I know. I miss you both too.'

She said nothing more, only wondered, as she often did, if they'd ever forgive her if they found out the truth.

* * *

Lea left her parents' home after breakfast, but not without a lot of gentle persuasion from them both for her to stay longer, and after that had failed, to commit to when she'd next see them.

Honestly, despite the sadness of saying goodbye, she felt much better for having seen them, for having talked through some of the issues on her mind, particularly Naomi. It'd mean, in theory at least, that she felt more prepared for reuniting with Callum.

She headed straight for his apartment. No point in going back to her place. She'd last had a text from him at eleven last night and could tell he was pretty wasted then by how gushing he was, and how poor his spelling was – bad even for him. And strangely, as she stood at the door to which she had a key, she paused a moment, thinking about what kind of state he'd be in this morning.

But then another much more disturbing thought struck her.

Was he alone inside?

Was he home at all or had he ended up someplace else?

Even though she had the key in her hand, she initially knocked on the door, as though to give him a get-out if he really was in bed with someone else, because quite frankly, if he was, she didn't want to see it.

No answer.

So she put those morose thoughts aside and slipped the key in the lock and opened up and paused again in the doorway. No sounds coming from inside.

But he should be home?

Now more ominous images spiralled in her mind...

She moved along the hall quiet as could be, past the open bedroom door. The bedsheets were ruffled but no one was in there.

'Babe!' she shouted, having had enough of the intrusive thoughts. 'You home?'

No answer, and so her worry only grew as she neared the living room.

But then... sound behind her. Creeping footsteps.

This was always the risk. The risk of the enemies from her job coming to sabotage her life in the cruellest possible way. As she spun around it was an image of her parents – as vulnerable as they were – that haunted her the most.

She caught sight of the looming figure and swung out her arm to bat away the outstretched hand. Still spinning she swiped the front leg of the person – a man – and thrust out her hands to topple him and only at that point focused on his face...

'Lea!' Callum shouted in shock as her hands shoved into his chest. Off balance with his foot uprooted, he went tumbling back, thumping into the sideboard.

The object he'd had pushed out towards her flew from his grip and bobbled along the floor.

'What the hell!' he shouted.

'Babe, I'm so sorry!' She rushed over to him. 'You surprised me. I didn't...' She couldn't finish the thought and reached out and initially it looked like he was about to swat her away, but then his face went from anger to surprise to… something else.

Her eyes drifted along the floor to the fallen object. Not a gun or a knife or any other kind of weapon as she'd at first feared as she spun around in attack mode.

A little black box.

He shuffled across and scooped it up and even as she rose up, gobsmacked, he stayed down.

'Not quite… how I'd planned it,' he said.

She said nothing. Was actually speechless for both good and bad.

'I've been sat looking out the window for hours. I had no idea what time you'd be back. I would have sat there all day like a mug.' He laughed nervously. She still couldn't find any words.

'You have no idea how much I missed you,' he said, playing with the box in his hand. 'And Lea… every time you're not here, it makes me realise just how much I *need* you to be part of my life.' He fumbled with the box now, making a meal of opening it up. 'Shit. I had so much good stuff to say. I think… I think maybe you knocked it all out of my head.' He scratched his forehead, looking so lost and vulnerable. So bloody sweet.

'Lea, will you marry me?'

And even though she knew the difficulties, the danger, the pretty much impossibility of what that meant, she didn't even hesitate before giving her answer. 'Yes! Yes, I'll marry you!'

13

GLOUCESTERSHIRE

Present day

Aaron and Callum sat in the car, outside the Simmonds's home, staring at the picture on Callum's phone.

'I don't get it,' Aaron said, looking really confused. 'It's just a sticker. Just the name and address of an art shop in Bristol.'

'No,' Callum said. 'It's not. It's the name. Adele.'

'*For you, Adele*,' Aaron said, reading the pencilled message written across one corner of the white sticker. 'She's probably the shop assistant or something?'

'Then call the number and check.'

Aaron didn't. Probably too scared of being proven wrong by his dumb brother.

'What are you suggesting it *actually* means then?' he said.

'It's a message from Lea. To me.'

'You've lost me. Just... try and explain.'

'She has a tattoo. It's these Chinese characters. They mean hope and light. The same characters were on that painting. Her dad said she brought that painting home from an overseas trip years ago.'

'She left you this message years ago because...?'

'No. A few weeks ago she took the painting away for it to be reframed. *That's* when I think this sticker was put there. The timing, the message...'

'But *how* is that a message to you?'

Callum briefly replayed the memories before answering. One from many years ago; one a bit more recent.

'You know I always struggled at school,' he started, not really sure how best to explain. Aaron sniffed as some sort of response. 'I never talked to you much about this kind of stuff. It was just too... belittling. But shit happened to me pretty much every single day. I just had to learn to deal with it. Expect it. There was this one time though... I was only eleven or twelve, first year of secondary school. We'd had this big assignment in English, and our teacher had taken our folders away to mark everything... Bearing in mind I was in the frigging bottom set, with all the other dumbarses, most of whom weren't actually stupid but just lazy, or troublemakers, or lazy troublemakers—'

'OK, OK, I get the picture.'

He didn't really. Aaron had been in the most advanced classes for everything. He had no idea what anything else was like.

'Anyway, it was a simple task as we walked in. Grab your folder from the pile on the teacher's desk and take it back to your seat. I don't even know why I did it because even if I struggled like mad to read properly, I knew what *my* name looked like, even if it doesn't look like it should to me. If that makes sense. But I picked up Adele's folder instead. The letters... To me they actually looked like how my name sounds. The l is... kinda the same, and the c, backwards, kind of looks like a d, and an a to me, upside down is kind of like an e, and...' He paused and looked across at his brother who seemed dumbfounded. After all this time he still just didn't understand, not at all.

No, he understood that there was problem, but he didn't understand how the problem could create such an issue over such a seemingly simple task. But that was Callum's life. Those simple tasks – recognising his own name, reading a simple phrase – were things that other people just did, without any thought at all. For Callum it was a constant battle.

And in the moment he didn't properly think things through... That's when shit went wrong. Like picking up a girl's folder rather than his own.

Or getting a construction crew to bolt steels on to a brick frame in the incorrect configuration with the wrong screws. Very different mistakes with different consequences but it all came from the same place.

'So you picked up someone else's folder?' Aaron said, quite blasé. 'That's it?'

'Well, yeah... but... you can't imagine the shit I had to deal with, the heckling, the name-calling, the bullying, all of the time. Not just because of this but every other thing too. This was before I was big enough to fend off a pack of rabid dogs.'

And once he was big, bulky, not only did the bullies back off, but – for that and perhaps other reasons too – he found a kind of acceptance within Aaron's circle of friends. But by that point he was sixteen and the mental damage of those earlier years was done.

'I'm sorry,' Aaron said. 'I'm sorry that I never... knew about stuff like that. That I never helped you with any of that. You should have told me.'

Callum had often thought the same thing. Perhaps he should have told his brother. But would it have really made a difference? Or would it only have added extra ammo into Aaron's arsenal, putting him even further ahead of his struggling sibling?

'Anyway. I told Lea about this stuff. I told her everything. And...' He closed his eyes, pictured her face. Found himself smiling about the memory. 'She took the piss out of me. Like, rolling on the floor laughing at me. She called me Adele non-stop for about two months. But she did it in a way that... made me feel better about it all. I don't even know how to explain that.'

'I still don't understand what you think this means, though. Why would she write that for you?'

'Let's go and find out.'

* * *

The shop was one of several in a row of terraces on an early 1900s high street on the outskirts of the city proper. Probably once a thriving area, the buildings looked down at heel now, with the establishments in the still-open units ranging from two barbers to a charity clothes shop to a grotty-looking e-vaping shop.

A small car park sat in front of a slightly larger Spar convenience store and Aaron pulled up there, both of them staring out of the window to the Bristol Art and Supply Co.

'So what now?'

'This isn't it,' Callum said.

'What isn't?'

'This isn't what she meant.'

He took out his phone and scanned the picture again.

'Wait a second...' He pulled the phone right up to his face, then pushed it over to his brother.

'What's the street number?' he asked.

Aaron looked at him curiously. 'You can't even read the numbers?'

Callum ground his teeth, although he was sure Aaron hadn't meant to insult him.

'Sorry,' Aaron said. 'I meant... like, I didn't even know if you had the same issue with numbers as with letters and words.'

His brother of over thirty years? He really should have known.

'It depends,' Callum said. 'Often numbers are easier than letters. There are only ten digits, and they're mostly unique except maybe six and nine and eight and zero. But my biggest issue is correctly identifying the order. The bigger the number, the harder it gets.'

Probably more explanation than was needed in this case, but Aaron had asked.

'When I plugged it into the satnav, I read out the name of the shop to the voice prompt. Not the address,' Callum added.

'It says 480,' Aaron said, staring at the picture on the phone screen.

'Yeah. I thought so too,' Callum responded and they both looked out to the art shop again and the plaque on the wall by the door with the three digits.

'400,' Aaron said. 'The shop is at 400, not 480.'

'On the sticker it's written over. She turned the zero into an eight.'

'So what's at 480?'

Both of them turned the other way, following the same thought process at the same time. A rare brotherly connection?

'Must be the other side of the crossroads,' Callum said.

Aaron was already releasing the handbrake as he'd said it. They headed across the lights and he pulled into the car park of the bank.

'480,' he said, nodding to the sign. 'You really think she planned this for you?'

'I'll soon find out. Wait here. Call me if you see anything suspicious.'

Callum went to get out but then paused. Thought. Opened the picture again. 'Just read out those numbers for me one more time?'

By which he meant the pencilled numbers right underneath the sticker. They looked like maybe they were the order number from the art store or something. Callum hoped it was something else altogether. Fourteen digits.

'Got it,' he said after Aaron had finished.

He couldn't read for shit, but his memory was damn good.

He headed out and into the bank. Not a national chain – in fact, he'd never heard of South-West First Bank. The stone building had an old-world appearance to it, with a lofty although cool-feeling interior, marble – or at least marble-effect – floor and gold embellishments here and there. A smartly dressed attendant smiled at Callum as he entered.

'Good morning, sir,' he said. 'Anything I can help you with?'

'Just come for my, erm... safe-deposit box?' Callum answered, trying his best to sound assured and calm. There was only a narrow choice of options for why Lea would send him here. A secret account with money in it? Possibly, but what would be the point and why the little clues from Lea leading to it? Money wasn't going to help him. Much more likely that she was taking him to information of some sort. Information would much more likely be in physical form, one way or another. So safe-deposit box was his guess.

'Certainly, sir,' the man said. 'If you go to my colleague over there, she'll assist you.'

He pointed towards a suited woman behind a desk in the far corner. Callum headed over there, looking over his shoulder as he went, making sure the guy hadn't alerted anyone or anything like that.

The woman looked up at him and smiled just before he reached her desk.

'Good morning. Can I help you?' she asked.

'Just come to access my box.'

'Certainly. What's the account number?'

He'd never had a safe-deposit box before, but he'd seen in films where, for privacy reasons he guessed, people only needed a number to access them, no name on the account or a need to show ID or anything like that. He wasn't sure if every bank everywhere dealt with their boxes in that manner, but he hoped that this one did. For obvious reasons.

He repeated the first eight numbers from the sequence that Aaron had told him. The woman typed into her computer but then frowned.

'Just give me that number once again, please?'

He repeated the sequence. She typed again. 'Sorry, sir, I don't have a record with that account number.'

'Oh, I... er,' he looked over his shoulder again, felt the beads of sweat forming on his neck and brow. Damn, he couldn't even pull off this simple task without flaking. He took out his phone. Opened the picture once more. He was certain the last six digits were a passcode because it was the same six digits he and Lea used for so many other things. The date he proposed to her. Except with the day as sixteen rather than nineteen because that was the dumb mistake he'd made the first time he'd set that as the number on his phone lock screen. So the first eight digits, he'd assumed, would be the account number.

He replayed the sequence Aaron had told him in his head. No, that wasn't what he saw at all.

And that was the point.

Lea had written this for *him*, not for Aaron or anyone else. She knew *exactly* the mistakes he'd make.

He read out the numbers again.

This time the woman smiled before getting up from her seat. 'This way, sir.'

He followed her into a room behind where two walls were taken up with row upon row of metallic boxes built into the walls.

'If you'd like to input your code,' she said, indicating one of boxes that was listed as 846D. At least, that's what he saw.

He typed the six digits into the panel on the box and a green light blinked. The woman smiled again and pulled a key up from the retractable chain on her side. She pushed a round-ended key into the lock on the door, twisted, and the green light blinked again and this time Callum heard a lock release too.

'The door'll be locked to outsiders,' she said, 'so you'll get privacy while you go through your things.' She turned and headed out.

He waited a moment, listening. For what, he didn't really know.

Then he grasped the box's door and pulled it open...

Empty.

Nothing at all.

'What the hell?' he said.

Didn't get the chance to decide on an answer before his phone buzzed in his pocket.

Aaron.

'Shit.'

He pushed the door closed and double checked it was locked, though he wasn't really sure why, before he rushed to the door. He flung it open. The woman pretty much jumped up from her seat.

'You're done? Everything's OK?'

He looked out across the foyer. All quiet... Normal.

'Done, thank you,' he said, trying to appear calm. He strode across the tiles, pushed open the doors to the outside, his phone buzzing in his pocket the whole way. He scanned the car park. Still didn't see anything untoward. No sirens, flashing lights, anything like that.

He caught sight of Aaron through the car window, phone pressed to his ear.

The brothers locked eyes. Callum started towards him, but Aaron ever so slightly shook his head.

Callum pulled the phone from his pocket. Answered the call.

Neither brother spoke. Callum could hear Aaron's deep breaths.

'Run,' he said. Almost a whisper.

Except before Callum could, he jolted when a gun barrel came into view from an unseen person in the back seat, shielded from view by the privacy glass. The barrel was pushed into Aaron's neck.

'Do anything stupid and your brother's dead,' came a voice from behind him. A female voice. One he recognised.

Jenn Hinch.

Before he'd moved a muscle, the barrel of a gun – at least that's what he imagined the object to be – was pressed into the small of his back. 'Now get in the car.'

14

Callum walked slowly, steadily, towards his brother's car. Aaron stared at him through the glass the whole way, his eyes wide in panic. The shaded glass in the back meant Callum couldn't see who held the gun, but he assumed Warren Brandt was back there – Hinch's chum who'd been in his house the day before. The police had said both of them had got away.

But how had they tracked Callum here?

They reached the passenger side of the car.

'Get in,' Hinch said before the pressure on Callum's back released.

Could he make a move?

The fact his hand trembled as he reached forward for the handle told him no. A fist fight was one thing, but fighting empty-handed against an armed and likely damn well-trained assailant? He was so far out of his depth.

But then the alternative of sitting inside the car, with both brothers at the mercy of Hinch and Brandt, didn't seem so great either. He really didn't see how that was going to end well.

Yet he still opened the door and took the seat and a moment later Hinch was in the back behind him.

Callum first glanced that way – confirming it was Brandt back there – then to his brother.

'You OK?'

'Fuck no,' Aaron said with something close to a chuckle, sounding way cockier than he looked.

'We don't want to hurt you,' Hinch said.

'Then how about you stop pointing guns at us,' Aaron snapped back.

A momentary standoff but then both backseat riders lowered their guns, holding them on their laps. Not quite out of sight, out of mind, but a bit better than before at least.

'But if you do anything stupid,' Brandt said, 'I'll put the first few bullets somewhere I know it'll hurt like hell without killing you. Make sure you get the point.'

'We get the point. What do you want?' Callum asked.

'Hang on!' Aaron said. *Way* cockier than he should be. He turned around in his seat, finding a fight Callum didn't realise his brother had. 'Would someone mind telling me what the fuck is going on? Who the hell are you two?'

Fair questions from Aaron's point of view. Although if his brother was in such a feisty mood, it did make Callum wonder how Brandt had got inside and behind Aaron in this first place. Perhaps the fight was only coming on now he had Callum next to him.

'Your brother can answer that one for you,' Hinch said, a little slyly, really.

Aaron set his glare on his brother.

'These are the two I told you about,' Callum said. 'They were at my house yesterday. Shot at the police when they arrived. They claimed to know Lea.'

'Claimed?' Hinch said. 'We didn't just know Lea, we worked with her. We're her friends.'

'Then why the hell are you holding us at gunpoint?' Aaron asked.

'One, to get you to listen,' Brandt said. 'Two, because last time we tried this with Callum the police showed up and started a firefight with us that got another of our friends killed.'

Silence. Callum replayed those moments. Had the police started the shooting? He hadn't thought so, but really couldn't be sure now, it'd all happened so fast, so unexpectedly.

'Tell us what you're doing here,' Hinch said.

'Actually, no,' Brandt interrupted. 'Tell us how you got away from the police yesterday. We saw you on the news last night, so we can only assume they didn't just let you go and that them naming you is to heap the pressure on.'

Callum thought about both demands before answering. 'I wasn't under arrest,' he said. 'I wasn't locked up or anything like that. So it's not like I escaped a maximum-security cell, is it? I took an opportunity and... left.'

'Seems like they probably didn't want you to leave, though, if you ask me.'

He said nothing to that.

'And what did they say about us?' Hinch asked. 'About what happened at your house?'

'Good question,' Callum said. 'Because interestingly, what didn't make the national news last night was that the police shot dead a man right outside my house after a gunfight with you two. No mention of you at all, as far as I know. Although I got the distinct impression they know who you are.'

Hinch and Brandt shared a look. 'Who'd you talk to?' Brandt asked.

'The detective who came to my door was called DCI Jasper. And I met a man who told me he worked for MI6. Andrew White.'

Another glance at each other.

'You know him?' Callum asked.

'What did you tell him about us?'

'I don't have anything to tell. But the impression was that I think he knows a lot about you both anyway. Which perhaps explains why he didn't need to ask me anything about you. And maybe even why your names aren't plastered over the news.'

A snort from Brandt.

'You shouldn't trust him,' Hinch said. 'Nor the police, given they're getting their orders from him.'

'But we should trust you two?' Aaron asked, sounding rightfully dubious.

Again no answer.

'You know Andrew White?' Callum asked again.

'We know who you're speaking about,' Hinch said. 'And yes, he works for MI6, but no, he's not on your side. Or our side.'

'But you two are MI6 too?'

'No, we're not,' Hinch said.

'But you said—'

'That we knew Lea. Worked with her. We never told you we worked for MI6.'

'Then who?'

'We can tell you everything you need to know about that later,' Hinch said. 'Right now, we need to know why you came here and what you found.'

Neither Callum nor Aaron said a word.

Brandt thumped the back of Aaron's seat.

'Seriously, we don't have time for crap. We know you're looking for something, Callum. You ran from the police, headed straight to your brother's house. Not to lay low, but to get some assistance because before long you were travelling across the country together. Next thing you're at Lea's parents' place. Then here. Explain that.'

'We were watching your brother's house,' Hinch said, as if the clarity was needed. 'When we saw the news breaking, we assumed it meant you'd got away from SO15. Assumed you might turn up in Berkshire given the proximity.'

Did that simple explanation make sense? Kind of, but it also made Callum feel really stupid if they'd figured out his moves so easily.

And if *they* had, why hadn't the police and White?

'And what... you've followed us all that time without us spotting you?' Aaron asked.

'We're good at this shit,' Brandt said. 'You two aren't. So why here?'

Callum pondered the question. He really didn't trust these two, no more but perhaps no less than Andrew White, but he also knew he couldn't bullshit this one away, given they'd followed his every move and given they still had the upper hand here.

It didn't mean he had to tell them *everything* though.

'Lea has a safe-deposit box here.'

'How'd you know that?'

'She was my wife.'

'So she told you to come here?' Hinch.

'She's dead. How could she tell me anything?'

'Not really what I meant.'

'What about the parents?' Brandt said. 'They have anything to do with this?'

'I don't really know what you're asking. Like me, her parents had absolutely no idea who Lea really was.'

'Then why'd you go there?' Brandt asked.

'Because she asked me to. If anything ever happened to her she wanted me to go see them.'

'So you *did* know—'

'I knew absolutely nothing!' Callum shouted. 'Nothing at all about Claire Simmonds. Only that Lea wanted me to go see her parents – Claire's parents – if something ever happened to her.'

Both Hinch and Brandt glared at him, obviously not believing his words, and he didn't know how else to persuade them. Given everything else that was transpiring, it really did sound like bullshit.

'They know nothing,' Callum said. 'They're not involved in anything. And we came here... I thought, maybe... maybe she'd left something here. A clue to what was going on. Who killed her and why. Or the information that everyone's telling me is now missing.'

'A message from the grave,' Brandt said, tapping his head. 'Makes sense.'

'No. Not from the grave, idiot. I think she knew she was in trouble before she was killed. And I thought maybe there was evidence of why here.'

'And what made you think that?' Hinch said. 'If she never told you anything.'

They really weren't buying into any of what he was saying, even if it was mostly true.

'Because for the past twenty-four hours I've had you two and the police and MI6 chasing me across the damn country telling me she had *something* that you all need! Something that got her killed. It doesn't take a fucking genius to put those pieces together and think maybe if she *did* have that something that she hid it somewhere!'

'OK,' Hinch said. 'So now tell us what she had here.'

'Nothing,' Callum said. 'There was nothing at all.'

An uncertain glance from Aaron, as though even he didn't believe that.

'You sure about that?' Brandt asked.

'Yes.'

'OK, you, out of the car,' Hinch said to Callum before opening her door. He didn't move until she tapped on his window with the butt of her gun.

He slowly got out, no sudden moves, even though he really wanted to do *something*.

'Face the car.'

He did so and she quickly patted him down. He only had his phone and his wallet. She didn't seem interested in either and after a brief look through each was finished.

'I told you,' he said to her. 'There was nothing.'

'Then show me. Inside.'

Callum turned around to face her but otherwise didn't make a move away.

'We haven't got all day, arsehole. Move!'

'Be quick,' Brandt called out, tapping on the glass with his gun before Callum and Hinch made their way towards the bank's entrance.

She walked by his side now, no sign of her weapon, and she seemed pretty nonchalant, confident. The exact opposite of how Callum felt.

He headed through the revolving door first. The same man greeted him on the other side.

'Forgot something,' Callum said with a smile.

No particular reaction to that, although his gaze did linger on Hinch for a second or two longer than necessary.

Soon they were both in front of the woman's desk in the corner.

'Oh. You're back?' she said, no doubting her suspicion. 'You're...'

'She's with me,' Callum said. 'We just needed to get something else.'

'OK,' the woman said, and Callum knew the look beyond him was to her colleague at the front door. They didn't like the situation. Something Callum or Hinch had done had already tipped them off. Did they know Hinch?

But how would they?

Callum glanced to her. A clandestine operative? She stuck out like a sore thumb, all edgy attitude.

'Please give me the account number again,' the woman said.

Callum passed the test at the first attempt, and the woman took them into the back room and moments later the box was unlocked and he and Hinch were alone.

'See for yourself,' he said to her.

She pulled the door open and took out the tray and looked inside.

'It doesn't make any sense,' she said.

Callum said nothing.

'She wouldn't have this box with nothing in it,' Hinch added.

Callum still held his tongue.

'And you're telling me you didn't already come here, clear it out?'

'If I did, then why would I be back here today?' he said.

'Then someone else did.'

'You know who?' Callum said. 'Because I certainly don't. And I'm guessing the bank aren't going to tell us.'

'No, they won't,' Hinch said. She sounded and looked even edgier than before. 'Let's go.'

They moved for the door, exited out into the foyer.

'You're all done this time?' the woman asked.

'I'm certain of it,' Callum said, although something about the way she'd asked the question...

The man at the front door stared at them as they made their way over.

'Get to the car as quickly as you can,' Hinch whispered.

Something was wrong.

And as they stepped out into the open, Callum saw the police car pulling into the car park. No siren, no flashing lights, but he'd bet his life the bank had called them.

Why?

'Move!' Hinch shouted, prodding him in the back to get him going. Not with the gun, just her hand. They began walking down the steps at the bank's entrance.

Two officers got out. They spotted Hinch and Callum straight away. No doubt why they were there.

At least it was only two police officers, not an all-out armed response unit. Two regular, unarmed police officers.

'Hey,' one of them shouted over, but both Hinch and Callum ignored him and kept moving for the car.

'Turn the fucking engine on, idiot,' Hinch whispered, as though Aaron would sense the instruction.

He didn't. But he'd definitely seen the police, by the panicked look on his face.

The next moment he flung his door open and kind of flopped out onto the floor, staying low as he scuttled towards the police.

'They've got guns!' he yelled.

The passenger door burst open next. Callum saw the gun before anything else of Brandt.

He fired. Two booming gunshots which sent both the police officers and Aaron cowering towards the squad car. Callum spun and shoved Hinch as hard as he could. She stumbled and tripped and banged down the remaining three steps into a heap as Callum raced forward to Brandt.

He fired another two shots towards the hunkered police before he realised Callum was bearing down on him. He couldn't adjust his aim quickly enough as Callum launched his foot to the door. It swung wildly on its hinges and slammed into Brandt, squashing him against the frame. Enough to stop him shooting. Not enough to stop him fighting. Callum went for the gun, but Brandt's grip was too tight and when the weapon blasted again, harmlessly into the air, Callum let go and darted away, towards the road.

Shouting behind him. *Stop*. More than one voice shouting that or similar. Hinch. His brother. The police too, perhaps.

He ran for his life. Where to? Right into the road. A car horn blasted. Tyres screeched. He was nearly at the other side. Then what?

No idea. But Aaron was safely with the police. Wasn't he?

He certainly didn't want to be. Not again.

'No!'

Another shout from behind. Hinch.

Callum would have ignored it. Would have kept on running were it not for the ominous thud a moment later. More screeching tyres. Another thud. Another. Those last two were metal on metal. Not like the first strike. The first strike was definitely a person being hit.

Callum stopped. Turned. Expected the worst. Expected to see his brother in a heap on the road, even though he'd already convinced himself he was safe with the police.

No. It was Brandt. A van had smacked into him, tossed him several yards away. Two other cars had shunted one another as they tried – unsuccessfully – to stop becoming involved.

Hinch rushed to her colleague. Scooped him from the ground. Waved her gun at the police officers and bystanders to keep them at bay.

She whipped around to Callum, thunder on her face. He thought she'd shoot him there and then...

Instead, she dragged Brandt, barely able to stand, towards their car.

Callum flinched when a car sprang into his periphery and slammed to a stop right by him.

'Callum, get in!' his brother shouted.

So Aaron wasn't with the police. What the fuck was going on?

Callum jumped in and Aaron floored it and they were off down the street. His eyes remained glued to the wing mirror as he watched the police car, the terrified police officers, the chaos in the road fade into the distance. No sign of Hinch or Brandt at all. Had they gone off in the opposite direction? On foot? In their car?

Certainly, they weren't on Callum and Aaron's tail.

Aaron flung the car around a corner, barely braking before accelerating off again.

Callum stared a few seconds longer, but no one was following them. They were in the clear.

But Callum strongly doubted it'd be for long.

'And what the hell do we do now?' Aaron asked, the anger in his voice clear. The question seemed a little rhetorical, as though he was saying there was *nothing* they could do that was going to make things better, keep them safe.

'I have an idea,' Callum said.

'You do?'

'Yeah, I do. But I don't think you're gonna like it.'

15

LONDON

Two years ago

Drizzle pattered down on Lea as she stood on the banks of the Thames, looking out across the murky brown water, her thoughts wandering, her personal life on her mind as much as her job.

Saying yes to marrying Callum was one thing, the easy thing, but figuring out how to tell her boss had been a much harder task, although actually one which had gone far more smoothly than Lea had expected. Not that she *had* to get Goldman's approval. There was nothing in Lea's contract of employment that specifically stated she couldn't have a relationship or marry. But there were so many reasons why so few field agents did. Predominantly because what *was* made very clear in the contract of employment was that anything and everything an agent did in the line of work was strictly classified, and couldn't be divulged to anyone, family members included, and the penalty for doing so ranged from immediate dismissal to a life sentence in jail. And, maybe not officially, but Lea wouldn't even put it past the big machine to simply have an offending agent quietly despatched under certain circumstances. Not that she had any specific evidence of that happening in the past, but still...

In any case, the upshot was that most field agents were young, most had no long-term relationship or spouse and it wasn't because they were all playing the field, but because of the obvious difficulties of living a double life.

Regardless, Lea had genuinely found love, whether for better or worse. Perhaps long term that meant the writing was on the wall for her life out in the field. But wasn't that an inevitability for all field agents? It was undoubtedly a young person's game, always had been and always would be.

Lea's nerves and hesitations about telling Goldman had ultimately been unfounded, because her boss had given her the nod of approval. Not that she seemed *happy* for Lea, but she'd said she wouldn't stand in Lea's way, so long as Lea stuck to the rules of engagement.

After the hurdle of getting Goldman's approval, Lea soon found out that everything that came after was *way* harder than she'd expected when she'd said yes to Callum six months ago. Firstly, *when* would they get married? Callum wanted sooner, she wanted later, because putting it off meant more time to properly prepare herself and not have to face the added challenges the new life would bring. Head in the sand, that sort of thing. Plus, he wanted big, she wanted as small and intimate as possible. Not for any romantic, idealistic reasons or anything like that, but because she literally had no clue how she could invite *anyone* she knew. Her parents? Absolutely not. Her MI6 colleagues and assets who were, sadly, about the only people she could consider anything close to friends of her own in recent times? But why would any of them even want to come and get caught up in Lea's world of lies?

Something would have to give. She'd said yes to Callum and she'd meant it and was determined to see it through. She just didn't know how, or when.

And, quite frankly, she had plenty of other things that she needed – hoped – to get through before she and Callum tied the knot.

Not least figuring out who had killed Naomi and why and catching up with the people who'd tried to have her killed too – possibly the *same* people.

And she'd make them all pay.

'Dreaming of your wedding dress again?' Denis said, startling her from her thoughts.

She turned to him but didn't respond immediately. She was annoyed both because she hadn't seen him arrive, too distracted – even though she was expecting him – and also because she actually *was* thinking about the wedding. Again. Plus, she hated the derogatory way that Denis always talked about it and Callum, as though he looked down on her future husband for his 'normal' life and saw Lea as lowering her standards to try to fit into that life.

Not that he'd said anything anywhere nearly as bluntly as that, but she just knew.

'How was Turkey?' she asked him.

He'd been in Istanbul the last two weeks on a new assignment that she knew little about. Nothing to do with the Iranians or what had happened in Toulouse or Cairo, he'd said. Everything on that front had gone quiet, both officially and unofficially. Lea hated that. And hated that even Denis seemed to have moved on despite what had happened to him.

'I didn't lose any more toes,' he said, smiling, relaxed. 'So that's a plus.'

'Maybe if you did even out your left and right at least so you wouldn't be zigzagging all over like a drunkard.'

She delivered that deadpan, still a little angered by his initial comment. To start with he scowled, as though not impressed by the quip, but then laughed and she soon relaxed too.

'I'm sensing you didn't ask me to come here to talk about Turkey,' he said. 'Or my toes.'

'And not my wedding either.'

'Any news on when the big day'll be?' he asked.

'What did I literally just say about that?'

'The plans are going that well, huh?'

She said nothing. Hated how he seemed to take pleasure in her discomfort.

'I'm sorry,' he said. 'You know I'm happy for you really.'

Funny way of showing it.

'And you know I do care for you,' he added.

'I know, Denis.'

'When two people have been through the things we have together...'

'I get it.'

Still, he let the comment sit there between them a few moments.

'So, back to the point,' he said. 'I'm guessing it's the *other* thing you wanted to talk about.'

'The Iranians.'

'Yeah.'

'It's like... everyone else has just forgotten about what happened. To you. To me.'

'But that's *because* it happened to you and me. Not them. MI6 isn't about resolving personal grudges. To everyone else... what happened to us was just... how it goes. Or something like that. And we still have no evidence any of those parties is up to anything that the British government would care about—'

Lea tutted. 'Naomi was killed.'

'And I'm sure MI6's actions have seen plenty of people we didn't like killed. Yours and my own too.'

'To help make the world a better, safer place.'

'According to MI6 and our government?'

'No, according to me. I do what I do because I know it helps. And... Denis, those people – Hadjam and the Iranians – I still think... they have to be doing something... *bad*.' She huffed, annoyed at herself for her failure to properly explain it. 'They must be, right? Otherwise, why the attacks on me and you at all?'

'If we knew the why—'

'Then MI6 would have given us, or the SAS or whoever the orders already to go and round them all up or take them all out.'

'But we haven't had that order—'

'And that's the fucking problem, Denis! *Why* haven't we had the order? Nobody else cares, and I can't stand it. I want to know what they were, *still are*, up to.'

The conversation paused. Denis held her eye, as though scouring her thoughts. She felt pretty sure he read them in that moment.

His gaze narrowed. 'Have you already been looking into this? On your own?' he asked.

'No.'

'But you *want* to. And you want me to help?'

'Yes. Because I think some of the answers I want are close to home.'

Quiet again. Staring at her again, reading her mind. Except this time, he didn't offer anything back.

'Hadjam's daughter is married to Omar Yousefi,' Lea said. 'The MP.'

'Who, as far as we're aware, has zero connection to any proscribed group. Even when we were looking into these people, he wasn't specifically a target.'

'Which is bullshit! His father-in-law is one step away from Islamists and that's a fact!'

'So MI6 should be rounding up everyone who's ever been connected to anyone who's connected to a terrorist group?'

'No. But... Well, yes! I mean, isn't that the purpose of MI6? To at least make sure everyone who fits that scenario is vetted?'

Denis shrugged, his nonchalance only further irritating her. 'Think we'd need a few more agents to get that job done any time in the next century or so.'

'You want to be like that? Then piss off. I can figure this out myself.'

She went to turn away but he grabbed her shoulder and pulled her back around. For a moment she thought he was about to...

No. He didn't do anything as stupid as that.

'I'm sorry,' he said. 'I'm not disagreeing with you. Not exactly. Just explaining why it is like it is.'

'Whatever.' She shrugged him off.

'So you're focusing on the MP? But what's the play? What is he up to? How is he connected to what happened to us?'

'I don't know! But that's what I'm going to find out. I *will* find out.'

Denis sighed and looked around them, as though more concerned now of the potential for eyes on them, eavesdroppers.

'You really want to not only go ahead with an unsanctioned move, but you want to make that move against a sitting UK Member of Parliament, on UK soil?'

When he said it like that, it did sound a *bit* risky. Ill thought-out.

'I'm not suggesting we go and snatch him, interrogate him. Light touch. Level two.'

Denis said nothing.

'I'm going to do it with or without you,' she said. 'But I thought, given your personal involvement in this, you'd want to help.'

'Lea, even if it wasn't personal for me, you *know* I'll help you.'

She smiled, relief more than anything.

'Just let me know when,' he said.

She tried not to laugh.

'Shit. What?'

'Are you busy... tonight?' she asked.

He was obviously trying his hardest to stay looking serious at the question. Failed after about three seconds before he laughed too.

'Looks like I am now,' he said.

* * *

Despite a spate of scandals over the misuse of ancillary benefits, and sometimes dodgy taxation too, it remained entirely usual for a UK MP to have a second home in London, either rented or owned, and largely paid for through the public purse, regardless of where in the country their constituency lay. Omar Yousefi held the constituency of East Riding in Yorkshire, although he certainly wasn't a native of that area. He'd been born to a relatively wealthy Iranian immigrant family in London – his father was a doctor – and had grown up there, gone to university in the city too. After that he'd worked in an investment bank for several years before starting his own investment company with a colleague. A company in which he still held a minority stake, despite selling a controlling interest to a larger competitor several years previously. A deal about which the details were never made public, but it was routinely considered that Yousefi and his partner had each taken away eight figures. And not low eight figures, either.

After that Yousefi had turned to politics, originally campaigning for the left wing – or occasionally centrist – Labour Party, and had found favour for his liberal stances on immigration, particularly in and around London's East End where he'd been born, and where the immigrant community, especially from the Middle East, continued to grow.

Despite that initial platform, before long he'd switched allegiances to the more right-wing Conservative Party and had changed his stances on numerous more liberal views around immigration, the welfare state, taxation. Quite why that change had taken place, Lea didn't know, but within a short time Yousefi had risen through the Conservatives with his clean-cut image and impeccable dress sense and his obvious charm and well-spoken manner. His rags to riches story (even if it wasn't really a 'rags' start to life, despite what the right-wing press tried to conjure) only added further appeal both within the party and to its base.

To swing voters too, apparently, as he'd pulled off something of a coup by winning the seat of Kensington for the Conservatives, one of very few London boroughs to vote right-wing in the election two cycles ago. His rising prominence had seen him earmarked for a future cabinet position, and so he'd been switched to the far more safe seat of East Riding for the next election, where it seemed almost impossible that the residents of the area wouldn't simply vote along usual party lines, even if Yousefi was clearly an outsider to the area – and not just because of his heritage.

Still, despite his growing importance, he hadn't lasted long in the role of Chancellor of the Exchequer for that government, though it was generally believed to be down to party in-fighting rather than his own personal performance. Regardless, his party lost the last election, even if he held his seat comfortably, though having not been selected for the shadow cabinet, he once again found himself on the backbenches.

But he remained a prominent force in his party, with some even suggesting he was a potential future leader.

Prior to his name coming up because of their interest in Hadjam, Lea hadn't really paid much attention to Yousefi's life or career. Politically speaking, she held no strong views on him. Personally speaking, she was massively suspicious, not just of his links to Hadjam but... about pretty much everything.

Even the simple fact that he'd been shipped up to Yorkshire, some 200 miles from the capital. Just the fact that he couldn't possibly lose that seat made the whole thing seem so bogus. And just look at where he lived here...

'If this is his second home, what the hell is his first?' Denis said, looking out of the car window.

The grey-brick Georgian townhouse in Knightsbridge sat on a short street of other near-identical townhouses, each probably worth ten million or more. Knightsbridge wasn't *that* far from Westminster, so she guessed it was plausible this place was a good location for carrying out his duties in the capital, but still...

'Maybe it isn't his second home,' Lea said. 'Maybe he counts it as his third. He's got a place out in Berkshire too. A few acres there for his wife's horses. I'm not sure about up in Yorkshire. I've not checked exactly where he lives there.'

'Oh, I've no doubt it's just a tiny flat above a shop or something.'

'Yeah. I imagine you're not even close to right.'

Denis scowled. 'A man of the people, eh?'

'Of course he is. Just depends on which people you mean.'

'And you're sure he's not here?' Denis asked.

'I'm sure. He's in Yorkshire. A gala of some sort.'

'And his wife?'

'With him.'

'Kids?'

'He only has one daughter and she's at university. Cambridge, obviously.'

'Why's that obvious?'

Lea sighed. 'Just seems like what you'd imagine for a man who lives like he does.'

'Servants?' Denis asked.

Lea laughed. Denis didn't.

'I was being serious,' he added.

'Yeah, I know. But no, he has no live-in servants. I've kept a close eye on this place for a couple of weeks now. There's a gardener to tend to the walled garden at the back, but he doesn't go through the house, has a key to get around the side. And there's a cleaner, once a week on Wednesday. But that's it.'

Denis sighed and looked out at the house again.

'And you figured a way in already?'

'Of course.'

He turned back to her and she held his eye, enjoying his impatience, his obvious curiosity as he awaited an answer.

'And?' he eventually said, and Lea chuckled as she reached into her pocket and withdrew the key.

'Front door, obviously.'

They both got out of the car, gave a quick glance along the quiet street. Not much going on around here at 9 p.m. on a weeknight. Yousefi's townhouse wasn't quite fully in darkness, with a couple of lights visible beyond the windows on the ground and second floor, but Lea was sure it was only a basic security measure.

They headed up the steps to the front door, side by side.

'And you got that how?' he asked.

'Newly cut. His wife goes to a gym around the corner from here. I followed her in there a few times, got a good idea of the layout, what she does, where she puts her things, how long she spends there. The last time I broke into her locker – they're pretty basic – and I took her key and caught an Uber to the nearest locksmith and got my own copy cut. Had hers back in her bag before she'd finished her shower.'

They reached the door. Lea looked over at Denis.

'What?' she asked.

'Just... you. I admire your... balls.'

'Not the best word, really?'

He rolled his eyes in response. Lea pushed the key into the lock, turned, opened the door.

A blip sounded out from the entry alarm.

'I hope you're about to tell me you know how to disable that?'

She smiled and followed the sound to the control panel on the inside wall. She input the six-digit code and the lights on the panel flashed green and the noise stopped.

Denis closed the door behind him.

'And the story for that?' he asked. Then his eyes narrowed in suspicion. 'Have you already been here?'

'No, actually. First time. But I've spent a bit of time following the cleaner too. I swiped her phone when she was eating lunch with a friend a few days ago, unlocked it using an old trick *you* taught me.'

'The iPhone one? You mean the one where you—?'

'That one, yeah. And, lucky for me, she had a message from a couple of years ago from Yousefi's wife with the code right there. I think sometimes people get just a little bit too complacent with these things.'

'Yeah. That, or they just don't expect MI6 agents to be swiping their phones while they're eating lunch, to search for access codes their employers gave them in good faith.'

'You know what? You're probably right. But they really should.'

Denis smiled. 'Let's get to it.'

Which didn't take them too long. In the modern world, so many people had become reliant on mobile data. Even if the opulent home had an office, there weren't exactly reams of paperwork – confidential, scandalous or otherwise. And even electronic data was becoming more and more mobile. Laptop, tablet, phone rather than desktop.

'Maybe we need to come back when he's actually here,' Denis said as Lea closed the last of the desk drawers and sighed, disappointed yet again.

'Yeah. I think maybe you're right. Although...'

Her eyes wandered around the room as she thought. Her gaze came to rest on a painting along the wall opposite the desk.

'You like it?' Denis asked.

'No idea what it is.'

'Probably something way more expensive than you or I could ever afford.'

'I don't doubt that.'

She moved over to the painting and carefully lifted it off the hook.

'Old school,' Denis said as they both stared at the door to the safe.

'Safe behind a painting?'

'Yeah.'

'It's an electronic lock though, so not that old school.'

'No. But all the easier to get into it.'

'Yep.'

'Want me to do the honours?' Denis asked with a smile.

'Go for it.'

It took him less than two minutes. Lea knew several common ways to break a standard electronic safe – the type used routinely in hotels and in people's homes. Some had override codes, some had a manual key entry behind a removable panel, while with others the control panel could be hacked into.

Which was exactly the case with Yousefi's safe. Like many such safes, there was a battery backup system should the unit lose power. That battery enclosure needed to be accessible for obvious reasons. But that access also gave easy access to the entire electronic system. Back door entry to manually override the system, if you knew how.

Denis pulled open the door and then turned to Lea.

'Happy?'

She stared inside. Quite a few items in there, from watches to bundles of cash, brown envelopes with papers. A couple of DVDs, flash drives. An old mobile phone.

'No, not happy,' she said.

'Because?'

'Because I didn't want to have to take anything. I wanted to get in and out without him knowing.'

'We still can,' he said, digging into the contents as she looked over her shoulder to the windows. 'I'm not in a rush. Are you? We can go through everything right here, right now.'

'I don't think that's going to be possible.'

'Because?'

She nodded up to the corner of the room. Then over into the opposite corner.

It only took Denis a few seconds to figure what she'd seen. Two cameras. Two quite different cameras.

'One of them's not connected to the main alarm system,' he said.

'I don't think so.'

One definitely was. The one in the corner to Lea's right afforded a view over the entire room, doorway included. It was the same one as in several other rooms. But the other... the other camera was a different model and directed down at the safe.

'You think he's looking at us right now?'

'Possibly.'

His look turned to more of a glare.

'When did you figure that out?' he asked.

'While you were cracking it.'

'You didn't think about warning me?'

'Didn't think there was much point until...'

She didn't bother to finish. The 'until' was made pretty obvious by the flashing blue lights outside.

'Let's get the fuck out of here,' Denis said.

But not before he'd scooped the contents from the safe and stuffed them into his backpack.

No sirens outside yet, which was a good sign, perhaps, but there remained no doubt why the police had turned up. Lea and Denis hotfooted it down the stairs and to the back door then sprinted outside.

'This way,' Lea said, tugging on Denis's jacket before she headed off to the right of the garden to the gate that led to a side access for several of the properties.

'Stop, police!' came the shout of a police officer all of ten yards in front of them as they moved out into the alley.

Neither Lea nor Denis stopped. In fact, both sped up and charged the unsuspecting officer. He had his baton out, but nothing he could do really in the confined space except swing it wildly at Denis who dodged easily before swiping the officer's legs and he tumbled to the ground.

Denis carried on past, Lea hopped over the floored police officer, and they emerged onto the road. Two police cars were on the street right in front of the property. Three more officers on foot there.

'Hey!' one of them shouted out to Lea and Denis. Not a very clear instruction, really, but it at least got the attention of his colleagues.

It didn't stop Lea or Denis though, and they rushed for the car, which sat roughly in the middle of them and the police. Lea and Denis got there first. She had the engine fired up as the quickest of the officers thumped onto the front of the car, as though he thought doing so would stop her from pulling away.

It kind of did, because instead she reversed, hard, and he slipped off just before she crashed into the car behind her. She flicked the gearstick into drive and thumped the accelerator and swung out into the road.

'Lea!' Denis shouted out.

But she'd already seen the next officer rushing to try and cut them off. She swerved and he dove out of the way just in time before her car side-swiped another vehicle on the other side of the road. A clattering impact but not enough to stop her. She gunned it to the end of the street, away from the officers, two of them pulling themselves from the ground. The third? She wasn't sure.

She swung left. Sirens behind them now. Soon the chasing car was in her view.

'You strapped in?' she asked Denis.

'This isn't my first rodeo, Lea. Not even my first with you.'

'Still, I'd recommend you hold on tight.'

As soon as she'd finished that sentence, she pumped the brake, tugged on the wheel and the back end of the car flew out to drift them around a right turn. Denis *was* strapped in, and was holding on, but not quite tightly enough and his head smacked off the window as she adjusted the steering and got them moving straight again.

'I did tell you,' she said.

He only smiled in response as she pushed the accelerator again and shot off down the street. She took the next left in the exact same manner. This time Denis was more ready for it.

She could have driven like that all night if she wanted, but she knew the safest thing to do was to ditch the car as soon as possible. Just over a mile later and she raced into a multi-storey car park while the police were out of sight and, lights off, sped up to the second floor. They jumped out and rushed for the stairwell and soon emerged on the street below.

Both took pause there in the cool night-time air, chests heaving with both exertion and excitement.

No sirens drifted over. No flashing lights anywhere in sight here.

'That was fun,' Lea said, adrenaline and endorphins surging.

'Always is with you. It's why we're so good together.'

His comment caught her a little off guard, her head fifty-fifty as to the intention behind it.

'You got a plan from here?' Denis asked.

'Take a deep dive into our MP's treasured items, of course.'

'You want some company?'

She thought about that one, pushed all the growing doubts away. 'Yeah. Why not.'

'Then let's get to it,' Denis said with an eager smile.

16

HAMPSHIRE

Present day

They'd hired the puny-engined VW Jetta in Aaron's name. Having escaped – if that was even the right word – from the bank near Bristol unscathed, they'd realised they needed to ditch Aaron's car sooner rather than later. The police would no doubt be out looking for them, Brandt and Hinch too, MI6, whoever the hell else wanted to catch up with Callum.

So they'd left Aaron's Mercedes in a sprawling Asda car park about ten miles south of the city, took an Uber back closer to the centre to a car hire place – an independent rather than a national chain – and had taken the cheapest option available. Not just to save money but because, ominously, Aaron had probably rightly suggested that if this one somehow got wrecked, or they had heat on them and had to dump it someplace before returning it, he wanted the least possible liability.

Still a hefty liability, if it came to that.

Either way, Callum knew the plan, both with the rental, and what came after, was far from foolproof. Everything they'd done had left yet another paper trail, not to mention witnesses at the bank and outside it. They had to expect heat at some point. But hopefully by that point he wouldn't even be in the country.

Once in the VW they'd initially travelled east, back to Berkshire. Not quite as far as Aaron's home, as Deena had met them out on the road, both because she didn't want Callum anywhere near her house and kids and because it simply saved them time. Callum had stayed in the car rather than attempt any kind of interaction with her. He knew she hated everything about the idea of Aaron and her helping him. But she still had.

And so, with what they needed in their possession – most importantly Aaron's passport – they headed back onto the road, south and a little bit west, aiming for Southampton. More specifically, the port there.

'Taking off like this...' Aaron started. Callum didn't bother to interject during the silence. 'What about your work?'

'I have no idea,' Callum said. He'd tried not to think about that at all. Was it really only yesterday he was last at the construction site? It felt like a lifetime ago. No doubt if he'd still had his old phone, he'd have been battling a plethora of messages and calls, and he did feel bad for leaving the team in the lurch. Perhaps a courtesy call or message to his foreman, Hall, or to Gloria would be worthwhile.

But not yet.

'How's it going, though?' Aaron asked. 'I mean... everything else aside, is it still want you want to do? Long term?'

A seriously odd question at this point in time.

'It pays.'

'It's good that you found something else. You know, other than rugby.'

Callum raised an eyebrow to show his distaste at the statement. He knew where it was coming from. The same place similar comments had come from for years, mostly from his parents.

You need to get a proper job. Things like that.

'I haven't seen your name on the team sheet in a while,' Aaron said.

'You bother to check?'

'I've always been bothered. I used to enjoy watching you.'

He'd never really said so.

'I still keep up with the results,' Aaron said. 'Still look out to see if you're playing.'

'I've barely played the last couple of years. It's a young man's sport.'

'You're only thirty-two.'

'Which means I've had more than a decade of being pummelled, battered and bruised all for a few quid here and there. It takes its toll pretty fast. Mentally as much as physically.'

Aaron glanced over. 'You were close to making it, you know. Really close.'

As if he knew. 'What is this?' Callum asked.

'What?'

'Why are we even talking about this? Now?'

Aaron looked offended. A little embarrassed. 'I guess... I guess we just don't get enough chances to talk. Not recently.'

'And whose fault is that?'

'You're blaming Deena?' Angrier now.

Callum didn't say anything. The answer was obvious.

'She's my wife. The mother of my kids.'

'Yeah. I get it. There's nothing for you to justify. It just is what it is.'

'She has good reason not to like you,' Aaron said.

'No, she doesn't. Not really. What happened before the wedding? However you spin it, you were as much to blame as me. If she'd wanted, she could have forgiven me like she forgave you. You could have had me as part of your lives still. Part of your kids' lives. You could have been part of mine and Lea's life too. Who knows... maybe something would have gone different for us two as well.'

'So now Deena's to blame for Lea's death?'

'Not what I said at all.'

'But it seemed like that's what you were suggesting.'

'Honestly? I'm not sure what I'm suggesting. But you want the truth? I wish I could go back. Fix *everything*. With you, Deena. Mum, Dad. But mostly with Lea. Thinking now... there were so many moments... where, looking back, maybe the signs were there. I mistook her moods, her emotions for work stress, time of the month, whatever. But maybe... it was always much bigger than that. And I could have helped if only I'd known. If I could have got her out of that life... she'd still be alive.'

'Maybe she didn't want out.'

'Now I'll never know.'

They went silent and Aaron took them off the motorway, their destination not far now, and Callum's nerves crept up with each passing moment, especially as nightfall wasn't far off, as though the dark would bring with it something sinister.

'You really think this is going to work?' Aaron asked him.

'I have to try.'

'But you really think there'll be something there for you?'

I love it here. This is the place, Cal. The place I feel most alive. Most free.

He could recall the moment, all of six weeks ago, so vividly. And not the only time she'd said something like that to him on the several occasions they'd visited that place. He remembered those moments for the very reason that they were such happy memories. But was there more to it than that? Had she been planting a seed in his head all along, in the same way she had done with the mention to him of the Simmonds family?

He had to hope so.

'At the least, if I'm out of the country, I'll feel safer. Less... on the run.'

'You won't be any less on the run. You think MI6 can't reach you still? Their whole purpose is in operating outside the UK. And not necessarily always above board. And you don't think the UK police can't involve anyone overseas either?'

'But why would they want to?' Callum said. 'I've done nothing wrong in their eyes. Even if there is some sort of conspiracy here with MI6, the government or... I don't know what, but there's no evidence I did anything wrong. So why the hell would the Portuguese police or anyone else outside the UK agree to hunt me down?'

'Because what Lea knew got her killed. And you're in her world now. So you need to be prepared.'

Callum understood that point, despite his words, which had been intended to comfort himself more than anything.

'It still doesn't make sense to me,' Aaron said.

'What doesn't?'

'That box being empty. Why give you the clues to go there if it was empty?'

'Because it *wasn't* empty,' Callum said. 'Just someone got there before us.'

'Brandt and Hinch?'

'It would make some sense. But then why would Hinch make me go in there to prove it was empty? Especially as it's likely that move raised the suspicions of the bank staff enough for them to call the police.'

'Which I'm not sure I buy either.'

'In what way?'

'I don't know. It's just... all these coincidences. Maybe that's not even the right word. But I don't like it.'

'Me neither.'

'There is one thing you need to seriously consider, though.'

'And that is?'

'There has to be *one* side who's telling you the truth. Who you can trust.'

Callum thought about that a moment.

'I'm serious,' Aaron said. 'So far, both times you've come across Brandt and Hinch? They've pulled guns on you. Both times the police have been on the scene too, and both times Brandt and Hinch have fired shots at the police.'

Aaron paused there, as though letting his point sink in. Callum chewed on it, replayed the key moments in his head.

'Whereas the police and the guy who told you he was from MI6? Firstly, they took you *away* from Brandt and Hinch. Then all they do is talk to you. Tell you about Lea. Even show you those pictures of people who could be involved. They offered to let you stay at a safe house. And when you attacked them—'

'I didn't attack them.'

'You told me you shoved the woman and elbowed the MI6 guy in the face. Kicked an officer in the balls.'

Callum said nothing.

'That's what you said, isn't it?'

'Yeah.'

'You did all that and then they just let you out of there?'

'Did they let me? I'm not so sure. And then that night they have my face on TV saying I'm a suspect in Lea's death.'

'But they didn't say suspect, did they?'

'They may as well have done.'

'Except maybe that's the point. You're not a suspect. They know it too. They really do just want to speak to you. To keep you safe while they figure things out.'

'You'd rather I just called the police now and have them come pick me up?'

'If it was me?' Aaron said.

'It kind of is you, now.'

'Not for long. But... if it was? You already know what I'd do.'

'Your lawyer friend. Yeah, yeah, we've done this one before.'

'And how do you know it wasn't the best idea from the start? Because so far, your way, you've been involved in a shoot-out this morning. There's a manhunt in place for you, and you're about to abscond to another country with false documents.'

'There's nothing false about your passport.'

'*My* passport. Exactly.'

Callum played with that document on his lap. Opened the picture page. Again. The brothers hardly had a twin-like resemblance, but they were clearly related. And in the picture, there was no indication of the size difference between the two, other than Callum's cheeks were that little bit more full. Nothing that wouldn't be seen as a reasonable change from a recent weight gain though. Unless there was a close scrutiny of the document, Callum could pass it off as his own.

They soon reached the port, no hitches. A good thing, even if it only made Callum all the more questioning. The area was more active than Callum had imagined it would be at this time of night. Lights twinkled and huge cranes whirred and clanked in the near distance, moving shipping containers on and off transport ships. Closer to them sat the passenger port, and a huge cruise ship busy with people queuing to board.

Aaron parked up and glanced over at Callum again. 'I've never been on a cruise,' he said, smiling.

'*You're* about to.'

Aaron laughed. 'I guess *I* am. But I still don't know if this is the stupidest idea or the cleverest.'

'Me neither.'

But it had made perfect sense to Callum when he'd first suggested it.

He needed to get out of the country. Specifically, he wanted to go to Portugal. To *their* place. Flying was the quickest route, but airports also had the most stringent security. He could have taken the Channel Tunnel – either driving or on the Eurostar train – to get to continental Europe, but that journey was slower and just... seemed like it had more potential for hiccups.

Slow? Well, the cruise ship wasn't exactly speedy, but they'd be at their first stop-off in Portugal in the morning. And in his mind... it just felt like the least-expected route for someone in his position to take. Not only slow, but the most expensive too: he'd had to fork out more than £2,000 for the seven-day trip. A ferry to the same area would have cost a couple of hundred, a flight not much more. He'd certainly never seen a film or read a book where someone on the run had chosen a cruise liner to escape.

Either the stupidest idea, or the cleverest.

And using Aaron's passport was just an extra layer of protection, Callum had decided. Was his name already on a 'no-fly' list or whatever such things were called? Possibly. Possibly Aaron's was too, but it was much less likely.

Aaron's phone was ringing. His wife, Callum knew by the way he answered.

'Hey... The police?' he said. 'But they didn't come in... OK... Don't worry. I'll be back soon... No. I'll be back tonight... Then go to your parents. I'll meet you there... I promise. Everything's fine here... Just go. I'll see you there.'

The call soon ended and Aaron sighed, his worry clear to see.

'You probably got most of that,' he said.

'The police went to your house?'

A nod.

'Did she get the names of the officers?'

'No. They were just two uniforms. Asking for me. And you. They didn't go inside but they're still there, waiting in a car.'

'She didn't tell them anything?'

Aaron shot him a glare. 'She doesn't *know* anything. Nothing that's going to harm you, anyway. But she's scared, Cal, and you can understand why. My *kids* are there.'

'I know. You've done more than enough for me,' Callum said. 'It's time for you to go back to them.'

The brothers sat in awkward silence a moment, as though neither knew what else to say or do. Were they supposed to shake hands? Hug?

In the end they did nothing before Callum grabbed his things and got out.

'I'll wait until you're boarded,' Aaron said before Callum closed the door and headed for the ship.

He only had a backpack and a small suitcase with him. The suitcase was pretty much a prop. He needed to at least look the part, and it was only partially filled with some cast-offs of Aaron's that Deena had earlier brought out to them which Callum may or may not use at some point. He also had £2,000 in cash. Again, Aaron's. Not because he didn't have his own money but because he was trying his hardest to not leave too much of a trail. At least not in his name.

He joined the queue of other travellers, mostly older couples, all smiles and eagerness.

Soon it was his turn to show his documents. His brother's passport, and a single ticket for a two-berth cabin, no frills. He held his breath. Risked a look here and there, scoping out for any sudden onrush of security or border guards or police or whatever else...

'Enjoy the trip,' the border guard said with a forced smile as he handed the documents back over.

Callum nodded and carried on, his legs initially stiff and his stride unnatural as he tried to find his usual rhythm. He reached the gangway and pulled out the phone and sent a simple text message to Aaron.

All good. Take care.

Then he turned the phone off and made his way on board.

17

Callum made his way through the warren of corridors and directly to his cabin on the fourth floor, wary of every person who came his way. The ship could accommodate a couple of thousand passengers, but it seemed like there was an almost equal amount of staff too, people just *everywhere*. It made him feel equally nervous and safer at the same time.

He kept his head down, kind of, but also made sure he was aware of his surroundings at every moment.

Is this how Lea had to live all the time? he wondered.

He reached his door and looked left and then right along the busy corridor. No one paid him any attention. He unlocked and opened the door and stepped in.

He sighed. He'd never been fond of cramped spaces. And this space felt even less inviting given the turmoil in his mind. He had two options: hide inside here until morning, or spend as much time out in the open, among other people as he could.

He sat down on the bed. After a few moments he took his shoes off and lay back.

Closed his eyes.

Tried to relax.

Didn't work at all. Even if the ship wasn't moving yet, with his eyes closed everything swirled.

No, he really didn't like cramped spaces, and sitting or lying in there... What was the saying? A sitting duck? Exactly what he'd be if someone turned up at his door to attack him.

He put his shoes back on and headed out.

* * *

The boat didn't leave the dock for another hour after Callum had boarded. Tension gripped him the whole time, so it was natural that his whole body relaxed as he watched the land disappear in the distance through the windows of the bar, serotonin released and rushing through his head making him feel almost lightheaded. For a short while. Until reality dawned. He was nowhere near in the clear out in the ocean, all alone. This was merely the first part of a very long step. And when he reached Portugal? It wasn't as though all his troubles would suddenly be over. He'd just be on to another phase of this taut and discomforting mission.

He ordered a beer from his stool at the bar. Took his time with it, because he knew it was a long night ahead and the last thing he needed was to be drunk. Except it was damn good, so before long he had a second, relaxing even more into the journey, particularly as the crowds around him livened up with people ready to enjoy the first night of their big escape.

By 10 p.m. the bar was jam-packed, a little loud in places where big groups were drinking together, but all in all, given the clientele on the upscale craft, it remained respectable.

A couple of times other people ordering at the bar had engaged him – a quick nod of the head or a smile, and one man had even tried to strike up a conversation about dolphin-watching while he waited for his and his wife's cocktails. Callum glanced over at them, a few tables away from his position. They were both probably in their fifties, all dressed up for the occasion: her with a summery dress, a diamond-encrusted necklace, hoop earrings, tasteful make-up; him in an expensive-looking shirt and trousers combo, a big gold signet ring on one finger. The cruise wasn't cheap, and it showed in the guests and their attire. The couple laughed and giggled with each other, stared into each other's eyes. A hand on the knee here, a squeeze of the side there. At one point the woman leaned over and pecked her husband on the neck, leaving a little red smudge there and Callum practically felt the goosebumps on his skin, imagining being in that moment. With Lea, obviously.

Watching them, so happy, so content in each other's company... It's what his and Lea's future should have been. It's what his and her present should have been.

Now there was *no* future. He'd never get back what had been taken from him.

But he'd damn well find out *why* it'd been taken from him.

'I'll have whatever he's having,' came a voice from beside him. A female voice. 'And get him another too.'

Callum froze, every bone and muscle in his body unmoving. Except the ones needed for him to switch his gaze from the couple to the mirror behind the bar.

Jenn Hinch was standing beside him.

He went to turn around on the stool to face her but then paused when she spoke again.

'Just keep it calm, big man, yeah? No need for a scene. It won't do either of us any good.'

He relaxed just a little, more so to ensure she realised he wasn't about to make a sudden move. Not just yet, anyway. He turned on the stool to properly face the bar and stared at her in the mirror.

The bartender put two beers down in front of them. Callum downed the remaining third of his old one.

'Funny time to be taking a cruise,' Hinch said, snide smile on her face.

Callum said nothing in return.

She chuckled. 'You know, I still can't figure out if it's genius or completely dumb as hell.'

Callum still said nothing but took his new beer and a long sip.

'You're alone?' he asked after putting his drink back down.

Her smile faded. 'Yeah. I am. You know why? Because right now

Warren is in hospital with a dislocated knee and a shattered pelvis. I don't know if he'll ever be able to walk properly again.'

'Should always look both ways before crossing the road.'

He resisted smiling at his own quip but still took just a little pleasure in seeing the annoyance on her face.

'You think it's funny? He's a good friend, and we've been through some big-time shit together. Now he's probably out of action for good.'

'My heart bleeds. You realise I lost my wife? I think my pain trumps yours. His too.'

'And like I told you before, she was also a friend of mine.'

'Hard to believe given both times I've met you you've pulled a gun on me.'

He looked at her hands, glanced at her side. She wore jeans and an open jacket and even if he saw no sign of a weapon, she could be carrying something still.

'I have no gun,' she said, as if to answer his thought. 'Didn't have time to figure a way to get it through security.'

'Lucky me. What do you want?'

'Believe it or not? To help you. It's what I've been trying to tell you every time I've seen you.'

'How'd you even follow me here?'

She sighed. 'I told you before, Callum – I'm good at this shit. And you're... really not. The biggest surprise is that I've seen no indication that anyone else is on your tail.'

'The police, you mean?'

'Among others. Listen, Callum... I get you trust me as much as you like me—'

'You think?'

'But I *am* trying to help you.'

There has to be one side who's telling you the truth. Who you can trust.

Aaron's words echoed in his mind. Except his brother had suggested it likely *wasn't* Brandt and Hinch he should trust.

'We've got a few hours to kill before we hit the next port,' Callum said. 'So why don't you start convincing me.'

'The next port? Leixoes. So that's where you're getting off?'

Damn it. How'd he given that away so easily? But he didn't confirm the obvious.

'What's there, Callum? I know you're not just running. You know something.'

He sipped his beer again.

'Callum! I can help you, but I need to know what the hell you're up to.'

'And I said you need to convince me about who you are. Because right now I trust you probably less than anyone I've ever met in my life. Is Jenn Hinch even your real name.'

A pause before she answered. 'Depends what you mean by real.'

'Not a good start.'

'It's my name as far as almost anyone anywhere is concerned. Kind of like how Lea Torrence wasn't really Lea Torrence.'

'So you're MI6 too? Is that what you're saying?'

'No. I'm not saying that.'

'Who *do* you work for then?'

'Callum... it's hard to explain to someone like...'

'Like me? What? I'm too dumb to understand?'

'No, this... just isn't your world.'

She was right about that.

'If you want the truth? The best way to explain what I do? I'm an asset. An intelligence asset. Not an agent.'

'A mercenary, you mean?'

'No. Not that. I hate that word. I'm not a gun for hire. Just someone who... gets around. Unofficially.'

She took a swig from her beer. Callum kept his eye on her, ever wary.

'I've known Lea for nearly six years,' Hinch said. 'Our paths first crossed... over something that you really don't need to know about. But we worked together regularly. I know you're only just figuring out now about Lea's... other life, but she really was a bloody good spy. For the very fact that she was so good at maintaining assets, whether it was for intel or something as simple as needing a translator to... more physical missions. Whatever she needed, she had people she could turn to.'

'And where do you fit on that spectrum? Between translator and assassin.'

'It's a pretty broad spectrum. And I like to think I sit across quite a lot of it.'

Was that supposed to make him feel better? He gulped as ominous thoughts flashed.

He tensed as she reached inside her jacket, but it was only for her phone. She unlocked the screen and tapped away and then turned it towards him.

A picture. He couldn't tell where, but it was sunny, hot, sand-coloured buildings behind the two figures in the foreground. Lea and Hinch. Both of them smiling.

'Not long after we first met,' Hinch said. She tapped away once more, before again showing Callum the screen. 'Some more.' She flicked through several others. A European city this time, he thought, though he couldn't immediately tell which one. 'And this... is the most recent.'

Callum stared at that one a little longer. No smile from Lea – she looked pensive, a little fed up. He thought he kind of recognised the square behind her.

He scoffed. 'You're an asset of a spy, and you walk around with photos of the two of you together, smiling, having fun?'

'Why wouldn't I? Even if we actually didn't like each other that much this'd be good cover to show two women who're simply friends.'

Kind of made sense. But it also seemed way too convenient.

'You don't believe these are real?' Hinch asked.

Is that what he was saying? He supposed it wouldn't be that hard to fake pictures like that with Photoshop or AI or whatever.

'I've already told you countless times, we were *friends*,' Hinch said. 'Even spies are allowed those.'

He dwelled on that as he drank. *Even spies are allowed friends*. In the same way that Lea was allowed a husband too. Except apparently the friends were in on her big secret, whereas he wasn't.

It made him feel all the more insignificant in Lea's life.

'Do you know about... whatever it is that got her killed?' he asked.

'Not much. I wasn't involved in that operation. But I know it'd been rumbling on for a long time.'

'Not much? So something?'

'Like I said, I know she'd been working on this thing for a long time. She'd got deeper into it, and it was causing problems.'

'Problems with who?'

'With the people she worked for.'

'I don't believe you,' he said.

'Callum, come on, I—'

'No, you listen to me. When you came to my house, one of the first things you and Brandt said to me was that Lea was killed because of information she had. Information that is now missing. You came to me because you thought I might know about it, have access to it. Now you're telling me you know next to nothing about what got her killed? It can't be both. One of those positions is a lie. Maybe it's both.'

Hinch didn't respond. She looked upset more than anything at Callum's blunt statement. Perhaps this woman was just so used to lying, or at least being scarce with the truth, that she couldn't even remember what story she'd told and when any more.

'I wasn't involved in the op,' Hinch said eventually. 'That's the truth. But I know something about what she was working on. And I am in this for her. I want to find the truth, and I want those responsible for her death punished.'

'You know *something*. Tell me!'

'I can't!' A couple of people looked over at the heightened conversation and Hinch gave him an imploring look. 'I'm sorry, but right now, I just can't. There's more at stake here than you realise. Please, can you just understand that?'

'No. I really can't. Not at all.'

'And what about you, anyway?' she said. 'Are you going to tell me why you're here? Where you're going when we get to Leixoes and why?'

He wiped at the condensation on his glass with his finger, leaving a neat trail.

'Thought so,' she said. 'Trust works both ways.'

He finished off his beer. He wouldn't have another tonight.

'But we can still help each other,' Hinch said. 'I know you don't want to do this alone. It's why you brought your brother into the mix, and I'm sure you'd have him here with you now if you could.'

'You're saying you want to tag along with me to wherever I'm going?' Callum asked.

'It's not such a bad idea if you think about it. I have way more experience than you do of evading the authorities and... just *everything* you're now involved in.'

'But if I turn around and tell you to piss off at any point? What then? You pull a weapon on me? Threaten me? Am I just your hostage until it suits you otherwise?'

'You're not a hostage. If I wanted you harmed or dead, you would be by now.'

Was that supposed to make him feel better?

'Callum, I'm only a threat to you when you try to put *me* in danger. That's the truth. You know what I'm saying makes sense.'

It didn't really. But sitting there in the middle of the ocean he didn't really have many options. Cry foul and the police would be on him, and there was no way he could escape from her without making a scene.

Not on here, anyway.

Once they were ashore?

That was a different prospect. One he'd have to mull over. And he had a few hours to do so.

'OK, you win,' he said. 'We'll stick together. For now.'

And he thought he did a pretty good job of sounding sincere.

18

LONDON

One and a half years ago

MI6 headquarters at Vauxhall Cross dominated the foreground as she approached, the looming structure an impressive and renowned architectural feat, even if the sheer sight of it sent shivers down her spine, given her own history – not of the building specifically, but because of what she knew it represented.

Coming here today represented a stumbling block. A stumbling block that if she could clear, would take a huge weight off her.

But it was a stumbling block that was several feet tall, and to get over it she'd be blindfolded and have her hands tied behind her back and her ankles roped together.

Or something like that.

Her thoughts whirled as she approached the doors. It'd been months since the break in at the home of MP Omar Yousefi, and the event had never made headlines. No images of Lea or Denis had been paraded on TV or the internet.

Was the quiet surprising to her?

Not exactly. But it did tell a story. It told her that Yousefi, for whatever reason, had wanted to keep the matter out of the public eye, and that the police were willing – and able – to go along with that.

Lea hoped that fact itself pointed to a nefarious influence from Yousefi, although she had no evidence of it. Not much evidence of anything, really, despite having spent as much of her spare time as she could over the last few months trawling through everything they'd taken from Yousefi's safe, and cross-matching anything even remotely intriguing across files and databases she had access to.

So far that work had yielded zero answers, zero clear evidence of dodgy deeds by Yousefi, although there remained plenty of threads which she'd like to continue to pull if given the chance.

The issue was, to get that chance, she really needed to be doing things out in the open. From an MI6 standpoint, at least.

And so, frustratingly, and more than a little apprehensively, she'd decided – with Denis's encouragement – that it was time to come clean to Goldman.

The plan was to gloss over the break-in as much as possible, and present the little that they'd found with as much vigour as possible, and hope that their boss would be intrigued enough – and not disappointed or angry enough – to give them the green light to carry on, and perhaps even with some additional help.

Denis was waiting for her outside the top-floor meeting room.

'You look… hassled,' he said, and without his usual smile of greeting which really didn't fill her with much confidence. Had he already decided this was a doomed proposal?

'Just not sure this is going to go how we want it to,' she said.

She stopped by him and took a moment to compose her thoughts. He put his hand to her shoulder – unexpected, but she didn't brush him off.

'You've got this,' he said.

'Is Goldman in there already?' Lea asked.

'Yeah.'

'Then let's get this done.'

* * *

'Are you totally fucking insane?' Goldman bellowed, rising from her chair, face contorting, cheeks burning red. All that was missing were fireballs coming from her mouth and laser beams from her eyes.

If she could have, she would have.

'Erica, I'm sorry,' Lea said. 'But it's not about what we did, but why we did it and what we found—'

'Of course it's about what you did! You damn idiots.'

She slumped back down in her chair, anger dissipating for despair.

'But... think about it,' Lea said. 'You didn't know about this, right? That Omar Yousefi, a sitting MP, had his home broken into?'

Only a quizzical look from Goldman in return.

'Why do you think that is?' Lea asked. 'The police were called there that night. They *chased* us across central London. Six months ago! And you haven't heard a single thing about this?'

'*That* is your big take away from all of this?' Goldman said dejectedly.

The room went silent for a few moments. Lea fought in her mind for what else she could say to bring her boss around, make her see things as Lea saw them.

She failed.

'Can you two be identified by the police?' Goldman asked.

'I doubt it,' Lea said. 'We were careful.'

'We're not amateurs,' Denis added.

Goldman shot him her death glare. 'You really don't believe so?'

'*We were careful*,' Lea said again. 'And you've heard nothing about this, and I've certainly not had a knock on the door yet, so—'

'I could have you both terminated right here, right now,' Goldman butted in. 'In fact, I'm struggling to find a good reason not to.'

'Because you know we did this with the best intentions,' Lea said.

'It's not about intentions!' Goldman shouted back. 'It's about laws, rules. Reputations. *My* reputation.'

'Our actions are on us, not you,' Denis said. 'We made the decision together. Whatever happens from here, it'll never come back to hurt you.'

Goldman shot him another glare. 'It doesn't work like that, *Romeo*. I'm guessing this was *her* idea and you just followed blindly?'

'No,' he said, stern. 'I did this because it was the right thing to do. You know yourself from our files on Hadjam and the Iranians that Yousefi does, most likely, know something. And if we're not the ones to find out what that is, then who?'

'*Know something?* What does that even mean? You have no evidence of his involvement with any person of interest. If it wasn't because of who his wife is he'd be nowhere near your thoughts.'

'That's a pretty big *because*, if you ask me,' Lea said.

'I did not ask you. And this is not how your jobs work. *You* do not get to decide on what missions to undertake and where without *my* authority.'

'We're sorry for that,' Lea said. 'There's no excuse. We should have briefed you first. But we're here now, telling you everything. We're not trying to hide—'

'I expected better from you,' Goldman said to her. 'I really did.'

The words stung and for a few moments Lea was flummoxed. She looked over at Denis as if for backup and he nodded to her. Telling her to carry on?

'The thing is, we have found something...' Lea rummaged in her satchel.

Although as she did so the word 'we' stuck in her head. Because it wasn't just her and Denis who had found this evidence. Lea had recently drafted in the services of Harpreet, a data analyst who worked for MI5, to help sift through the reams of data, and to take the deep dive further. Harpreet was probably the best analyst Lea had ever met, which meant her work was in high demand. So high, in fact, that unless she actually liked you, any request for her services would be pushed to the bottom of a never-ending backlog of work.

Just as well that Harpreet owed Lea a few favours, plus they genuinely got along.

But Lea certainly wouldn't be mentioning the cross-agency assistance, given Goldman's mood.

'Please,' Goldman said. 'I don't even want to know what you've got. The best thing for you to do is destroy *everything* you took from that house.'

'But we can't destroy our knowledge,' Lea said, undeterred now as she pulled out the papers and put them on the desk in front of her.

Goldman continued to glower but at least didn't have another comeback. Yet.

'Please,' Lea said. 'Just... let me explain what we found.'

Goldman thought about it then sighed. 'I'll give you thirty seconds. If you haven't convinced me in that time, you'll burn those papers, and I never want to hear about this matter ever again.'

Lea gulped. Thirty seconds? She was already set up to fail.

'We've identified several unknown parties who Yousefi has either received money from or sent money too. Often round-sum amounts ranging from five thousand pounds to half a million—'

'*Unknown* parties?' Goldman interjected. 'You're going to have to do better than this.'

'They're unknown because there are so many layers to unpick. Offshore LLCs that we haven't been able to get behind, individuals with what look to be obviously coded identities. We have text messages on a burner phone, talking about *Ithaca* that appears to link up with at least two of the payments to Yousefi that—'

'Time's up,' Goldman said.

Lea's shoulders fell.

'If I could just—'

'No,' Goldman said. 'You can't. I only have one question for you, and I need a clear answer.'

'Yes?'

'Have you found *any* evidence that Yousefi is personally involved with any criminal activity, or has involvement with any of the parties from the Iran investigation, other than because of who he's married to?'

'No. Nothing direct, but these parties, the transactions, the mention of Ithaca—'

Goldman held her hand up to stop Lea.

'Just so we're clear, you said *no*. You have *zero* evidence to link Yousefi to activities relevant to MI6 investigations, current or past?'

'We have no direct, *clear* evidence, but—'

'Then destroy everything you took, and I mean that. I'll forget about the indiscretion, for the sole reason that I understand the personal toll past events have taken on you both. But this is the end of it—'

'And what if we *do* find evidence that links to Yousefi to the Iranians and to—?'

'Then come back to me and show me. But you *won't* find that evidence by targeting Yousefi directly, in this country, without my say-so. And you do understand the Iranian investigation remains sidelined?'

Goldman stared at her, waiting for a response, but Lea didn't answer.

'We understand,' Denis said. 'Sorry for putting you in this position.'

Goldman turned her wrath on him. 'Tell me, Denis, if you weren't so eager to impress *her* all the time... would you ever have done something as stupid as this?'

He didn't answer. Lea said nothing either, even if the comment was obviously designed to rile both her and her colleague.

'We're done here,' Goldman added.

Lea couldn't get out of her seat quick enough. She stormed to the door. Stormed down the corridor.

'Lea, wait!' Denis shouted.

She didn't. She reached the lifts. Hit the call button. Was standing inside pushing the door close button over and over when Denis barged his way inside.

'I'm sorry,' he said when the doors had closed behind him.

'For not backing me up?'

His eyes pinched in distaste. 'You think I haven't got your back?'

'You barely said a word in there.'

'I didn't see the point. Goldman had already made her mind up. You saw that, right? Nothing we said would have changed anything.'

Lea didn't respond but turned away from him.

Denis hit the emergency stop button and the lift rocked to a halt.

'What are you doing?' Lea said, moving towards the panel but Denis blocked her.

'You really think I don't have your back?'

He was angry. With her. Well, she was angry with him. With everything, really.

'I'd do anything for you,' he said. 'I mean that.'

'Can we just go?' she said to him.

'No. Not until you understand—'

'Then what are we going to do from here?' she asked him.

He didn't answer.

'Will you still help me? Because I won't just give up.'

'You heard what Goldman said. We can't—'

'So you *won't* help me. You just said you'd do *anything* for me.'

'Lea, please—'

'Can we just go!' she shouted, glaring at him. And for a moment he looked really angry too.

Then he reached forward, closed his eyes. Planted his lips on hers.

He should have realised within the first millisecond that he'd misread the situation. Instead, he doubled down and pushed himself closer, pushed his lips more firmly onto hers as though willing for a better response.

She thumped his side. Not hard. Just hard enough. He spluttered and stepped back... She expected to see anger. But he just looked really embarrassed. A little... destroyed.

'Don't ever do that again,' she said to him.

'Lea, I'm sorry, I—'

'Can we just go?'

He slumped as he turned and pushed the button. The lift carried on down without another word from either of them. When the doors opened Lea brushed past him and was out like a whippet.

'Lea!' Denis shouted out.

She kept going.

'Lea, please!'

But she paid him no attention as she carried on out.

19

SOMERSET

One year ago

Visiting her parents the morning of the wedding was about the hardest thing Lea had ever done in her life, and that was saying something. She'd been with them for only a couple of hours, had taken off the engagement ring on her way up the drive, quickly smoothing the indented flesh on her finger as though to help further erode, disguise, hide reality from them. While she was there, they'd talked, smiled, laughed, reminisced. They'd really wanted her to stay longer but she insisted she couldn't because she needed to be out of the country.

Not a lie. She and Callum would be on a flight to Portugal – their happy place – first thing in the morning.

But that wasn't really the point.

She felt cruel, having to lie to them about *this*, perhaps the most important day of her life, and probably one of the most important in theirs if they'd known.

The big problem was that this way of living had been cemented years ago, and there was no way back now. Not everyone who worked for MI6 had to live a bogus existence. It was a choice. A choice Lea had made at the age of only twenty-one when she'd been suggested for work overseas as a field agent, at a time when to her the world, especially the world her new paymasters could show her, seemed so exciting and diverse. The only drawback? Or not the only one, but certainly one of the biggest, was that she had to leave Claire Simmonds behind and become someone else entirely. Lea Torrence. But doing so simply opened so many different doors for the types of assignments she could be given, because it all came down to very simple concepts of security and risk. With a false identity, Lea was able to take on much riskier assignments, knowing that those she loved the most were left protected by their disassociation.

It had seemed like a no-brainer to a twenty-one-year-old, eyes wide open at what the world had to show her.

And it *had* been worth it. She'd done so much in the last few years, so much for the greater good. But now... there really was no turning back.

A knock on the door. Lea took one last look in the mirror, satisfied with her hair, make-up, the hired dress, and got up from the chair and moved to the door. She opened up. Goldman.

'Wow. You look... stunning.'

Honestly, Lea felt it. Goldman... She looked pretty good too. With her hair loose – did she have some extensions too? – and make-up and a tasteful light blue dress she looked so... normal. So unlike her normal self, at least. Helped by the coloured contact lenses too. But today she wasn't Erica Goldman, either the MI6 variety, or the BTS Consulting variety. Today she was Pauline Torrence, Lea's mother. The only member of Lea's 'family' who'd be attending the small ceremony.

'Hi, Mum,' Lea said and after a brief silence they both burst out laughing.

'Come on, let's go.'

Goldman smiled and Lea grabbed her purse and they headed out, made their way down to the hotel lobby, the silence becoming more awkward. Was it sad that Lea's boss had to be here to play this role today? Very. But actually, Goldman knew Lea as well as anyone else in her life, so it was also fitting in many ways, even if their relationship had always been on a professional level, no real social interactions. And the sad truth was that the only other option would have been to hire an actor which would have been ridiculous. This was still Lea's day. She didn't want strangers here.

She just wished there'd been a way to get her real parents here. She was an only child and because of a variety of issues from deaths to fall outs, they were now the only family she had. And it wasn't like she had a big friend group either. Only assets and people at MI6 really, a small number of whom – mainly from the office-based teams in London – she'd invited to the evening reception later so that it appeared she was something approaching normal to Callum and his family and guests.

Lea and Goldman moved out across the reception area of the hotel, a boutique establishment on the outskirts of Bath. A pleasant hotel, with a stunning manicured country garden, but it really wasn't the kind of place Lea had envisaged getting married in over the years. Too small. Too plain. Except, in her conversations with Callum, it was exactly the type of place she'd insisted she'd be most comfortable with.

And despite pressure on him for something bigger, more spectacular, which she knew came mostly from his mum and aunt, Lea had won out. The main reason for his capitulation had been her compromise of getting married sooner rather than later. Because she really did want to marry him, even if she'd dragged her feet for the best part of eighteen months, unsure how they could ever make it work. Now a certain part of her just wanted to get it over and done with so she and Callum could move on.

A horrible way to think about her own wedding, but that was the reality.

They reached the entrance to the Prince Philip Suite. A grand name for a space that often doubled as a basic meeting room for small conferences. But it did have ornate fixtures from the beamed ceiling to the big stone fireplace. The doors were open. Lea spotted Callum at the desk by the fireplace, talking to the registrar. He realised she was there and turned and beamed at her and came over.

'Lea...' was all he said as he took in her dress before he reached forward and planted his lips on her cheek. Well, he'd aimed for her mouth but she twisted her head away so he didn't smudge her lipstick. 'You look *amazing*.' He turned to Goldman. 'And you must be Pauline.'

Goldman held out her hand and Lea tried not to cringe. She'd dreaded this first interaction. Dreaded the idea of any interaction between the two of them.

Callum shook her hand, more than a little awkwardly, although Goldman looked anything but.

'How was the flight over?' he asked her. Because Pauline Torrence now lived in Spain. Keep her out of sight, out of mind.

'A bit boring,' Goldman said. 'No TVs on a short hop like that.'

'Andalusia, right?'

'Yes. A small white-washed village up in the mountains. Heaven on earth.'

'Can't wait to visit it. I love that area.'

'Oh, that would be lovely,' Goldman said, unfazed. 'You know, you look even better than the pictures Lea sent me. Really nice. Big and strong, just like Lea told me.'

She actually had the audacity to squeeze his bicep. Lea would have words with her later...

Callum smirked, was obviously flattered. 'It's just a shame her dad couldn't be here too,' he said.

Referencing the fact that Lea Torrence's father had passed away three years ago from a heart attack.

'Come on,' he said, checking his watch. 'Let me do a couple of quick intros before we get started.'

And it *was* quick, because there were only a small number of people inside the room. If his mum had got her way, she'd have filled this place out three or four times over with friends and cousins and whatevers. Callum hadn't even invited his brother, although Lea knew there was a lot of tension between the two of them, even if he'd never fully opened up to her about why. Instead it was only his parents, who now lived in Cumbria a few hours' drive away, and his best man, Ollie, a fellow rugby nut who'd known Callum since they were in their teens, even if they rarely saw each other these days given Ollie had moved to Ireland to be closer to his wife's family.

Cosy. And everyone looked so happy, at ease.

So very nearly perfect, really.

'You ready?' Callum asked her, and looking into his eyes in that moment, it was so easy to bury every single trouble that bubbled away.

'Yes.'

She took his hand, and they made their way to the registrar.

* * *

The evening reception in the local town hall had a few more people. Five turned up from 'BTS', but with other halves and kids that meant twelve. Pretty much every single person who'd ever been associated with Callum's rugby club made an appearance as well, which easily took the numbers into the forties, fifties, mostly big, brawny men who guzzled beer like it was the last chance they'd ever get.

Not a problem to Lea. Even if she'd met barely a quarter of the people who were at her wedding, it was amazing. She couldn't remember ever being in a room so full of people just living life and happy to be there. Happy *for* her. And Callum, obviously, but as the bride she really was the belle of the ball, everyone wanting to greet her, congratulate her, compliment her.

Callum wasn't holding back. Encouraged by his old teammates he was becoming more and more animated as the alcohol kicked in, the dance floor a rowdy – in a fun way – mess by nightfall. Even Goldman was having a good time. Lea wasn't sure she'd ever seen her boss smile like this before. Apparently, the man she was chatting to, and had been pretty flirty with for a while now, was Jim, a widower who used to be the manager at Riverdale RFC. Goldman seemed to be forgetting she was actually a happily married woman and not a widow herself.

Lea broke away from the group on the dance floor and started towards Goldman, only realising then just how wobbly her legs were, how much her head spun.

Goldman spotted her coming and dropped the flirty pout, looked wary like a teenager caught out by her parents. But then Lea paused, a few steps away from her boss. Because Goldman had glanced to her left to look at the man who'd just walked into the room.

Denis.

He nodded to Lea, went straight to the bar.

Lea carried on to Goldman who moved forward, away from old Jim.

'What the hell is he doing here?' Lea asked.

'Nothing to do with me,' Goldman said. 'But... why *wouldn't* he be here?'

Lea didn't say anything to that. Just kind of glared at Goldman.

'What?' her boss challenged.

'Just make sure you... you know. Don't do anything stupid here.'

She looked over at Jim who smiled and winked.

'I think I'm old enough, experienced enough to make those kind of calls myself. Don't you?' Goldman said.

Although the words were more than a little slurred, and after she'd finished them, she downed the rest of her glass of champagne and tootled off towards the toilets.

Lea caught Jim's eye. He winked at her too.

She had bigger problems than worrying about her boss canoodling with that guy.

Although really it wasn't the idea of Goldman cheating on her husband that bothered her, as much as the fact that the more drunk Goldman got, the more likely it was she'd slip up somehow.

And now Denis was here.

Damn, this whole fucking thing was like a ticking time bomb ready to explode.

Or was that just Lea?

She went over to the bar, smiles and pats on the shoulder every couple of steps. Denis already had a pint of beer in his hand, standing with his back to the party.

She stepped up beside him.

'What are you doing here?' she asked him.

He downed most of his beer rather than answer.

'Denis, I—'

'Denis? Don't you want to give me a made-up name instead?'

'If you've come here to—'

'What?' he said, staring at her, challenging.

'Cause trouble.'

'Why would I do that?'

She didn't answer.

'Although I am pretty pissed off I didn't get an invite. After everything we've been through together.'

'Yeah. Because today is all about you.'

He finished his beer and signalled the bartender for another. And Lea could tell the one he'd just had wasn't his first.

'What are you trying to prove?' she asked him.

'Why are you talking to me like I'm a problem?' he asked, genuine bitterness now.

'Denis, it's not that. But you *know* how hard this is for me. Because I've told you exactly that!'

'You have? I must have forgotten, because I've hardly seen you the last six months. I've started to wonder if you're deliberately avoiding me now, making sure we never get assigned on anything together.'

'That's not true, I—'

'You think me being here jeopardises your big day?'

'It *does*. Whether that's your intention or not.'

Denis grabbed his new beer and glugged it as he looked over at the dance floor. To Callum. Dancing like an overconfident idiot, in all honesty. But a damn happy one.

'I'm still more than a little shocked it's *that* guy who made you question everything you are.'

And she really didn't like the way he said that.

'You think you're better than him?' Lea challenged.

'Doesn't matter what I think.'

'Actually, it does,' she said. 'Because... you're still one of the most important people in my life. I *trust* you with my life, Denis. I just wish you'd be happy for me.'

'I am. But don't forget this impacts me too. Like you say, we still work in the field together. We need to rely on each other, like we have in the past. Can you still do that now that—'

She put her hand on his. '*Nothing* changes today,' she said. 'We're a team. Same as always.'

She pulled her hand away again.

'Please, just... let me have this day.'

He snorted and shook his head with obvious disdain.

'I'm disappointed you think I'd come here to screw things up for you,' he said.

She didn't get a chance to respond before Callum bounded over.

'Hey, princess,' he said, coming up behind Lea and wrapping his hands around her waist. He nuzzled into her neck and any other time or place, and she would have welcomed his touch so badly.

'Hey,' she said.

Callum pulled back and glanced over at Denis and the inevitable eureka moment came.

'Wait. Aren't you...?'

'I'm Denis.'

An unsure handshake followed. Unsure on Callum's part, at least.

'Weren't you in...?'

'Toulouse? Yeah. Good memory.'

'That... was a while ago, but I'm pretty good at faces,' Callum said. 'But... you two didn't really know each other back then, did you?'

He directed the question at Lea.

'No,' she said. 'We didn't. But it turned out Denis works for BTS too. That's why he was there in Toulouse, at the same conference. We'd just never met before. We've crossed paths a few times recently.'

'That's right,' Denis said, loving every moment of the awkwardness.

'Funny, though,' Callum said. 'I've not heard Lea mention anything about you since then. And look now. Here you are at my wedding.'

'Ha! Yeah, here I am.' Denis raised his glass in toast, acting oblivious to Callum's more hostile tone. 'To the bride and groom.'

Neither Lea nor Callum had a glass to raise.

'You know what, though, Callum?' Denis said.

'What?'

'I've heard a lot about *you* since then. I feel like I've known you forever. She never stops yapping about you.'

Denis laughed. Callum didn't. He received a tap on his shoulder. His gang wanted him – and Lea – back on the dance floor.

'It's nice that you came,' Callum said, ever the gent, before he was whisked away.

'Be there in a sec!' Lea called out to the group, before she turned back to Denis.

'I don't think he likes me,' Denis said, barely hiding his delight.

She opened her mouth to speak but the chorus of calls from the dance floor stopped her.

'Please, just... stay out of trouble,' she said to Denis.

'You know me,' he said, raising his glass again before she was dragged away.

20

LEIXOES

Present day

It took forever for the cruise ship to dock, for the staff to do whatever the hell it was they had to do before passengers were allowed to disembark for the excursions. Callum hadn't quite been at the front of the queue, which actually surprised him given how early he'd arrived. Not because he was hoping to get a run on Hinch – although it had crossed his mind a thousand times or so – but because he just wanted off. As soon as possible.

He and Hinch hadn't exactly arranged to meet, as he'd simply assumed she'd find him. Which she had, while the boat was still floating towards the dock. They barely spoke a word to each other as they waited.

Finally, the time came and Callum, Hinch by his side, was walking down the gangway to the dock, enjoying the early-morning salty air.

His legs felt like jelly for the first few steps when he reached the concrete – not him steadying his sea legs, but because of his continued uncertainty as to what he should do next.

Nothing. He did absolutely nothing. Just carried on walking, walking until they were on the road outside the port.

'And what's your plan now, genius?' Hinch asked, smirking, as though enjoying his discomfort, his indecisiveness, his obvious lack of a clear plan. At least, he had no clear plan now that *she* was with him.

He didn't answer, too busy thinking.

'Are you going to tell me what we're doing here?' she asked.

'We need to rent a car. It's a couple of hours' drive.'

'Drive where?'

'Into the mountains.'

It looked like she was going to say something else to that but then didn't. At least not until she'd obviously had enough of his lack of action.

'Don't let me stop you,' she said. 'We need a car. Why don't you go find us one?'

Which meant she was expecting him to put it in his name. Sneaky?

'Don't you have like a... fake ID or something you could use so it's not so... obvious?' he said. 'The police are looking for me, remember.'

She laughed. 'Of course I do. All you had to do was ask.'

* * *

An hour later and she was driving the little Fiat 500 east, away from the coast, and towards the Serra da Lousã mountains. Callum was familiar with the route – at least once out of the city, because had never headed there from the port before – but he'd asked Hinch to drive regardless as he wanted her and her hands occupied. She didn't question that. But she did question him. A lot.

'Tell me about the bank,' she said.

Not the first time she'd asked him, but he'd tried his best to fob her off before.

'What about it?'

'You knew Lea had a safe-deposit box there.'

'Not until yesterday.'

'Then how did you find out?'

'She... I figured it out. I found a receipt. Sort of.'

'A receipt? Who gives a receipt for a safe-deposit box?'

'Not a receipt. A record.'

'You're not a very convincing liar.'

'I'm not lying! I just...'

'Don't want to tell the truth? At least not all of it.'

'Look, it's you people who came to me, suggesting that I must know about Lea's work. That either she left something with me or at least told me where I could find it.'

'Did she?'

'No! Haven't you figured that out by now?'

She didn't respond.

'But it is possible that... she left some clues.'

A curious glance over at him.

'Clues? As to where she hid the intel?'

'I don't know. Clues... They might be deliberate or maybe they're not at all, and it's just a trail she left accidentally. I really don't know.'

Although he definitely thought it more likely to be deliberate, given the message on the back of that painting, which *had* to be intended for him. Didn't it? The amended address too. The fact Lea had reframed that picture in the first place.

It was all designed for *him*, surely?

But why hadn't she just told him something!

'And?' Hinch said.

'And what?'

'It felt like you were explaining something to me. And then just decided to quit instead.'

'I found she had that safe-deposit box. I didn't know about it before. I went to the bank, and—'

'How'd you know the security code for the box?' He opened his mouth to answer but she beat him to it. 'Wait. I know. There was a receipt for that too?'

'You're teasing me,' he said.

'Am I?' she said, smiling.

'You think this is funny?'

He said that without enough ill-feeling to wipe the petty smirk away.

'I figured out the passcode because I know my wife.'

And he said those words with real belief, even though it was becoming more and more apparent that he didn't know his wife at all.

'It doesn't make sense though, does it?' he said.

'What?'

'That it was empty. Did she... not have time to put in there whatever it was she'd intended to?'

'Possible, isn't it?' Hinch said. 'Perhaps she was *intending* to leave a trail to what she knew. For you, or whoever else. But never got the chance to finish it. But then...'

'Then what?'

'I don't believe that, and I'm pretty sure you don't either.'

'Why?'

'Because here we are in this tin can car travelling into the mountains in Portugal. So you want to tell me about that? What clue are you following this time?'

'A hunch, not a clue,' he said, turning to stare out of the window as memories whirled. 'A wishful hunch.'

If that even made sense.

'This place means something to you.'

'To us both.'

'Go on?'

'We've been here several times. It's... our happy place.'

He cringed at his own words but how else to describe it? It's literally what she'd told him so many times. Faithfully, he'd thought. But maybe not.

'But what is it?' Hinch asked. 'Hotel? Villa?'

'A villa. On its own, looking out over the hills, vineyards. It's serene, peaceful, beautiful.'

He battled his emotions, trying to stay in control.

'I know this probably doesn't give much comfort to you right now but... I can see how much she meant to you.'

Callum didn't respond.

'But do you really think she would have left something here for you? Why? When?'

'Like I said, it's a hunch. Just like she told me to go see her parents, although... I didn't know they were *her* parents. But that's how I figured out the bank thing. And last time we were here… it was only a few weeks ago. And the *way* she told me, that this was *the* place.'

Hinch looked really dubious, which only made him doubt himself even more.

'Have you booked it?' she asked.

'No. I didn't want to leave a trail. But I did check if it was available. And it is. So it should be empty.'

'And you were going to just break in?' she asked, making it sound as though she thought the idea was hilarious.

'I hadn't quite got that far, at least not in terms of the how. But yeah, basically.'

'Lucky you've got me here then. Would you believe it's something I've got a lot of experience in?'

He said nothing to that. In fact, neither of them said anything for a good while, and soon Hinch was winding the car along the twisting roads on a heavy incline to their destination. Finally, she turned a corner, headed on through open gates and onto a yellow dirt track, the white-washed villa, red terracotta roof tiles looking glorious and pristine against the deep blue sky in the near distance.

'Wow,' Hinch said.

Callum agreed. Every time he came here, that initial view took his breath away. But this time it also filled him with an almost overwhelming sadness.

Hinch parked up, shut the engine down. Callum got out first, then paused.

So quiet up here. Serene. Isolated.

He'd become way too comfortable in Hinch's presence on the ride here but now he realised how stupid that might be. Out here, alone, with a spy? A rogue asset? Mercenary? Whatever the hell she was.

Hinch got out the car too and glanced at him over the roof, obviously realising he was torn about something.

'Are we good?' she asked.

'Yeah.'

'Now wouldn't be a good time for you to go getting any silly thoughts.'

'About what?'

'About anything. I'll get us inside. We'll take a look around. We'll scour every inch if we have to. But you'll stay in my sight for the whole time and not do anything stupid. Yeah?'

'Whatever you say.'

'I like that answer,' she said with a wink. She looked around at the house, the grounds. 'It's pretty. I see why you like it. And... it's quiet. Looks like you were right about it being empty.'

They made their way up to the front door, Hinch a little fidgety.

'Any alarm?' she asked.

'Not the last time I was here. Just a simple lock on the front door, same for the back and for the door to the kitchen on the side. Guess they don't get too many burglaries around here.'

'Just the way I like it,' Hinch said. She dug in her pocket and took out what looked like something between tweezers and a hair clip.

'Always prepared, huh?' Callum said.

'You'd better believe it. Close your eyes and count to ten.'

'You don't want me to see how you do it?'

'You can if you want. Just wanted to test myself.'

He closed his eyes. But... not really.

He'd counted to eight before he heard the click and saw Hinch push down on the handle. He opened his eyes fully and noted the wide smile on her face.

'Not bad, eh?'

He didn't respond but pushed the door further open and took in the familiar sight.

'After you,' she said.

Callum stepped inside and sucked in the cool air of the interior. A little musty. A little... unusual. Not quite the same as he'd expected. As if—

'Why don't you give me a quick tour first, then we'll start searching.'

'OK. This... is the entrance hall.'

Hinch nodded and pursed her lips. 'You know, I think you might be right.'

Callum turned and walked off rather than respond to that. He headed along, the entrance to the kitchen to his left, the main living room on his right, unease growing with each step.

He stopped.

'What is it?' Hinch asked.

The smell. The *feel*.

'We're... not alone,' Callum whispered. 'I think someone's here.'

He nodded to the kitchen doorway, all of two steps from them.

'It's OK,' she said to him, nodding.

Callum froze. But what he should have done was barge through her, trample her head as he rushed out of there. Instead, he fucking froze.

'It's OK,' Hinch said again, calming, like someone would with a wild animal. 'Just... keep going.'

And for some reason he did. Mainly because he actually *wanted* to know what he was walking into before he went on any kind of attack.

Although in the end there was no kind of attack at all. Instead, he simply froze once more when he reached the kitchen doorway and saw the man inside.

A man he recognised.

Lea's 'colleague', Denis.

'Good to see you again, Cal.'

21

'Why does it feel like we've been here before?' Callum said, subtly stepping further into the kitchen, circling around the island, keeping the opposite side to Denis as Hinch took up the space in the doorway. His eyes flicked around the room. A door – an exit to outside – lay to his right. But if he made a dash for it, where would he even go? Hinch had the key for the car, and it was a hell of a long way to run to safety.

Knife block, on the far end of the island.

So he was going to stab these two to death?

'I think he means the time Warren and I were at his house,' Hinch said. 'How we surprised him there.'

'Yeah,' Callum said. 'That's exactly what I meant.' He shot a steely glare at Hinch. 'What the hell was the point of the charade? Picking the lock, walking me in here, like...'

'Like what?' Denis said, looking amused. Smug.

'Just why?' Callum said. 'You knew he was here, waiting?'

'Yes,' Hinch said. 'But how was I supposed to explain that to you before? Would you have gladly walked inside still?'

'So you wanted me inside first, nowhere to run, before springing this latest twist. Do you people ever tell the truth about *anything*?'

'Yes,' Hinch said. 'About wanting to help you.'

'So you…' Callum said to Denis. 'You…'

'Work for MI6,' Denis said. 'Always have done. At least, since we first crossed paths.'

Toulouse. That's when Callum had first met this guy. He felt like a fool all over again thinking back to those days. Back then Lea had claimed Denis was just at the same conference as her. That they hadn't even known each other until that point.

Then the next time Callum had seen him was at his and Lea's wedding. And he hadn't got the vibe that she was particularly welcoming of his presence that day…

'How did you even know to be here?' Callum asked.

Denis smiled again, so damn confident and full of himself. 'It wasn't that hard, really,' he said. 'I was already on the continent. I had Warren and Jenn back home trying to find you, trying to find out whatever they could about what was happening. I hear you've been quite hard to pin down.'

He laughed at that. Apparently Hinch found it funny too. Callum didn't.

'When she said you'd boarded that cruise? I guessed you'd be coming here. Two hours ago, she sent me a text to confirm it, when you put the address into the satnav. But I was already ahead of you both by that point.'

Callum's temperature was rising, anger building, because the villa was anything but stuffy.

I guessed you'd be coming here.

'You know this place?' Callum asked.

'The villa? Not specifically. The area? I've been before, yes. And I know you and Lea came here often.'

'Yeah. I'm sure you know everything about us. About me. About her.'

'You don't need to sound so bitter,' Denis said. 'We were colleagues. Pretty much partners. The first time you two came here… there wasn't *exactly* an ulterior motive. But I was in the country too. We'd arranged to meet an asset here. The vacation, travelling with you, was good cover for her.'

Callum didn't say anything, lost for words as his brain scrambled for answers, scrambled to make sense of the memories he had which he was now so unsure about.

The first time he and Lea had come here? One of the best long weekends of his entire damn life. She'd been so happy, relaxed. They'd eaten great food, drank *so* much local beer and wine, sunbathed, read, lazed in and by the pool.

She'd taken a trip to a day spa... a treat to unwind. He'd been happy to sit by the pool by himself for a few hours – he hated massages.

He'd been played. Then. How many other fucking times?

'Don't beat yourself up,' Denis said, still enjoying every moment of Callum's discomfort. 'It's just who she was. A damn good agent.'

'A manipulative liar,' Callum said, and immediately felt bad for it. And the insult seemed to knock some of Denis's smugness away too, as though *he* was Lea's great defender.

'She was conflicted,' Denis said. 'Because of *you*.'

Callum snarled. Would happily have hopped over the island at that point and smashed his fist into Denis's gut at the insinuation that *he* was the cause of whatever problems Lea had.

He didn't. And not just because he wasn't a man of violence, but because he was way too wary of what these two were capable of.

A thought struck him. 'Wait,' he said. '*You* were there? In Bucharest?'

'Yes.'

'You're the missing agent?'

No answer or even indication this time, but Callum still felt that was kind of the same thing as saying yes.

'So you know exactly what she was doing there,' he added. 'What you *both* were doing there. And why she was killed.'

'I know a lot more than most people,' Denis said. 'That's for sure. But I don't know everything.'

'You know who killed her?' Callum asked.

A nod.

'You know why?'

'That's more complicated.'

'Are you going to tell me what the hell is going on?' Callum asked.

'I will,' Denis said. His gaze flicked from Callum to the knife block which Callum had edged towards. 'But why don't we go sit down... somewhere more comfortable.'

* * *

The living room, with a gorgeous mountain view and patio doors opening out on to the swimming pool, definitely should have been more comfortable than the kitchen, but Callum really wasn't feeling it.

Still, he had taken a seat, propped forward in an armchair as though ready to spring into action should he need to, decide to. Denis sat across a coffee table from him. Hinch stood sentry by the doorway, like she often did.

'I understand from Jenn that the police spoke to you already?' Denis said.

'Yes.'

'I tried to get her and Warren to you before they did. If I could have been there myself, I would have been. So I apologise for how this has all been thrown on to you.'

Callum didn't respond, but Denis's words didn't really feel like any kind of heartfelt apology.

'Did anyone from MI5 or MI6 speak to you too?' Denis asked.

'Haven't your minions already filled you in on this?'

'I'm not anybody's minion, idiot,' Hinch said, looking genuinely offended.

'I'm asking *you* to fill me in,' Denis said.

'Then yes. A man claiming to be from MI6 spoke to me. He said his name was Andrew White.'

Denis said nothing. Showed no reaction, no recognition at all.

'Do you know him?' Callum prompted.

'Yes.'

'And is he really from MI6?'

'He is.'

'And is he a good guy in this or a bad guy?'

'You're expecting there to be a very clear-cut distinction between the two. In my world there often isn't. But right now... White is a man probably best avoided. For all of us in this room.'

'Is that answer supposed to make me feel better? Because it really doesn't.'

'I'm just trying to be honest with you.'

Callum resisted laughing at that ludicrous statement.

'What did White say to you? Ask you?'

'He told me Lea was on an operation in Bucharest. That it went wrong. She was killed. Another agent... who I now believe to be you, went missing. Along with some intelligence. Intelligence that supposedly got Lea killed in the first place. Does that sound about right?'

'It's definitely one way to spin it.'

'So do *you* have this mysterious information?'

'No,' Denis said.

'But you know what it is?'

'Yes and no.'

'Are you going to explain that?'

'In time. But first let's finish your story. We were talking about White.'

'There's not much else to say. He believed, like you people seem to, that perhaps Lea had given this intel to me somehow. Or hidden it somewhere only I'd know about.'

Callum paused to see if Denis or Hinch would make a comment on that point, but neither did.

'He told me little about the mission Lea was on but did put several faces in front of me.'

A raised eyebrow from Denis to Hinch who shook her head.

'What faces?' Denis asked.

'They're in my bag.'

The rucksack he'd brought with him for this 'day trip' from the cruise. He'd left the suitcase in the cabin. He wondered now how that would play out. How long before the cruise line identified that two of its passengers never reboarded at Leixoes? And what would they do then? Alert the authorities? The police?

'Go get it,' Denis said to Hinch, and off she went.

Denis and Callum sat in silence. Crazy thoughts whirred in Callum's head about making a move while it was one on one. But he didn't, and soon Hinch was back. She tossed the bag to Callum, and he pulled the photos out and placed them on the coffee table. Denis took them and perused while Hinch hovered over his shoulder.

'You know them?' Callum asked.

'Yes,' Denis said. 'I'm sure by now, if White didn't already tell you, that you've figured the connection between Hadjam and the MP Omar Yousefi.'

'Yes.'

'And I can tell you the other men are, one way or another, connected to the Iranian government.'

'And these are the men who got Lea killed?'

'Perhaps not directly, but yes.'

'Why?'

'It's complicated.'

'Because of Yousefi? He's corrupt? Is that it?'

'I'm damn certain he is. But there's more to it than that. Much, much more.'

Callum sighed. 'But I'm realising you're not going to be telling me about that.'

'Because it's more complex than you could imagine, Callum. Just trust—'

'Trust? Trust what? You two? The lies Lea told me? White? How can I trust anything that any one of you has ever said or done to me?'

And Denis didn't even try to convince him, only sat there silently a moment. 'Anything else from White?'

'No.'

'How'd you get away? Given you've been named as a wanted man, I can only assume they didn't willingly let you go.'

'Or maybe they did, for the very reason that they wanted to follow me, to see what I'd do next.'

Denis nodded, as though he believed that part of the explanation to be correct, although he didn't seem at all bothered by the idea.

'And why did you come here?' he asked.

Callum briefly explained. The visit to Lea's parents. The painting and its hidden message. The empty safe-deposit box. The idea that if Lea had left him something, it – or at least a clue to it – could be here in Portugal.

Denis smiled. 'You're actually pretty good at this. A couple of days and you're already thinking like us.'

'I'm *nothing* like you.'

The smile faded as quickly as it had appeared. 'Well, you were right to come here,' Denis said.

'Because?'

'Because she *did* leave something for you. Didn't even take me that long to find it.' He reached into his pocket and took out a mobile phone which he held aloft like it was a trophy he'd won.

'Where?' Callum asked.

'Hidden. But not so well hidden. Perhaps that's only because Lea and I think so alike though.'

Callum cringed at that comment. Another dig at him? 'How'd you know that's for me?'

'Listen for yourself.'

Denis tossed the phone, and Callum grabbed it and unlocked the screen. A pretty basic phone, much like the one he'd bought yesterday. No contacts, no calls received or made, no messages, no browser history. Only a single voice note.

Callum hit the play button and put the phone to his ear.

And then he heard her voice.

His heart pounded against his ribs, the beats so hard he thought the bones would smash.

'*Callum... if you're listening to this... the first thing I want to say is I'm sorry. Sorry for everything. The lies, what you're going through now. I hope you'll forgive me. There's one thing you have to know... my love for you was real...*' A longer pause this time and he could hear her breathing still, and... was she sobbing? '*I know you're very confused. And it's very likely, if you're listening to this, that your life is in danger, and it's because of me. And for that, I... I hope you can forgive me. But I can still help you, so listen very carefully...*' Another pause. Silent this time. '*Find Denis Petit... You have to find him.*'

Confused, Callum looked at the phone. The voicemail had ended. He rewound the last few seconds and listened again.

'I don't... understand,' Callum said.

'She wanted us to do this together,' Denis said.

Callum ignored him, listened to the whole of the message again. Then he pushed the device out across to Denis, but he shook his head.

'You keep that. It was meant for you.'

'And you found it—'

'Here, in the villa. Behind a false panel in the wardrobe.'

Callum looked from Denis to Hinch. She was giving nothing away, but he wondered again how much she really knew about what was happening, about Denis and Lea at all.

'There must be more to it,' Callum said.

'More to what?'

'To... the clues she was leaving me. Everything was just... to come and find you?'

'No,' Denis said. 'I don't believe that. I think she probably really did intend to leave you more. Perhaps files, papers, I don't know. That deposit box... maybe she never got around to filling it.'

'Or maybe someone else got there before me.'

Denis hunched his shoulders.

'*You?*' Callum questioned.

'I've not been anywhere near England. Probably not a very good idea right now.'

Callum looked at Hinch.

'Not me,' she said. 'I was too busy following you around.'

'I get you're confused,' Denis said. 'Frustrated. Angry. Upset.'

'You don't know the half of it.'

'I do. Because I'm all of those things too.'

Callum disagreed, strongly, but he didn't bother to argue.

'And I *can* help you, Callum. We need to help each other now.'

'How?'

'You want answers to what happened? So do I.'

'You were there,' Callum said. 'You know exactly what happened.'

'Correct. We were taking part in an exchange. The intel Lea had—'

'On the MP? The Iranians?'

'Yes. We were swapping that intel for a prisoner. An American asset. But we were blindsided. The whole exchange was a set-up.'

'So you don't have the intelligence now?'

'No. But there's more, Callum, so I want you to listen really carefully to what I'm about to say. What about I'm about to propose.'

'OK?' Callum said, his stomach knotting with unwelcome thoughts.

'I know the people we met with. The main man. I know where we can find him.'

'You think he still has the intel? Is that what you're saying?'

'I think we could follow breadcrumbs that Lea may or may not have left for you... or we can go straight to the source. Find the intel we need, hand it over to the right people, and find the bastards who attacked her and me.'

Callum was nodding. Why was he nodding...? Because revenge, payback, whatever it was, really did sound good to him.

'But... you *had* that intel. So you surely already know what it is?' Callum said. 'And if the whole purpose of the exchange was to give that intel to these people... isn't that what happened?'

The thought had made sense in his head but it didn't really as he tried to explain it.

'Attacking us was *not* part of the deal,' Denis said. 'And I'll be candid... I didn't know everything Lea had found. I was helping her, but the intel was hers. It appears now... she most likely didn't bring everything she had to that exchange, which means what she had was far more damaging than she'd told me. If it gets into the wrong hands...'

'Damaging to who?' Callum asked.

'To people a lot more powerful than you or me. But there's one more thing, Callum.'

'What?'

'You haven't *seen* Lea's body, have you?'

'No. It's only been two days, and she was in Bucharest and...'

The penny dropped. His heart was ready to explode with hope. Or was it despair? He didn't know which or why.

'And it's because it's too soon?' Denis suggested. 'The remains haven't been repatriated yet? Or something else.'

'Something else?'

'Callum, put the pieces together. You're her husband, but you've seen no body, and I'm guessing there was no proposal for you to go to Bucharest to identify her.'

'No, but—'

'I saw her lying on the floor, hurt, but... dead?'

'You saw her lying on the floor hurt and... what? You ran away?'

'Wrong question right now. Callum, I'm trying to tell you... this might not be a revenge mission. It might be a rescue mission, because...'

'Because?'

'Because I think there's a very good chance that Lea is still alive.'

22

EIGHT MONTHS AGO

Lea had left Callum in bed, snuck out of the house in the dark at a little past 5 a.m. on a Monday morning to catch the train east to London. She'd been queasy all weekend and the rattling train only made matters worse. She tried to sleep through the journey but simply couldn't, which only left her mind rumbling as much as her belly.

She'd been home less than forty-eight hours, and in all had been on the go for several weeks between home, the capital and overseas, never quite sure how long she'd be staying at her next destination. She was finally making progress on the Iranian investigation, but that progress came at a snail's pace, and at big personal cost, with Lea eking out what otherwise would have been personal time in order to meet Goldman's demands on other official assignments, her boss – most people – unaware of her moonlighting.

Both she and Callum struggled to remain upbeat each time she had to rush away from home again at short notice. His big problem? He was too damn nice. Why wouldn't he just put his foot down and tell her no more? Tell her that she needed to be home more often, with him, so they could live as a real married couple. And if she didn't then he'd leave. If he did that...

No, who was she kidding? She couldn't stop. Not yet. But soon. It had to be soon.

In any case, the call the night before to head to London had been unexpected. She'd hoped for three or four days at home, but Goldman had demanded her presence at Vauxhall Cross the next morning. A demand like that usually meant bad news. Lea didn't know why that'd be the case this time, and in fact had a lot of good findings to discuss with her boss. But that didn't stop the nerves creeping in as she neared the capital. Those nerves ramped several notches as she walked along towards HQ. Up to the top floor. The same meeting room she'd been in a few months ago, with Denis, when she'd last been berated by her boss.

No sign of Denis waiting for her outside today. She'd not heard from him for a couple of weeks. He was still being distant with her, and, quite frankly, if he wanted to sulk because she was now happily married, putting to death any notions he had of bedding her himself, then he could.

A bit harsh perhaps, to think like that about a man she'd shared so much with, but it seemed like it was his choice to distance himself from her, not the other way around.

She reached the closed door and banished the uneasy thoughts of her colleague from her mind, prepped herself, then knocked.

'Come in,' Goldman called out.

Lea opened the door. Paused. Not just Goldman inside. Denis was already there too. A surprise, but not unfathomable. The really big shock was the other person sitting in the room, beside Goldman. A man she'd not met in person before, but who she knew an increasing amount about.

Omar Yousefi.

Her stomach growled, as if in anger at the turn-up.

'Lea, please take a seat,' Goldman said.

Lea did so, fighting off the renewed wave of nausea to take the seat opposite Denis, with Goldman and Yousefi on the adjacent end of the table.

'This is her?' Yousefi said with disdain. Straight to the point, no attempt at any pleasantries.

'This is another of my agents, Lea Torrence.'

'What's going on?' Lea asked.

Yousefi huffed. 'Is that the best you can do? Plead ignorance? I thought you people were supposed to be expert actors.'

He shook his head.

'Lea, Mr Yousefi is here because—'

'Because apparently you two weren't satisfied with ransacking my home here in London, stealing my things, you've now gone and done the same thing at two of my other places as well. Right under my nose. The last time while my wife was home alone *sleeping*.'

'What are you talking about?' Lea said, eyes flitting around the room. 'I haven't...'

She stopped the protest when Yousefi angrily shoved two photographs across the table. Lea didn't need to pick them up to see what they were: images from a home security camera. Two shadowy figures with baseball caps. Looked to be a man and a woman, roaming through a home office. Not the one in Knightsbridge though.

'This was from two nights ago,' Goldman said. 'From Mr Yousefi's home in Yorkshire.'

'It sure as hell looks like *you* two,' Yousefi said. 'Exactly the same as the other time.'

'That is *not* me,' Lea said.

'Yeah, and *he* said the same thing.' He jabbed a finger at Denis. 'But how am I supposed to believe two people who lie about everything for a living?'

'That. Is. *Not*. Me,' Lea said. 'Two nights ago? I was home, not in Yorkshire.'

'You have any witnesses to that,' Yousefi said. Stated, rather than actually asking a question he expected an answer to. 'Because—'

'Actually, yes, I do have a witness for that. But I don't need to tell you anything about the circumstances because it's none of your damn business. I wasn't in Yorkshire two days ago. I've never been to your home there.'

'Oh, but you're not denying you broke into my house here or in Berkshire?'

Lea didn't answer that.

'Mr Yousefi's come here today to clear the air,' Goldman said. 'He has every right to have you prosecuted—'

'It wasn't me!' Lea shouted.

'And I already told them it wasn't me either,' Denis added, sounding bored rather than pissed off or put on the spot.

'Will you two let me finish?' Goldman said.

Lea and Denis didn't say anything.

'Mr Yousefi has come here as a courtesy, and you can argue all you like, quibble over who did what and when, but I'm going to make this very clear and simple for you both. Neither of you is to go anywhere near Mr Yousefi, his properties, his family members at all. At. All. And if you do, you won't just lose your jobs here, you'll be behind bars. Have I made that clear enough?'

'Yes,' Denis said with a little salute that made Yousefi's face twist with renewed rage.

'Yeah,' Lea added. 'That's clear.'

And apparently Yousefi didn't have much more to say because less than two minutes later he was out of the door.

Silence in the room for a little while.

'It really wasn't me,' Lea said, to Goldman as much as to Denis.

'Same,' he added.

Goldman sighed. 'Right now, I don't know if I believe either of you. But I think the point has been made.'

'He shouldn't have been here,' Lea said. 'You shouldn't have brought him here.'

'Excuse me?'

'He's seen our faces. He knows our names. You just exposed two MI6 agents to a potential enemy of the state!'

Goldman balled her fist and thumped the desk, causing Lea to jump in shock.

'*I* just saved you from a prison sentence.'

That. Or she'd just put her and Denis's lives further at risk. But Lea didn't bother to try to get Goldman to see that.

'Is there anything else?' Goldman asked, and Denis shuffled in his seat as though he was already done and ready to go.

'Actually, yes,' Lea said.

A surprised look from the other two.

Goldman sighed as though that wasn't the answer she wanted. 'To do with the Iranians?'

'Yes.'

Goldman sighed again. 'If this has anything to do with information you gained from—'

'It wasn't me at his home!' Lea shouted again. 'I haven't directly targeted Yousefi at all since you last told me not to. But that doesn't mean I haven't been pursuing the other parties when I can, the foreign parties, Hadjam, Azmoun, Taremi, the other Iranians.'

Goldman groaned but said nothing. Not the worst response under the circumstances.

'And I think I *have* found a link to Yousefi. It might even explain why he's now so keen to put himself in front of you because he knows I'm close to something. Something big.'

Goldman pretty much growled at the mention of the MP as though even saying his name was now off limits.

'Give me something tangible,' Goldman said. 'Or we're done here.'

'I told you before about the references to Ithaca?'

'And?'

'I think... the most likely explanation is that it refers to a clandestine op, being run by the Iranian Revolutionary Guard. I've been concentrating on trails of money, originating from companies linked to the Iranian government. One of them is Integrated Electronics Industries. The same company Hossein Taremi works for. Remember? He was one of the men who met with Hadjam in Toulouse.'

'I remember. But what are you suggesting?'

'I'm not suggesting, I'm telling you what I've found. There's money coming from state-sponsored entities in Iran, flowing into Europe to various parties. Abdul Hadjam is one of the beneficiaries of this money. But so is Omar Yousefi, although not directly. And I didn't find that by raiding his home. I found it by following the money from its source.'

'Payments for what?' Goldman asked.

Lea sighed. 'I don't know exactly. But the codename Ithaca crops up again and again and—'

'But you have no idea what Ithaca *is*?'

'No. Not yet.'

'So this could all just be entirely legitimate? Business deals? Funding?'

'No! Think about who these people are. There's more to it than that, I just don't—'

'Have any evidence to support that theory?'

Lea slumped, didn't bother to confirm.

Goldman shook her head. 'Then come back to me when you do. And in the meantime? Stay the hell away from Omar Yousefi.'

* * *

Lea's gut rumbled as she stepped out into the corridor. It'd been on edge for the whole meeting. No, several days now, really. She paused and held her tummy and hoped it'd pass.

Denis stopped by her side.

'Lea, I—'

'Just a minute.'

She rushed off.

'Lea!'

She strode down the corridor, into the bathroom, flung the door open and was on her knees just in time as she retched and vomit spewed out into the toilet bowl. She retched over and over, each one a little less fierce than the one that preceded it.

Several gags later and her tensed-up body relaxed, the nausea finally dissipating.

For now.

She flushed the toilet and got back to her feet and washed her hands and face. Glanced at herself in the mirror. White as a sheet, eyes all blood-shot, skin blotchy. She looked as bad as she felt.

She moved back outside and groaned inwardly when she saw Denis was still there waiting.

'You OK?' he asked.

'I'm fine. So come on, tell me – was it you?'

'Are you serious? Of course it wasn't me. I assumed it was you, though.'

Lea didn't respond.

'You're really telling me it wasn't?' he asked.

'It definitely wasn't. I was at home in bed with Callum two nights ago.'

A slight cringe from Denis at that.

'Then who the hell was it?' he asked.

'A very good question. It... definitely looked like it could have been us two.'

'You think we're being set up?'

By whom, or for what reason, she had no idea, and Denis's lack of an answer suggested neither did he.

'Sounds like you've been making inroads though,' he said. 'You could have told me about that. Could have asked for my help.'

'I knew you had other stuff on.'

'Lea... can't things just... be like they were between us?'

She thought about that and really didn't know what the answer should be.

'Of course,' she said. 'I—'

But then she paused again as another wave of nausea hit. She hunched over, put her hand to the wall as if she needed the help to hold her up. She squeezed her eyes shut and hoped the feeling would pass. It had to, there was surely nothing left inside her right now.

And it did. Yet when she straightened up, Denis was staring at her curiously.

'Eat something dodgy?' he asked.

'No, I...'

'You're pregnant,' he said.

How the hell did he know?

She didn't answer.

'I'm right, aren't I? Because it just seems like you'd do anything right now to screw your career up.'

She still said nothing.

'So?' he prompted.

She nodded.

'I'm taking it Goldman doesn't know?'

'No. I only found out a few days ago.'

Denis humphed, his eyes narrowing as his detective brain whirred.

'Does *Callum* know?' he asked.

Lea went to push past him, but he stood his ground.

'Denis...'

'He doesn't, does he?'

She didn't answer.

'Which means you didn't plan this. And you're not sure about it.'

She hated everything about this conversation. He could read her so easily, but he had no right to!

'I haven't told him yet,' Lea said. 'Not because I don't want to have a family with him but because... because now is the worst possible timing.'

Denis laughed. 'Should've been more careful, then.'

She thumped his arm. Quite hard. Although the smile it somehow elicited from him seemed to help lighten her own mood. A bit of their old chemistry – *professional* chemistry – returning.

'You want to know the truth?' she said. 'I messed up. I've been on the pill for so long and... I lost track of my prescription. I've been chasing leads all over the damn world and just ran out. Only for a few bloody days. But I was home and... and now this. I should have just told him *no*, but... Damn it.'

Denis laughed. 'Thanks for the details. He's obviously a real charmer.' His smile faltered then dropped away. 'But seriously... you're not keeping it, right? You can't. Goldman—'

'This has nothing to do with Goldman.'

'It has *everything* to do with her. And me. Our jobs. You're not a fucking office-based accountant.'

'You don't need to tell me that, I—'

'Seriously, Lea, think about it. You're off chasing bad people across continents, and you're not just putting your life in danger, but that baby's too.'

'I'm aware of—'

'And think about it from *my* point of view—'

'Would you listen to yourself—'

'I'm only saying what you already know. If I'm out in the field with you, and we're put in a situation and I *know* you've got a baby inside you... Fucking hell. You really want to give me that added responsibility? Me, or any other agent?'

Lea put her head in her hands. She'd already had the exact same conversation in her head over and over. She really hated the way she was having to do it with Denis though, his view clouded by his ulterior intentions. At least in her mind.

'I know,' she said. She just wanted to go now.

'So you're going to get rid of it? Because if you don't, you're gonna have to tell Goldman so she can think about how to deal with it. You. You tell her, or I will.'

She clenched her teeth, channelling anger. So much for rekindled chemistry.

'You're going to, right?' he prompted.

'Yes,' she admitted. 'Like you said, I have to.'

'It's the right call. I've still got your back, Lea. You know that. I'll always have it.'

She didn't say anything, just brushed past him and away down the corridor, not wanting him to see the moment the tears began to fall.

23

BRISTOL

Five weeks ago

Lea lay on the sofa in Callum's arms, her body aligned with his, her back pressed up against him as he slowly breathed in, out. Asleep. He'd been asleep for at least the last ten minutes – she could just tell by the way he was breathing so softly, contentedly. That was fine, she was content there too.

Which was part of the problem. She was so content in moments like these that she wished there wasn't anything else.

But today, tonight, wasn't just any other night for the two of them. Today was *the* day.

Nine months since...

Of course, she had no idea if she would have given birth today, but it still held significance in her mind and even before she'd gone to the clinic on that horrible day several months ago, she'd mentally marked out this date. And then since the clinic, she'd dreaded this day arriving the closer and closer it got to reality.

At least she'd been home for it. She'd made sure of it, really. Not that Callum had any idea at all – not of the pregnancy, the termination or the turmoil that Lea had gone through before, during and after.

She should have told him. She wished she could have, but she just hadn't been able to bring herself to do it. Now... it was too late, even though she felt immensely cruel.

She sighed and Callum shuffled and she turned away from the TV to nuzzle further into him – it wasn't as though she was paying attention to the TV, anyway.

She got a shock when she looked up to find his eyes were open and he was staring down at her.

'You're awake,' she said, smiling and reaching up to kiss his chin.

'I've been awake the whole time,' he said, eyelids flickering as he battled to bring himself around.

She laughed at him, and he pulled away a little to sit up as though that was the only way he'd manage to stay awake.

'Sorry,' he said. 'It's just been a hell of a week.'

'I know.'

'No, you don't,' he said. 'It's not fair on you. You only get a day or two here and there and look at me? Tired out and snoring on the sofa like a bison at... Shit, it's not even nine.'

'Cal, it's perfect. *This*... this is what I look forward to.'

He raised an eyebrow as though he really didn't know if she was being serious or not.

'You really should set higher expectations,' he said. 'For us, for me.'

And even though she knew he'd meant that as a light-hearted comment, the words still stung, for all sorts of reasons she couldn't explain to him.

'What is it?' he asked, taking her hand, obviously reading the signs.

She felt tears welling but fought them back.

'I'm just getting sick of it,' she said.

'Work?'

She nodded. 'This is the last project. I promise you. Once I get through this... I'm done.'

'It's got that bad?'

She nodded again.

'But you've worked so hard for it. There's no pressure from me—'

'So you don't *want* me to be around more?'

This time *she'd* meant to be light-hearted, but her tone had been all wrong and Callum winced.

'You know that isn't true,' he said. 'But... your career—'

'It's just a job. My *life* is with you now. I'll be done soon, I promise. I'll be home all the time. We'll start a family. Then you'll *never* be able to get rid of me.'

He laughed but then just kind of sat there looking shocked. 'You want to... A family? Like... kids?'

'Yes, idiot,' she said, slapping his arm but then had a wave of doubt as though perhaps she'd really misread the whole situation. 'You... you do want that too, don't you?'

He didn't respond. At least, not in words. Instead, he kind of pounced on her, smothered her, wrapped her up in his big hulking arms and planted his lips on her lips, cheeks, neck, shoulders. 'It's what I want most in this world.'

She closed her eyes, causing a tear to fall from each, and in that moment, she had no idea whether it was from the sheer joy of the moment, the prospect of a happy future, or the utter distress of the potentially devastating uncertainty she knew still lay ahead.

* * *

Two days later
London

She sat on the bench in the warm morning sunshine, watching the throngs of walkers, joggers heading along the paths, the groups on the expansive grass fields doing yoga, playing football. So many people, all so seemingly carefree.

Carefree. Is that what others saw in her?

She spotted Denis when he was a couple of hundred yards away and kept an eye on him as he neared, noting his casual stride, the relaxed look on his face. She wanted so badly to trust this man, to still have him by her side in times of need.

She really wasn't sure she could. At least, not like in the past.

'You want a coffee?' he asked when he reached her, nodding to the food van a few yards away.

'I'm good,' she said.

He shrugged and remained hovering.

'Want to take a walk?' he suggested.

'Yeah, why not.'

So off they went, heading north, the sun beaming down on them.

'Not heard from you much recently,' he said.

'I know. Nothing personal.'

'I'm sensing given we're meeting out here like this that you've got something to tell me. Or ask me. Something that couldn't be done over the phone.'

'Yeah.'

'So spit it out.'

'The Iranians—'

'You're still obsessing over that?'

'Why wouldn't I be?' she asked. 'And why aren't you?'

'Because life's too short. They'll come back into our arena if there's a reason.'

'Well, how about I give you a reason.'

He stopped walking and turned to face her.

'Ithaca,' she said.

'Ithaca?'

'That was the code word I'd seen references to, over and over, remember?'

'With the money trails from Iran? You said you thought it was a clandestine op that—'

'I was wrong.'

His eyes pinched. He was doubtful. Perhaps a little suspicious too.

'I don't think it's an operation, or the name of a company, or a group or anything like that.'

'Then what?'

'It's a person.'

Even more suspicious now. 'Who?'

'That's what I need to find out. But... I think... I think it's someone who works for MI6.'

'A mole?'

She nodded.

'You have evidence?'

'It fits a lot of what I know.'

'Which is what, exactly?'

'I think...' She paused, looked around. Not because she was necessarily that concerned about being spied on, but because of the doubts swirling in her mind. *Could she trust this man?* 'This isn't about the Iranians. Or not... not only about the Iranians. It's about a whole sphere of influence being built up in the UK, in the West, by outside powers.'

'From the Middle East, you mean?'

'Yes.'

'Which is something we've been aware of for decades, and—'

'I'm not talking about sovereign funds investing in real estate, sports teams, big businesses. This is something much more shadowy. Dirty.'

'For what end?'

'I don't know. But what I do know is that people are getting rich from this. But people are dying too. Powerful people.'

'Because of Ithaca?'

'Yes.'

He tugged on her arm to get her moving again.

'Explain.'

'If I'm right... one thing I've found is that Ithaca is selling out assets to the Iranians, to others. Just over the last six months I've linked the deaths of three prominent Russians to Ithaca. Two oligarchs, one a powerful FSB figure. The official line from inside MI6 is that they were taken out *by* Russia. But I don't think that's the case.'

'Why would the Iranians, Hadjam, whoever, be killing Russians? They're allies.'

'On the surface, perhaps. And it might not all make sense, but I'm just telling you what I've found.'

'And this links back to Yousefi too?' Denis asked.

A slight pause as she pondered how to answer. 'I've found no *direct* link. But I think there's a way we can get closer to the truth. Perhaps even identify Ithaca.'

'OK?'

'I think I might know someone who received money for a hit that was orchestrated by Ithaca. But it didn't go to plan and...'

'And what?'

'It's more the *who* than the what.'

'Then who?'

'Alexander Anderson.'

Denis didn't say anything, but she knew he was clenching his jaw tightly at hearing that name. Anderson was a man they both had history with. But Denis more so. Anderson was an American, a former Marine who had the will, perhaps the physical ability, but not necessarily the mental stability to make it with any mainstream intelligence agency. Not officially, anyway. Still a very useful man though, and so he was an asset of the CIA, MI6 to name two agencies who were keen to outsource dirty work to someone at least one step removed from their regular agents. But rumours had circled for years that Anderson would, in fact, do pretty much anything for pretty much anyone if the money was there.

'Anderson's last known whereabouts were Romania, a month ago,' Lea said. 'The only vague intel anywhere within MI6 is that the CIA had sent him to Europe to despatch a Russian oligarch, Petr Ivanov, in Hungary. Except Ivanov survived the assassination attempt and Anderson went missing. The most common assumption was that he'd been picked up by the FSB, not just because of that attempted hit, but because... well, it's Alexander Anderson.'

Denis still said nothing.

'Did you know about any of that?' she asked him.

'I'd heard about the Hungary thing. That he'd gone missing. But if the Russians had him then they would have either tried to bargain a swap for his release by now, or he'd simply have turned up dead.'

'Exactly. So I don't think the whole of that story is true. Well, perhaps the part about him trying to kill Ivanov is, which is what we need to speak to him about. I want to know who really put him up to it, because I'm sure it wasn't the CIA.'

'How do you know this isn't just something that our higher-ups instructed? Above board, but not for us to know about?'

'Because... it doesn't fit with everything else I've seen. Everything else that's happened.'

'Perhaps you're only seeing what you want to see.'

'And what if I'm not?'

Denis sighed and shook his head.

'I don't know, Lea. I feel like I'm only getting half a story from you.'

Probably not even a quarter, she thought but didn't say.

'Maybe if you showed me everything you have—'

'I'm telling you what I know,' Lea said. 'And if you help me get Anderson back—'

'From who? You said the FSB probably don't really have him after all.'

'But I think I know who might.'

Denis's face soured further. 'Right. So this is the reason you've come to me. Not as a sounding board or anything like that.'

'The rumour is that Anderson never left Romania. That one person, specifically, was responsible for taking him. And still has him.'

'And that is?'

'Yuri Kozak.'

Denis stopped walking again. He turned to face Lea, his face all twisted in distaste, and she knew why. Yuri Kozak. Another name very familiar to them both. At the simplest level Kozak was a gang leader responsible for smuggling drugs, weapons and people across Europe. But he was also an FSB asset, whose activities were believed to be sponsored at least in part by the Russian government in order to help sow chaos in Western countries. Both Lea and Denis had crossed paths with him before, but Denis in a far more personal way. Two years ago, he'd spent several months befriending Kozak before eventually being sent to meet the man with a bag full of half a million euros – a 'gift' for Kozak in exchange for him providing intel on FSB activities.

He'd taken the cash and had his henchman put a gun to Denis's head to encourage him out of there. Had never provided a thing of value to Denis or anyone else in MI6 since then.

But maybe they just hadn't offered him enough in the first place. Kozak had no real loyalty to the Kremlin, only to whoever offered him the best deal, or at least who he could *extort* the most from.

'You know Kozak better than I do,' Lea said.

'Know him? He screwed me. Led me along with promises, promises, until the day I showed up at his door with half a million euros. Which he stole, just like that. I was lucky to walk away without a bullet in my head.'

'Or maybe he didn't put a bullet in your head because he really does like you.'

Denis scoffed. 'He doesn't *like* anyone.'

'I can find a way to reach out to him myself if I need to,' Lea said. 'Go and meet him myself to broker a deal, if I must... but... I was hoping you'd want in. That you'd help me.'

Denis took a few moments before answering. 'Where and when?'

'We should do it as soon as possible, because the information I already have on Ithaca... it's only a matter of time before whoever it is realises how close I'm getting.'

'You want to do a deal with Yuri Kozak? If you haven't got a *lot* of cash, you better have a damn strong hand to play.'

Lea smiled. 'I think I might just have exactly that.'

24

BUCHAREST

Present day

Callum never did figure out what transport Denis had used to get to the villa in Portugal, but the three of them crammed into Hinch's rented Fiat for the long journey east, each of them taking shifts behind the wheel in a mammoth drive of over thirty-six hours – driving by far the safest option, even if it was also the most arduous. At least on the European continent traversing borders was simple as long as they stuck to Schengen countries, because between those countries there really was *no* border. A good thing, considering both Callum and Denis were being pursued by MI6 and others.

Was Hinch too?

The point was, the drive went by without incident, but the drawn-out time in the car also gave Callum way too much time to think, which only got his head all tied up in ever-increasing knots.

'The last time I saw *him* was at my wedding,' Callum said to Hinch, who sat alongside in the front as he took the latest stint behind the wheel, while Denis was in the back, his eyes closed. He'd been like that for more than an hour although Callum didn't really know if he was actually asleep or not.

'Yeah?' Hinch said, a little unsure as though she didn't know why Callum was bringing that up with her.

'I have to say, I didn't like the fact he turned up. Because I sensed *Lea* didn't appreciate him being there either.'

'You'd have to ask him about that.'

'They were close?' Callum asked.

'You'd have to ask him about that.'

'*You* weren't at the wedding.'

'And? Is this because you still don't believe Lea and I were friends?'

'Just saying.'

'Her parents weren't there either. Or any members of her real family. Doesn't mean she didn't care for them. Or vice versa.'

'Did she ever talk to you much about me?'

No immediate answer.

'That wasn't our style,' Hinch said.

'Convenient.'

'No. Just the way it is. Was. You might have figured by now that neither of us was... normal. And there was little normal about our relationship. We certainly weren't girly types either. We didn't see each other as friends to go out dancing with, to gossip with, to get our nails done with.'

'Not cloak and dagger enough for either of you?'

'Well... yeah.'

Callum sighed.

'But yes, she did talk about you. I know she loved you, and I know she struggled trying to figure out a way to make you two work with her job. From what I understand... she very nearly quit after Toulouse.'

'You know about Toulouse?'

'The basics.'

'Toulouse was how this all started,' Denis said, and as Callum glanced into the rearview mirror Denis opened his eyes. So he *had* been pretending.

'What started?' Callum said.

'With the Iranians. That was the first time we'd had them under watch. We didn't even know why then. But even in the short time we were there they figured out we were on to them, and they tried to take Lea out.'

Callum gulped. 'Those kids...'

'Weren't trying to rob her. They were trying to kill her.'

Should that make him feel better? Knowing he'd saved her life that day? Because it really didn't. It only once again showed how little he understood her and her life.

'It affected her badly,' Denis said. 'Mentally, more than physically. And meeting you really didn't help matters. We nearly lost a very good agent because she found an easy, convenient way to escape reality.'

Callum gripped the steering wheel a little more tightly, Denis's bitterness pretty damn clear, and surely intended to rile Callum.

'She took months off work,' he continued. 'And maybe she would have never come back given she'd found a happy, simple life with you. But then I got kidnapped, chasing those same damn people while she was back in England screwing you. Not just me, another agent too. Naomi. Someone less experienced than Lea and... it was *her* fault. Lea would never have messed up like Naomi did. Unfortunately, she paid the ultimate price. Naomi was killed. I probably would have been too if Lea hadn't agreed to return to help get me back.'

Callum said nothing – speechless, really, at the talk of kidnappings, killings.

Hadn't White said MI6 hardly ever got into violent scrapes in real life? So either that was a lie, or perhaps White simply wasn't really a field agent like Denis and Lea were. Had been.

'So you could say *you're* responsible for what happened to Lea,' Callum said. 'If you hadn't been kidnapped maybe she'd never have returned. Would still be at home with me, safe and happy.'

'No. What happened to Lea is because someone in MI6 stabbed her in the back. Me too.'

'White?'

'He's involved, but there're people more powerful than him making it happen.'

'Why though?' Callum asked. 'What is this even about?'

Denis sighed as though building up to a reveal. Or deciding how much truth and how much bullshit he'd give this time.

'Intelligence is our currency,' he said. 'We deal with it. We make friends through it, enemies. It can start wars and end them. People like you... really have no idea what the world is like behind the facade you live in.'

'You think you're so much better than me, don't you?'

'I know I am,' Denis said. 'Because I know what I've contributed to this world.'

Callum said nothing to that.

'We don't deal in good and bad as you think of it. Sometimes the people you thought were your enemy turn out to be your ally. And vice versa. To put it simply, when we first started looking at the Iranians, we were looking for evidence of the most obvious theories. Links to Islamist groups, perhaps planned terror attacks even, funding for either of those. But what we actually found was something else. And we don't even know what the ultimate end goal of this group was, but we found, among other things, that they were actively sabotaging Russian interests.'

'Interests in what?'

'In all manner of things. Politics, investments, even within the intelligence community itself. We had known Russian assets were being eliminated, and it being made to look like the UK and the US were responsible. Most likely to create a greater divide between Russia and the West, while further assimilating Iran and other countries from the region into all levels of European life, from immigrants fleeing wars through to people making decisions for governments.'

'Why?' Callum asked.

Denis tutted. 'You're not going to be able to figure this one out, Callum. I told you already, this is so much bigger than you. So this is all you need to know. This group was prepared to hurt its own allies to further their aims, political or financial or otherwise, and they were using key figures from within the UK government and intelligence community to do it.'

'And you know who?' Callum asked. 'That MP? Yousefi?'

'Probably yes. But it likely didn't start or stop with him. He's just a pawn for more powerful figures. In Bucharest we were supposed to be meeting with a Russian asset, hand him the evidence of Iranian sabotage. One, to clear-up that it wasn't us, but two because we actually knew that the man they were holding prisoner was someone who'd been involved in that sabotage. And he could help blow open the scandal for us.'

'That... makes no sense. If he was the key... the Russians already had him and...'

He lost the train of thought.

'It doesn't make sense to you,' Denis said. 'But that doesn't mean it's not true. Except the exchange was a set-up. The man we were meeting, Yuri Kozak, attacked us. That could be because he was directly involved with the Iranian group himself, or it could simply be because he's a fucking back-stabbing prick. In fact, I know he's the latter, I just don't know if that's what he was in this case. I ran. It's the only thing I could have done. Before I'd even had time to consider what it all meant, I got word from a... source, back home, that they believed Lea had hidden some of the intel. And that only makes sense to me in one scenario.'

'What do you mean?'

'They know the data taken from that exchange was incomplete. Which means Lea must have hidden the rest of what she had. That's why I sent Warren and Jenn after you. It's why others are looking for you.'

'So she was actually planning to dupe this Russian guy? That's what you're saying? She didn't even have the intel she'd promised?'

'It's possible.'

Why would she do that?

But then another thought struck Callum.

'You... could have gone straight after this man,' he said. 'Especially if you thought he had Lea still. Why did you wait until now?'

'Why take the time to save *your* damn life?' Denis said.

'That's not what I meant, I—'

'It's been barely three days. Not such a long time, especially when everything, my whole *life*, went to shit so quickly. I won't apologise that my number one priority was getting away from that exchange alive. It doesn't mean there was ever any doubt that I'd be going back after Kozak sooner rather than later, whether he had Lea or not.'

'And you really do think he has her?'

'Yes. Because how else would these people know about details like that deposit box?'

Callum gulped. 'They could only know about that if...'

'Best not to think about how they're getting that kind of information.'

'And you know where this Kozak is?'

'Not yet,' Denis said. 'Not precisely, anyway. But we will before the end of the night.'

* * *

The evening was chilly, and a shiver ran through Callum as he and Hinch looked out from their perch at the top of the three-storey building – although it was equally likely that the shiver was from nerves as it was from the cold.

'Do you know who he's meeting?' Callum asked.

'Not personally.'

Callum waited for more but got none.

'But... is it a friend? An ally? Someone dangerous?'

'Everyone can be dangerous.'

'Not what I meant, and you know it.'

She turned to him, and he could just make out her amused look in the thin moonlight.

'Are you scared?' she asked.

'Are you?'

'Do I look or sound it?'

She didn't. Not at all.

'But if it does go wrong... what do we do? Is he armed? Are you?'

'Yes,' she answered, although it wasn't really much of an answer given he'd asked three questions.

He continued to stare at her and even though she wasn't directly looking now she obviously got the point. She sighed and turned back to him.

'If I were to give this meeting a percentage of it going to shit? It'd be below 10 per cent. Which is pretty damn good for these sorts of things. And if it does go to shit? My number one choice is for you and me to take off.'

She faced away again but Callum wasn't quite done, although it took him a few seconds to properly form the question.

'Is that *normal* for you people? Your colleague, friend is in trouble, and your number one instinct is to just run? *Never leave a man behind.* Isn't there an unspoken rule like that, like in the army?'

'I'm not a man. And we're not the army.'

'Not my point.'

'Your point was pointless. Like Denis said to you before, people like us... we're worth more alive than dead. Being captured? Worst possible outcome. Not just for us, but for everyone we know. Unless I know for sure I can help, it's not worth the risk.'

'So if we're not going to help him, why are we here watching at all?'

She didn't answer that.

Callum opened his mouth to say something else, but Hinch cut him off with a wave of her hand.

'I see him.'

And Callum saw him too. Denis. Walking away from them, along the street, hands in his pockets, head down.

He paused between two buildings, turned to face the street, to face... them?... then he backstepped and simply disappeared into the blackness.

Creepy as hell. Callum shivered again.

They were only waiting, watching, for another five minutes before another figure came into view from the opposite direction, heading along the street towards them. Callum glanced from the new arrival to the black spot where Denis had vanished, over and over. Still no sign of Denis before the figure stopped right where Denis had been minutes before. The figure looked left and right along the street, obviously nervy. Took a step forward. Reached into a pocket and drew out... something. Something that was passed off into the darkness. Moments later, empty-handed, the figure turned and walked off in the same direction they'd arrived from.

They were out of sight moments later. Still no sign of Denis.

Hinch's phone buzzed. She lifted it from her pocket. Listened for all of five seconds before she faced Callum.

'We've got it,' she said. 'We're done here.'

She slipped the phone away and peeled from the spot.

Callum's gaze remained fixed on the blackness. Still no sign of Denis down there.

'He's on his way to the car already. Move.'

A renewed shiver gripping him, Callum turned and followed her.

25

Denis turned the car's headlights off half a mile from their destination, the poor-quality street lighting and the touch and go moonlight poking through the increasing cloud cover their only illumination of the area around them. They were west of central Bucharest by about ten miles. Callum had no idea what this area was: rich, poor, safe, dangerous. They'd passed through various residential and industrial areas, and this was definitely more of the latter, although high-rise apartment blocks were visible in the near distance as Denis brought the car to a rolling stop.

'Is that it?' Callum said from the back seat, straining to see properly in the darkness, though it looked to be a warehouse of sorts about a hundred yards ahead of them.

'This is it,' Denis said.

'Is this what you were expecting? Why... why would he be here... at night?'

'You thought we were going to attack this guy at his home?'

'It's quarter past midnight... Yeah, I guess I thought we'd be going to his home.'

'If he's got Lea, he's hardly going to be keeping her in his guest bedroom.'

'No, but I—'

'The information I was given is that he's here tonight. Awaiting a shipment. It's a frequently used drop point of his.'

'A shipment of what?'

'Who cares?'

'Me. I mean... if this is something illicit, drugs, weapons, aren't there going to be others here with him? They'll be armed, and—'

'That's why first we sit and wait. Make sure we're happy before we go in.'

'And when they turn guns on us—'

Denis huffed and turned around to face Callum. 'If you're so unsure about helping, then you can stay here. Or go someplace else. But I'm going in *there*, tonight. I'm going to confront this piece of shit, and I'm either going to get Lea back, or at least find out where she is.'

Callum considered that a moment. Was he scared? Yes. Damn right he was. Was he prepared to push himself through regardless? Absolutely. This was for Lea. He had no choice.

'You two both have weapons?' Callum asked.

'Yes,' Hinch said, although Callum kind of knew that already as he'd seen them slyly prepping their handguns, packing spare magazines, before they'd headed here tonight.

'And... do I get one?'

Now it was Hinch's turn to spin around to glare at him.

'You ever fired a gun before?' she asked.

'Air rifle. At the fair. Think I won a pink teddy bear.'

'A *real* gun?'

'No.'

'Ever even held one before?'

'No, b—'

'Then you don't get one. This isn't the fair, and there are no pink teddies to shoot here.'

'You never know.'

'Yeah, I do. We don't need a twitchy finger getting us all killed.'

'Then what do you expect me to do?'

'Follow my lead,' Denis said. 'Do everything I tell you to do. You got that?'

'Yeah, got it,' Callum said, trying not to sound as scolded as he felt. 'So what do we do now?'

'You shut up and stay back there. Wait.'

'You got it, boss.'

* * *

And they waited for over an hour, all of them in the car, although they weren't just using their eyes to spy on the warehouse in front of them. Hinch had a mini drone which she'd sent up into the air not long after they'd arrived – although only after Denis had pulled the car off the street into a quiet side entrance to the next building along. From there they had only a side-on view of the front of the warehouse, but with the drone they had a full three-sixty from above, not to mention thermal images to show bodies in and around the place.

Five bodies to start with, all inside the warehouse. Until a truck arrived twenty minutes after they had. That truck had a driver, two passengers, who'd met on the outside of the warehouse with three people from inside. Several crates were taken from the truck, into the warehouse, before the vehicle and its people had retreated. The exchange had taken the best part of a nervy forty minutes, the shadowy figures all but impossible to make out from where the three of them sat, but it had started and ended without apparent incident.

'It's only a matter of time before the others leave,' Hinch said.

'Yeah,' Denis said. 'So let's get in there.'

'Five against three?' Callum said.

'Pretty good odds, really,' Hinch said.

'Do you think... Is one of the five Lea?'

So hard to tell from the glimpses he had of the thermal images on Hinch's laptop screen, but it seemed to him at least that all five of the bodies inside the warehouse had been moving around freely. No indication of any of them being tied up, captive.

'No,' Denis said. 'But there could be a basement, or another room inside that the camera can't get a read on. We'll soon find out.'

He opened his door and got out, Hinch followed. Callum waited only a couple of seconds, a final silent pep talk in his head, before he pushed the door open and stepped outside.

'Stay behind me,' Denis said to Callum and the two of them edged towards the chain-link fence in front of them, while Hinch scuttled off to the right, soon lost in darkness.

'Where's she going?' Callum whispered.

'Saw a McDonald's nearby. She'll be back with some nuggets soon enough.'

Callum didn't bother to say anything more.

They reached the fence, and Denis drew out his handgun, held it in a double-handed grip as they edged alongside towards the roadside.

'We're just going to walk in through the front?' Callum asked.

'Just follow me,' Denis hissed back. 'That's all you have to do.'

They pulled in through the open gates and then Denis scuttled quickly to one of the two parked cars in front of the building. Callum did the same and slammed to a stop behind a big 4x4, his breathing already heavy, although it was from anticipation rather than exertion.

'On three we go for the door,' Denis said. 'You stand to the right, I go to the left. We wait for Hinch to get in position. When I give you the signal, open the door for me, then wait there, outside, for anyone coming out.'

'And if anyone comes out—'

'Callum, I've seen you in action before. You're six foot whatever and who knows how many stone. Smash them in the face before they know you're there and keep them on the ground.'

He obviously realised Callum didn't really feel too confident about that because he sighed and looked around.

'There. Grab that brick. You act quick enough, no one's getting up from you cracking that into their skull.'

Denis didn't wait for a response before he scurried off, keeping low. Callum only hesitated a moment before he picked up the brick and set off after him. They pulled up against the door. Callum took long, quiet breaths, trying to get his thoughts under control as much as his breathing. He pushed his head back against the metal wall. Could hear voices beyond.

Were they about to come outside?

No. The voices became quieter again.

A light buzzing sound from Denis. He looked at his watch.

'Now,' he said to Callum and a moment later there was a booming crash from the other side of the warehouse. Hinch?

Callum reached forward and pulled the door handle down and pushed the door open, then quickly moved back out of the way. Denis barrelled inside, gun raised.

Shouting. Banging.

Callum flinched when a gun blasted. Jolted when three other shots rattled in quick succession. More than one weapon fired, his brain figured, given the different sounds.

More gunshots echoed. Shouts of pain. Shouts of anger.

Footsteps.

Heavy footsteps. Getting closer.

He held the brick up at the ready. A figure bolted out. Callum hesitated...

What if it was Denis? Hinch?

Lea.

No. It wasn't. The man jerked in response, realising someone was there. Spun. Snarl on his face.

Gun in his hand.

Whoomph.

Callum lunged forward and swiped the brick into the side of the man's head. The squelch and crack on contact made his insides twist. A portion of skull above the man's right eye socket caved, and he kind of just stood there, staring, looking confused as blood poured...

So Callum smacked him again, and this time he crumpled to the ground.

The brick nearly slipped from his grip, he was so shaky. Not just his hand, but his whole arm, his legs. He stumbled back and pressed up against the wall and stared down at the unmoving man, blood streaming from the ugly gash on the side of his head, his right eye mangled beneath bone and flesh.

Footsteps the other side of the door again. Softer, quieter this time. The shaking all through Callum's body stopped as he found a super focus he didn't know he had. At least not for situations like this. He slowly raised the brick up to head height, ready to smash down again, even if the thought of it made him want to puke.

The footsteps stopped, close by the other side of the wall.

'Callum?' came Hinch's soft voice.

He slumped with relief.

'I'm here,' he said.

She stepped out, looking from the fallen man and up to him.

'I thought for a moment that was you down there.'

'I'm good,' he said.

'Come on, it's done.'

He followed her inside but stopped dead a couple of steps into the warehouse to survey the damage. Three bloodied bodies lay on the ground around the space.

'Are they...?'

'Dead?' Hinch said. 'Yes.'

'Callum, get over here,' Denis shouted from across the room, standing in the door to what looked like an office. 'Jenn, keep watch.'

She nodded in response. Callum made his way over, his gaze not able to leave the bodies as he stepped around them. Only when he'd passed them could his head conjure the question he wanted to ask so badly.

'Is... she here?'

'I don't know yet,' Denis said. 'That's what we need to find out.'

Callum reached the door and looked inside at the man on the chair, his head bowed, his hands behind him – tied? – and blood dripping from his hairline onto him and the floor around below.

'Callum, meet Yuri Kozak.'

Denis strode up to him and grabbed him by the hair to lift his head.

The captive found Callum's eye and then some strength and launched a tirade of angry Russian – or whatever it was – Callum's way.

When he was done, he spat a bloody globule onto the floor and Denis burst out laughing.

'I don't think he likes you very much.'

Then he swiped the butt of his gun against Kozak's jaw and Callum winced as blood flew loose from the guy's mouth. A tooth too which rattled along the concrete floor.

'Where is she?' Denis boomed, his jolliness gone, replaced by a monstrous rage in a flash, his face red and contorted, a vein pulsing at the side of his head.

'W-what?' Kozak stammered. 'Who!'

Denis crouched down and grabbed Kozak by the neck, choked him. Kozak's face bulged, turned purple, his eyes looked like they'd pop. He scrabbled with his feet before Denis yanked him from the chair and smacked him down onto the floor. A crack of bone – his wrist, arm behind him, perhaps? Denis continued to choke him, ground his knee into the guy's groin.

'Where is she? Where's Lea?'

'Denis,' Callum said, edging forward before Denis sent him a death glare to keep him back.

He smacked Kozak's head into the floor before finally letting go and Kozak coughed and spluttered and wheezed.

'Where is she?' Denis said again, sounding only a little bit calmer.

'She's dead!' Kozak yelled. 'You know she's dead!'

'Liar!'

Denis launched his foot into Kozak's gut.

'Callum, take this,' he said before he tossed the gun through the air.

Callum made a meal of catching the weapon. It bounced in his grip like he was holding a red-hot piece of iron. He finally righted the thing, pointed the barrel at the floor.

'She's *not* dead,' Denis said, crouching down to Kozak. 'I know she's not.' He reached inside his jacket and took out a hunting knife. 'I have three questions for you. And for every one that you give me an answer to that I don't like? I'm going to cut a part off you.'

Rage-filled Russian spewed from Kozak's mouth again.

Not quite what Callum had expected from the prone man. He'd expected begging, pleading, and he could tell the response only further angered Denis.

'Let's start,' Denis said. 'The questions. One, where is Lea? Two, where's the intel she gave you before you turned on us? Three, who the fuck paid you to betray us?'

But rather than answer, Kozak chuckled. A light, pretty quiet chuckle to start but it got louder, more vociferous.

'What is this? Denis, Denis, Denis. I always knew you were a snake... but this? What is *this*?'

'You're not going to give me any answers?'

'You know the answers!'

The two men stared off. Kozak said nothing more.

'Thank you,' Denis said. 'For giving me this opportunity.'

He slammed his fist onto Kozak's head before flipping him over and snipping through the rope holding his wrists together. He prised a hand away, pulled the arm straight and tight, holding it between his legs, his feet pushed onto Kozak's shoulder and under his armpit to keep him at bay. It looked like a wrestling move to Callum – an arm bar?

'Little finger first,' Denis said as he readied the knife.

'Hey,' came the voice from the door. Callum jumped in shock and twisted the gun that way before his brain caught up and realised it was only Hinch.

'What!' Denis screamed at her.

'I think we've got company. A vehicle approaching...' She looked at her watch. 'About half a mile out.'

How did she know that? The drone?

'Shit,' Denis said. 'Watch the entrance. We'll take this fucker with us.'

She nodded and dashed off, and Callum opened his mouth to ask a question but as he turned back to Denis, he saw Kozak making the move. How, Callum had no idea, but he twisted his body around and pulled out of Denis's grip and—

'Denis, watch out!'

Kozak grabbed him and twisted around onto his back and Denis flopped on top of him, the rope that had held his wrists together earlier now pulled tight around Denis's neck throttling him.

'Shoot... him!' Denis choked.

Callum waved the gun about, trying to find a sure shot. Leg? Arm? Head?

'Shoot!' Denis yelled and a moment later managed to somehow pull away and to the side and Callum finally pulled the trigger...

He couldn't move. Couldn't breathe. A thin trail of smoke wafted up from the end of the barrel. Both men in front of him lay still too. A neat hole in the side of Kozak's head oozed blood.

'Shit!' Hinch said, bursting into the room. She rushed to Denis and turned him over. 'You're fine. You're fine. Come on.'

She pulled him up. Glanced over at Callum. 'Would you stop just standing there and help me!'

Callum dropped the gun and—

'You need that! Get it.'

He scooped it back up, stared at it, had no idea what to do with it.

'Fuck's sake, Callum. Come on.'

She already had Denis up and was pulling him to the door.

'If you see anything moving out there, shoot it.'

Callum nodded, couldn't find any other response.

He followed them out into the main room. Then outside into the night.

'Where the fuck are they?' Hinch said, as much to herself as to anyone else, and she got no answer.

She got moving again, Callum a step behind, gun still in his hand. After a few more steps, Denis found the strength and focus to pull away from Hinch's grip.

'I'm fine. I'm fine,' he said to her.

He turned to Callum, rage barely contained in his eyes.

'Give it to me.'

Callum did so and for a moment both men paused and Callum really thought the guy was about to lift the weapon and put it to his skull.

'Get to the car,' Denis said before carrying on.

Soon all three were there. Hinch got into the driver's seat, Denis up front beside her. Callum sank into the back. His stomach curdled as she pulled away, images of the man he'd smashed in the head, the man he'd *shot* in the head, swirling.

Hinch floored the accelerator. The warehouse soon faded into the distance.

'Looks like we're in the clear,' she said.

Callum said nothing. Denis huffed.

'She wasn't there,' Denis said to no one in particular.

'She never was,' Callum said.

Denis whipped around. 'I guess given you shot Kozak in the head, we may never know.'

'You told me...'

He didn't bother with the rest of the sentence. Didn't seem to be much point.

'Just get us the hell out of here,' Denis said to Hinch.

And Callum couldn't have agreed more.

26

ATHENS

One week ago

The top of the Acropolis was just about visible beyond the roofs of the buildings in front of them as Lea and Denis made their way along the shaded streets on an otherwise scorching morning.

'Seems kind of apt us being here to meet Yuri, don't you think?' Denis said to her.

'Because?'

'Ithaca? You know the story?'

'Not really. Something to do with Odysseus?'

'Yeah. Homer's Odyssey. Ithaca is the land Odysseus came from, which may or may not be the same place as modern-day Ithaca.'

'But we're not in Ithaca.'

'We're in Greece. Close enough.'

'And I don't see any correlation between us being here and that story,' Lea said.

'But if you think Ithaca really is a person... a *rat* in our system... don't you think there's a reason that name was chosen?'

She glanced over at him and wished she knew what he was thinking at that moment.

'Ithaca was, is a place, not a person, so... I don't really know what it'd mean,' Lea said.

'Well, it *could* have a meaning,' he said. 'Or maybe it doesn't. But for Odysseus... the whole story is about his years-long struggle to return home and take back rule of Ithaca, which he believes is rightfully his. I don't know but... it could fit.'

Lea hadn't thought of it like that. Perhaps it did make sense. Although the reality was that the only reason they were in Greece and not Romania or anywhere else was because Kozak was already here. Vacation, supposedly, but Lea would bet everything she had on him also being here for a hustle or five. That's just the way people like Kozak operated.

'He's already here,' she said as they rounded the corner and the cafe came into view. A trendy corner cafe with a bunch of outdoor tables and umbrellas to shield from the sun. Most tables were taken. Yuri sat alone, grey linen suit, sunglasses on as he sipped a coffee.

Yuri sat alone, but he wasn't alone.

'Looks like he trusts us as much as we trust him,' Denis said, obviously spotting the guards too. Three in total at other tables in the cafe. Two together – a man and a woman – and a third man sitting on his own. Each of them was just that bit too well-positioned with both the street and Yuri in their full view, and their manner that bit too stiff, eyeballs flitting all over. Not to mention not one of them had both hands in view. Which meant they had weapons, barely concealed beneath the tables.

'Three of them?' Lea said, just to confirm she hadn't missed anything.

'Plus the 4x4 at your two o'clock,' Denis said.

A pristine black 4x4, stopped where it shouldn't have been in a no parking zone. The glass was tinted but Lea could just make out the form of a driver in the front. More people in the back too, possibly? Or perhaps it was just Yuri's quick getaway if he needed it.

Lea and Denis reached Yuri's table, and they sat down without being invited, both of them side on to their host so they had the street in sight, and the three guards too.

'It's been a long time,' Yuri said in his Belarusian accent. He sat back in his seat, smirking as though he was already enjoying this.

'Yeah,' Denis said. 'And if we get this done, perhaps it'll be even longer next time. Probably good for us all, right?'

Yuri laughed. 'You think? I don't know. I guess I'd miss you guys. A *little* bit.'

'You brought quite the crew,' Denis said, looking at the stooges.

'Did I?' Yuri switched his gaze to Lea. He peeled his sunglasses off and pouted as though impressed with what he saw in front of him. Lea's insides curdled a little. 'Have we met?'

'Yes,' Lea said. 'We have.'

'Strange. I thought I'd remember such a pretty face. Especially when it has a figure to go with it.'

'Why don't we get to the point,' Denis said.

'Please do. You said I have something you need.'

'Someone, not something,' Lea said. 'Alexander Anderson.'

Kozak shrugged and turned out his hands. 'I don't know who that is. Or what you mean when you say I *have* him.'

'Yuri, let's do this the simple way,' Denis said. 'There doesn't need to be a game. You give us Anderson, and we'll make it worth your while. A simple trade.'

'I can't trade what I don't have.'

'You *do* have him,' Lea said, leaning in towards the table, the movement perhaps a bit too sudden as it resulted in both the man and woman across the way twitching as though ready to pounce.

'This is what we know,' she said. 'A few weeks ago, Anderson found himself in Hungary. To kill Petr Ivanov. He failed. Not like him, and I don't know the full details of what went wrong there, but he fled to Romania, and he's not been seen since. Because *you* snatched him.'

'Petr Ivanov? I've never even heard of him. Why would I care?'

Denis sighed, his frustration showing. Lea was feeling it too. The charade was unnecessary, but Yuri seemed to have his heart set on it, nonetheless.

'I'm guessing you took him because you knew the FSB were looking for him,' Lea said. 'And you thought not only would they pay a nice price, but that maybe the favour would get you back on something like good terms with them. We all know that things haven't been quite so rosy between you and them since word got out that you were being buttered up by MI6.'

Denis squirmed in his seat a little, as though uncomfortable at Lea bringing that up, but Yuri only grew in confidence.

'You think that damaged my reputation? Silly little girl.'

'I actually *do* think it damaged you. You're just too arrogant to admit it to me. A silly little girl.'

Yuri glowered at Denis. 'Why'd you bring this bitch with you?'

'Because she's damn good at what she does,' Denis said.

'She needs something big and meaty to fill that nice mouth with to stop all the yapping.'

Lea didn't bite back. No point.

'I think you should hear her out,' Denis said.

'So she's in charge of you?' Yuri said, shaking his head in disappointment. 'To think I nearly went into business with you.'

'Maybe you still will.'

'You took Anderson, but the FSB didn't want him. Right?' Lea said. 'Or didn't offer enough for him. Yet. And so, weeks later, you're sitting on a rotting asset, probably wondering why the hell you bothered in the first place.'

'And now you're here to set me free from this… mess? How very gracious of you both.'

'But if you want to get back on the good side of the FSB, I have *plenty* of intel that they'd be gagging for,' Lea said. 'Information you can give to them, if you like.'

Denis shot her a look. She hadn't explicitly explained this part to him. That she was prepared to offer this intel.

'What if I told you that Ivanov isn't the only one,' Lea said.

'Only one what?'

Now she had his interest.

'Not the only person with links to the Kremlin who's been assassinated over the last six months. Because of the same group of people. The people paying Anderson. People who are supposed to be allies of Russia.'

Yuri paused, considering the question. Looked more sullen now. 'You have evidence of this?'

'Yes.'

'Are you going to tell me who these people are?'

'I'll give you all the evidence I have. If you give us Anderson.'

'So you want this man... Who was it again?'

'Alexander Anderson.'

'Because he knows who these people are?'

'Does he?' Lea said. 'At most he knows one person. The person who paid him. But this goes much deeper.'

'Then why is he so important to you if he knows so little?'

An obvious question, really. But Lea couldn't answer it without giving too much away. She needed Anderson to help identify Ithaca. Of course, Yuri, if he was minded to, could likely torture that information out of Anderson himself, then go after Ithaca and get them to identify all the Iranians and other parties who'd been sabotaging Russian interests. If he wanted to. But Lea was offering him a much simpler solution.

'I'm trying to make your life easy, Yuri. Give us Anderson, I'll give you evidence that's taken us years to put together, and you get it all without any hard work, without any risk, without any bloodshed. Plus, I'll throw in €200,000 if you really need the sweetener.'

Kozak nodded. 'I guess that wouldn't actually be a bad deal for me. It's just a shame I don't know who Alexander Anderson is. But thanks for coming to meet with me.'

Kozak got up from his chair. Lea reached out and grabbed his arm as he smoothed down his suit jacket, causing the guards to jolt again and she spotted the tip of a gun barrel poke up from one of the tables, but Yuri sent a look of calm to his people.

'We'll only be here tonight,' Lea said. 'We're going to travel directly to Romania in the morning. We'll give you two days. If you haven't called by then to agree to my terms, we'll just get Anderson from you another way. And that way you don't get any money. Just a big fucking mess. And maybe your life, if you're lucky.'

He whipped his hand away but then forced a smile as he looked from Lea to Denis.

'I like her,' he said. 'You should have sent her last time. Maybe we'd already have been dealing with each other by now.'

Denis didn't respond but Lea could tell he was clenching his jaw.

'So you'll call me, yeah?' Lea said, handing him a business card – one of the ones she had for BTS consulting.

'You know what? Perhaps I will.'

He walked off, across the street and into the SUV, the three goons trailing a couple of yards behind. Neither Lea or Denis spoke until the car had pulled away and was out of sight.

'Am I supposed to feel used about now?' Denis said, obviously trying to lighten the mood a little although she could tell he didn't really mean it. 'You should have told me everything you know. It would have helped.'

'Maybe,' she said.

'I hope you know what you're doing,' he said. 'Because if this goes wrong... You're dealing with some bad, dangerous people here. And I'm not just talking about Yuri Kozak.'

No. He was talking about Ithaca, the Iranians.

'Yeah, I know,' she said. 'I guess we'll soon find out.'

* * *

Lea stood outside the hotel on another warm, sunny morning. She was expecting a call. Hoped to be finished with it before Denis was due to meet her in fifteen minutes for their ride to the airport. Her heart rate steadily increased as each second ticked by, anticipation growing.

She read the message again.

I found something. It's big.

The message had come from an unknown number, but Lea knew exactly who that number belonged to: Harpreet, from MI5.

Harpreet had been instrumental in putting many of the pieces together in Lea's work on the Iranians, Yousefi, Ithaca over many months now. And all on the quiet, because Lea still had no authority to be operating – or even having others operating on her behalf – on UK soil. But she really did trust Harpreet, which was a lot more than could be said for some of Lea's closer colleagues.

Lea reread the message one more time then deleted it. She needed to be careful from here. More careful than she'd ever been before. Not just with Yuri Kozak but with people who she thought of as colleagues and even friends.

The phone buzzed in her hand. She didn't check who it was before answering.

'It's me,' said Harpreet.

'What have you got?' Lea asked.

'I think I found who you're looking for.'

Her heart thudded even more quickly, more powerfully now.

'Stay on the line, I'll send the images to your Dropbox.'

Because by this stage Lea didn't want any of the evidence directly on her devices. Too risky now.

It only took her a few seconds to open the browser and input the details, and by the time she'd done so the cache of images was already waiting for her. She opened the first and stared.

'To explain,' Harpreet began, 'when we last spoke you'd asked me to concentrate on Yousefi...'

Which wasn't such a bad thing, right? Goldman had told Lea to stay away from Yousefi. She hadn't specifically said she couldn't get intel from others getting close to him. Although she really had been telling the truth about not being involved in the break-in at his home in Yorkshire. She still had no idea who'd done that.

But, for the last several months, she'd had him followed on and off by a couple of low-level assets, had reams and reams of photos and notes of the people he'd met with, where and when.

Most of it was useless to her. But she'd first struck gold a couple of months ago when an image had been sent to her of Yousefi meeting none other than Ali Azmoun – the Iranian government official. A potentially fully explainable encounter? Yes, potentially. Except it was at that point that Lea had first brought Harpreet into the fold. Harpreet, the expert data analyst. In her role for MI5, she had access to just about every database that the government and its agencies had access to, not to mention that of every police force. And anything she didn't have direct authority to access, she'd at least consider 'finding a way' if the right person asked her.

In this case, Harpreet had first cross-matched flight manifest records to CCTV images from both Heathrow and Gatwick airports, plus a small handful of private airfields in London both before and after the day Azmoun had met with Yousefi. That trawl had revealed that Azmoun had landed in the UK on a regular civilian flight to Gatwick, but using false documents. And he hadn't arrived alone, but with Mohammed Jalali, from the Iranian Revolutionary Guard.

So probably not such an above-board visit to the UK after all.

And so Harpreet had gone on a further search of CCTV records from in and around London. There were many opponents to the increasing 'big brother' nature of surveillance across the UK, but quite honestly, from Lea's point of view, it was a huge win for police forces and intelligence agencies. Law-abiding citizens generally had little to worry about. The government wasn't about to keep a record of what sandwich Peter Smith bought from Tesco every lunchtime. But swathes of city streets and roadways covered by cameras made life for criminals that little bit more difficult, and the lives of law enforcement and the like that little bit easier. And that was a good thing, wasn't it?

The result? Harpreet had closely followed both Azmoun's and Jalali's movements in and around London in the three days they'd been there. While the latter hadn't been anywhere near Omar Yousefi – a bit of a disappointment to Lea, who was still determined to pin dirt on the MP – he had met up with someone else with a very interesting background.

Alexander Anderson. Not long before his trip to Hungary.

Coincidence? Absolutely not.

Together with the money flows, that was the evidence – or, at least, the tipping point – which had sent Lea to Greece in the first place.

But apparently Harpreet now had more.

Much more.

'You're seeing what I'm seeing?' Harpreet asked as Lea clicked in and out of several of the photos.

'Yes.'

The pictures were from two different locations. Each of them featured either Jalali or Anderson, but also someone else. Someone Lea knew very well.

'This could be Ithaca,' Harpreet said.

Lea said nothing.

'I don't know what you want me to do with this but—'

'Do nothing,' Lea said. 'You should do nothing more. It's in my Dropbox now so you delete everything you have. Delete all messages between us. Delete the records of our phone calls. I didn't get this from you.'

'But Lea, this is—'

'You've done more than enough. All you can do now is to protect yourself, because if this comes out, you're in as much danger as I am now.'

'Lea, I—'

'Good morning,' came Denis's voice from behind her and Lea jolted in shock and then quickly killed the call, closed the browser as she turned to Denis.

'Morning,' she said.

'Are you... OK?' he asked.

'Why wouldn't I be?'

'You look like you've seen a ghost,' he said, a little too jolly.

A ghost. Perhaps not a bad way to describe it.

'Seriously, what's up?' he said, suspicion only growing.

'It's nothing. I'm just... missing home. Missing Callum.'

He shook his head. Disdain. 'That guy really doesn't deserve you.'

'Yes, he does.'

Denis rolled his eyes. 'Are you ready?'

'Yeah.'

'Then let's get going.'

Romania their next stop. Not a long journey but it'd feel a hell of a lot more fraught now. Not to mention the job she still had to do when they got there.

She'd try her hardest to relax. Try her hardest not to think about the revelation from the images Harpreet had just sent her.

Instead, as they sat in the taxi on the way to the airport, she thought of Callum. Not about how she missed him, how she longed to be home with him, but about the measures she'd already put into place recently as she got closer and closer to the truth about the mole in the midst of MI6.

Now doubts swirled in her mind.

Had she done enough?

Would he know what to do?

She had no choice but to hope the answer to both was yes.

27

BUCHAREST

Present day

The safe house was located in a regular apartment building in the centre of the city. Not only was the eight-storey stone building regular-looking, but so was the apartment itself except for the reinforced metal door with hefty bolts on the inside, with nothing inside but basic functional furniture in a basic functional space. They each had a bedroom, but Callum had barely slept at all. Had barely even closed his eyes because every time he did all he could see were the bloodied faces from earlier in the night.

Still, he wasn't the first out of his room in the morning. Hinch was already dressed and drinking coffee in the open-plan living area when Callum emerged. He paused outside the door to Denis's room on his way over there. Could hear him speaking to someone.

'He's always on the phone,' Callum said as he headed over towards Hinch.

'Yeah.'

'Any idea who he's speaking to?'

'None. If he wanted me to know he'd tell me.'

Callum huffed. 'So that's how things work between the two of you? He says jump, you say how high? But you're not really on the inside with him, are you? You don't ever get to really make decisions with him. And I bet he never really tells you exactly what's happening.'

'What is this?' Hinch asked, looking all twisty.

'You told me you were friends with Lea. That you two were close. As close as people like you could be, at least.'

'And? Are you questioning that? *Again*.'

'Actually, this time, my question is... who were you closer to? Lea or Denis?'

Her eyes pinched with intrigue, and she glanced beyond him to the corridor, as though questioning whether Denis might be listening to the conversation.

'Lea,' she said. 'Definitely Lea. But only because I knew her better. Had worked with her more.'

'You trust Denis?'

'I'm sensing you don't.'

'The thing is... Actually, it's not just one thing. I've been lying awake pretty much all night, and *every*thing stinks.'

He was about to start explaining that but then didn't know where to start. And really didn't know if this was even the right person to be telling this to. But if not Hinch, then who else? And if he was dead wrong... he'd surely find out pretty soon.

'You can trust me, Callum. I only ever wanted to help Lea. That's why I'm here. Not for Denis and not for you.'

'But she's dead, isn't she?' Callum said.

Hinch sighed. 'I think so, yes.'

'And when Denis said otherwise? Did you... believe him then?'

'I wanted to. I'm sure you did to. But I doubted it. Based off the information I'd received. But... you never know with these things.'

'No. She's dead,' Callum said. 'I really wanted to believe she wasn't, because I can't face the idea of never seeing her again, but... it just isn't true.'

'I'm afraid I think you're right.'

'So the big question is why did Denis say that?'

'Because... because maybe he *wants* there to be a chance? If we haven't seen the body... it *could* mean something.'

Callum shook his head. 'No. It's something else.'

'Then what?'

'He knows way too much about what happened to Lea, but he's telling us next to nothing. Unless *you're* in the know?'

A voice at the back of his head told him to not do it. To not spew his crazy ideas.

It didn't win.

'I think,' he started, 'that voice message from Lea... It just didn't sound right. I listened to it over and over and... it's like it had been manipulated. It's not that hard to do these days, right?'

'Manipulated how? Why?'

'At the end she said, *find Denis Petit... You have to find him*. But it just didn't sound right to me. It was too abrupt. Too little information. Almost like some of the message had been cut out or... spliced differently or something. But what if she wasn't sending me to him because he'd help, but because... *he's* the one responsible. She was *warning* me.'

'Then... what'd be the point of him seeking you out at all?' Hinch said. 'Having me involved in that too? What'd be the point in us coming all this way to Romania?'

'Because he's worried he can still be exposed. That maybe Lea really did leave me something. The empty deposit box? What if *he* emptied it? Perhaps the phone was actually in there, with the message for me. But he took it. And then when we're in Portugal? He gets us both trekking all this way, not to find Lea, but to confront Yuri Kozak.'

'For what purpose? Revenge?'

'Maybe. But... what if it's because maybe Kozak knows too much? He knows Denis is corrupt or a double agent or whatever it is. Maybe even... maybe even Denis planned that whole thing last night.'

'Planned what? For *you* to kill Kozak?'

Callum replayed those moments in his head a couple of times over, like he had been doing on and off for hours. 'Yes.'

'That's... an interesting theory.'

'He had Kozak secured. I saw what Denis was capable of. There was no way Kozak was slipping out accidentally. And the fact Denis had only moments before given me the gun... He set me up. He set me up to kill Kozak and—'

The door behind him opened and Callum quickly shut his mouth and tried his best to do a good job of being calm and collected.

He was pretty sure he screwed that up given the suspicion on Denis's face as he entered the room.

'You two OK?' he asked.

Callum looked to Hinch for confirmation. Hoped she'd say the right thing. Worried that maybe he'd made a horrible misjudgement and she'd throw him under the bus there and then.

He'd charge at Denis. Take him out, get to the door and flee.

'We're just hungry,' Hinch said. 'There's nothing good to eat. Why don't you go get us something?'

Denis's face scrunched like he'd stepped in dog shit. 'Why me?'

'Because we can't send Callum out there given... everything. And you know Bucharest a *lot* better than I do.'

Denis looked like he didn't agree, but... 'OK,' he said. 'But we're not staying here long. I've got another source who thinks she knows where Lea could be. We'll head to them today.'

He didn't say anything more, and not long after he was gone.

Callum toyed with that parting comment.

'You don't believe him?' Hinch asked.

'I want to, but... no.'

'Then what do you want to do?' she asked. 'If we stay, we at least get to see what he's got planned next.'

'Yeah. Which could be an ambush and our gruesome deaths.'

Hinch gulped, a reaction which only made Callum all the more worried.

'We have to find out if he's lying,' Callum said. 'About that phone, the message, Kozak.'

'But *why* would he lie?'

'I said already. Maybe he's the one.'

'Ithaca?' Hinch said.

'Wait... what?'

'Nothing,' Hinch said, shaking her head, her reaction making it very clear that it definitely *wasn't* nothing.

'That's what he said to Kozak,' Callum said. 'Ithaca. What's Ithaca?'

Hinch sighed. 'Not what. Who. From what he's told me, Ithaca is a mole in MI6. It's who he and Lea were pursuing, trying to identity. Are you seriously trying to tell me it's *him*? That everything he was doing with Lea, and since, was a charade?'

'It's... possible, isn't it?'

She looked scared. He'd never seen that look on her before. 'We don't have much time,' she said.

She scuttled past him, to the corridor, into Denis's room. By the time Callum got there she was already searching through Denis's belongings – backpack, suitcase.

'He's taken his phone with him,' she said. 'But he left his tablet.' She picked it up and hit the screen. 'Locked.'

'Can you crack it?'

'Not in the few minutes we've got.' She sighed and put it back on the bed and looked around the room. 'You go through his bags and I'll go through the drawers.'

'Looking for what?'

'*Any*thing.'

Two minutes. Three. Callum checked his watch nearly every ten seconds, unable not to as his nerves steadily crept up and up. If Denis caught them... What would he do? Shoot them on the spot? Beg forgiveness? Try to talk his way out of it, protesting his innocence?

Talk his way out of what? Callum had no evidence for anything he'd said to Hinch! Only a gut feeling.

'What the hell is this?' Hinch said.

Callum turned to her. She held up a single piece of paper with big typed letters across it, only a few words in total.

'What does it say?' he asked.

'Look,' she said, pushing it closer to him.

'Just... tell me what it says.'

She frowned but then looked down at the paper again and read it out loud. 'Sara Louise Barnet.'

'Sara Lou... Give me that.'

He pretty much snatched it from her and stared down at the words. He tried his hardest to decipher the short string of letters. It certainly looked consistent with what Hinch had said.

'Who's Sara Louise Barnet?' she asked.

'She... isn't anyone. It's... from Lea. To me.'

'But... what is it?'

'Denis took this. When he took that phone, this was probably with it. He's played me the whole time. Played you too.'

Hinch winced at that. 'But what's the message? If not a person, then what?'

'It's a place.'

'Do you know where?'

'Yes.'

'Is it... far?'

Callum smiled at that. Was it ironic? Something like that.

'Pretty far.'

'OK. Let's get the hell out of here.'

28

Yes, he trusted Jenn Hinch more than he now trusted Denis Petit, but he didn't *fully* trust her. How could he? She'd already lied to him multiple times. But stuck with both in Bucharest, as reality dawned, he'd had no choice but to play a risky hand and hope it paid off.

And it looked like it had. At least for now.

Without Hinch's help, he'd likely never have found the opportunity to rummage through Denis's things like they had. Likely would never have found that note.

'So what's your theory?' Hinch asked as she drove them back west, in a newly rented VW Polo. The Fiat remained in Bucharest and would until the rental company or the authorities recovered it. Callum had no idea what kind of liability Hinch would face for that, but she didn't seem perturbed by the fact, as though ditching cars here, there and everywhere was perfectly normal. 'Callum?'

'My theory about what?'

'That note. When he got it.'

'Most likely from the safe-deposit box. The phone and the note were in there.'

'But how? Denis hasn't been back to England—'

'Says who? Him?'

No answer from Hinch.

'I said to him before I didn't understand his delay in going back after Kozak. Particularly if he really thought Lea was still with him. But that delay gave him easily enough time to sneak in and out of the country.'

'But... how would he have known about—?'

'I don't know! I don't... I'm not used to thinking like this. To having to consider that everything I'm seeing and hearing is a lie and...'

'You're actually getting pretty good at it though,' Hinch said. She glanced over, smiling, and he felt the comment was genuine rather than mocking.

'I don't really *want* to be good at this.'

'Could the phone and the message, or one or the other, have been in the house in Portugal?' Hinch suggested. 'Denis said that's where he found the phone.'

'I don't think so.'

'Why? That's where we're going back to now, isn't it?'

'Yes, but...' He thought then sighed, frustration and anger taking over. 'I should have combed through that house myself. I took it on his word that he'd found the phone there. But either way, that note was definitely not there. It wouldn't make sense.'

'Are you going to tell me what it means then? The message? What's Sara Louise Barnet?'

He closed his eyes and shook his head. 'It doesn't matter. It's... stupid. Hard to explain.'

'And we've got about thirty hours of driving ahead of us. I'm pretty sure you can find a way to explain it in that time.'

'You know I'm dyslexic, right?'

She paused before answering. 'Yes.'

'Lea told you?'

'Yeah. But it's not like I know much about what it means for you.'

She said that in such a way as to suggest perhaps she did, but Callum didn't bother to question it.

'I've always struggled with reading, writing, numbers. It's hard to explain the ins and outs but letters and words don't look to me like they should *sound*, if that makes sense.'

'I guess.'

'So quite often I'll try and read something, and I'll just say something completely different to what it actually is. I'll say the word I think it looks like. It's hard, and... I never really had anyone to help me. But Lea did. In a way. Because she'd try to unscramble my thinking, try to see how *I* would see words. She got pretty good at it.'

'That message—'

'Barnet. You know the place?'

'In London?'

'Yeah. Now this is really stupid and... this part isn't even anything to do with my dyslexia, it's just... dumb.'

'OK?'

His cheeks were blushing before he'd even started. What an idiot. Although at the time it'd just been a sweet moment between a loving couple.

'We were driving and she was desperate for the loo, and she asked me to find the closest place to stop at, and I read the road sign and for once I actually got the thing right.'

'Barnet?'

'Barnet. Except, I said "Barnet, next stop", or something like that, and I've no idea how that got confused in Lea's mind because she's normally so switched on and... Maybe she was distracted by driving and needing the toilet, but she thought I said *barn at the next stop*.' He smiled to himself at the daft memory. 'She was confused when we pulled off and couldn't see the barn she was looking for. I don't even know *what* the hell she was looking for... Like a farm shop or something? I don't know. It doesn't even make sense when I try to explain it... but it just became a thing between us. Whenever we were on a trip and we were looking to stop somewhere it'd always be *the barn at such a place*. *Barnet* this, *Barnet* that.'

He stopped and held the memories a moment, tried to hold them as long as he could but reality soon pushed them away.

'I still don't get it,' Hinch said. 'Are we looking for a barn or not?'

'In this case, yes, we are. Sara Louise. The villa we were at? It's in the Serra da Lousã mountains. Sara Louise. That's the closest I got when trying to read it the first time. Get it?'

She sighed. 'And there's a barn there? That's what we're looking for. What's so special about the barn?'

He thought about that before answering. 'You know what? That's a memory just for me and her. But yeah, it's special.'

She pulled a face. 'OK. Enough said. I think I get the picture.'

They both chuckled at that. Though after they'd finished, she let out another sigh.

'What?' he asked.

'I can just imagine... a man like Denis? He's been scouring the world for Sara Louise Barnet the last few days.' Then her face fell. 'Shit. I hope he didn't find anyone called that.'

Her face went all serious, but only for a moment before she was laughing again.

'You should have seen your look. I'm sure... Whatever Denis is, he's not that thick. I'm sure the Sara Louise Barnets of the world are totally fine.'

'But I'd bet you anything Denis isn't. He'll know why we ran. And he'll come after us, won't he?'

'Yes.'

'And I've already seen what he's capable of.'

'Yes. Me too. And we've given him no reason to think we're headed right back to Portugal but... whatever's there for us in Barnet... we get it and we leave.'

'Agreed. But... leave to go where?'

'We'll worry about that later. Let's see what we find there first.'

29

Nightfall was still two hours away when they finally arrived back in the mountains of Portugal, although as they climbed the twisting incline to the final destination, the clouds became thicker and thicker, the scene darker and darker, and when they were still a couple of miles out the heavens opened with sheets of rain drilling down onto the car and all around. The wipers of the VW leaped across the glass at breakneck speed, water cascaded down the sides of the road, not far off pushing them backwards.

'Just as well we're not still in the Fiat,' Callum said. 'Think we'd have been swept away.'

He squinted as he looked ahead, as though doing so would better help him to see through the rain. Hinch took the final corner and pulled in through the open gates and the villa came into view.

The villa, and the vehicle that was parked up at the front.

'Shit,' Hinch said, stomping the brake. 'There's someone here.'

Callum said nothing as he stared ahead.

'Where's the barn?' Hinch asked. 'Can we take the car right there? If not, how close can we get?'

Callum still said nothing but stared over at her. It didn't take her long to get it, but he could tell she had by the look of disgust that spread across her face.

'You sneaky bastard,' she said. 'Who did you call? *When* did you call?'

'It was a long journey here,' he said.

'Who is it?' she asked.

'I had to be cautious,' he said. 'It's nothing personal.'

'Yeah, fucking right. *Who is it?*'

'Andrew White. Jenn... I didn't do this to snare you. If you want to take off... You've helped me more than enough. But I had to do it. With Denis chasing me down? I need as much help as I can get.'

She pursed her lips and shook her head, his words doing little to appease her.

'But I'd like you to stay for this,' he said. 'Stay until we've figured out exactly what Lea left here and why.'

'White won't be alone,' Hinch said.

'I know.'

'Did you already tell him about the barn?'

'No. Just to be here.'

Hinch seemed to consider that.

'It's up to you,' Callum said. 'But you've been saying all along you wanted to help Lea.'

She remained undecided but the fact she hadn't immediately attacked him or tried to flee told him a lot. Yet before she said anything the door to the villa opened and White emerged. Not alone, as Hinch had suggested. Another man walked with him, a man Callum didn't recognise. He held an umbrella over both their heads as they scurried across, hopping over puddles widening by the second across the gravel drive.

Callum wound his window down and White crouched to peer inside.

'Jenn Hinch,' he said with a satisfied grin. 'Nice to see you again.'

She said nothing.

'Come on, let's get inside and out of this damn rain.'

Callum glanced over at Hinch. She still looked really unsure. 'I'll park by the house,' she said.

White and his companion stood back and Hinch slowly rolled the car forward.

'I hope you know what you're doing,' she said to Callum. He didn't respond. 'I'll leave the key in the car in case we need to make a quick escape.'

He didn't question that and soon they were parked. White had already moved back inside, the front door to the villa remaining open as if to invite Callum and Hinch in, but his friend – still holding on to the umbrella – stayed outside, stationed behind the VW as though he'd stop it himself if Hinch tried to speed away. Callum got out and rushed to the door and only when he got there out of the rain did he glance back to the man, mind still churning.

'Get in!' Hinch shouted and pretty much barged into him and they both stumbled into the hall. For a moment, both were chuckling, relaxed before Hinch too looked back at the man outside.

She said nothing before she closed the door.

'In here,' White said, poking his head out the kitchen.

Callum headed that way, but he stopped to do a double take when he reached the doorway.

White wasn't alone in the room, but this time Callum did recognise the person – the woman – with him: Lea's mother.

Not the real Mrs Simmonds, of course, but the woman who'd been at the wedding pretending to be Lea's mother.

'*You*,' was the best Callum could think to say to her.

'Hello, Callum,' she said with a relaxed smile on her face. 'Can I just start by saying how sorry I am for your loss.'

Callum didn't respond, and the woman's attention was soon stolen when Hinch walked in.

'Jenn Hinch? What a surprise.'

'Isn't it?' Hinch said, moving around Callum, them on one side of the island, White and the woman the other.

'My name... my real name, is Erica Goldman,' the woman said. 'I was Lea's superior. Her handler, her mentor. Not exactly her mother...' She laughed at that. 'But not far off it in many ways.'

Callum glanced between Hinch and Goldman. Hinch looked even more uncomfortable now than before.

'You two know each other?' he asked.

Goldman beat Hinch to the answer.

'Yes. We both know Jenn. She's a reliable asset and has been for many years. I'm sure you've seen that for yourself. I know Lea placed a lot of trust in her at various times. And I know you're probably conflicted right now, Jenn, given you also hold loyalty to Denis Petit.'

Hinch shook her head. 'Maybe. Until I realised he'd been lying to me. And most likely had a hand in Lea's death,' she said.

'Yes,' Goldman said. 'About that. Callum, it seems you really have been busy since you last spoke to Andrew. Want to tell us about that? And about why you brought us here?'

Callum briefly explained, telling most of the truth as he saw it, from the message on the painting, to the empty safe-deposit box, to the voice-mail from Lea, to the raid on the warehouse where Yuri Kozak had been killed. No, where *Callum* had killed Yuri Kozak.

Before either said a word in response, White turned to Goldman. 'He doesn't know.'

'Know what?' Callum asked.

White dug in his pocket and pulled out his phone, tapped away before turning the screen to Callum. He took a step closer. He only needed to see the headline and the picture beneath it to understand.

He turned to Hinch who'd edged further away from the island, still looking uneasy. 'I knew it,' he said to her. 'Denis *wanted* me to kill Kozak. He made sure the gun was in my hand. Now I'm wanted for murder.'

She didn't respond. Callum turned back to Goldman and White. 'You know, he had the balls to try to convince me that Lea was still alive. That we were going to go there to rescue her.'

Goldman shook her head morosely. 'No, Callum. She's not alive. I can assure you of that. And I'm so very, very sorry.'

'It's Denis,' Callum concluded. 'He's the one you're looking for. The one Lea was looking for. Ithaca? He killed her because she found out the truth. That he was selling secrets of... whatever it was.'

'And you think she left what she'd found here? For you?' White said.

Callum nodded.

'In this house? Because we've already searched high and low and found nothing.'

Interesting. How long had they been here?

'No, not in the house. It's—'

He turned to Hinch, who'd moved even further from him, closer to the side door. Although it wasn't her movement that had stopped Callum, but the vibrating of her phone. An incoming message or call.

'Are you going to take that?' White asked her.

Hinch said nothing. A knot tightened in Callum's stomach. The pleading look she gave him...

'What did you do?' he asked.

She gave no response.

'Denis,' he said. 'He's... here?'

Hinch nodded, looked desperate.

'She told him where to look,' Callum said to White and Goldman. 'The barn on the east side.'

Moments ago, she'd questioned him about sneakily contacting White on the way here. But she'd done the exact same thing with Denis.

'Back in the safe house...' Callum said to Hinch, thinking out loud as anger took hold. 'The note from Lea. You didn't find it among Denis's things at all.'

Her hand edged towards her jacket. 'Ah, ah,' White said, moving his own hand into position, although neither of them drew a weapon. 'Think this through, Hinch. We're not your enemy.'

'*You* had the note already,' Callum said to her, still completing the thought process. 'Because *you* stole it. That and the phone, from the deposit box. You gave both to Denis when we arrived here. But you never told me anything about either of those items all that time we were travelling together.'

She nodded, ever so slightly. An answer, if not an explanation. How would she even have known about the box, how to get in it?

Questions for another time, if that time ever came.

'Why?'

'Because... I'm trying to find the truth, Callum. Just like you. But... I have to do it my way.'

'Except you've lied to me at every opportunity.' He smacked his temple, angered at being suckered in. And not just one time but over and over and over.

There was a gunshot outside, not too far away, and it stole everyone's attention.

Callum whipped around to White and Goldman, who had a phone to her ear.

'We got him,' she said after a few moments. 'Caught red-handed.'

'Callum, down!' White shouted, but before he'd moved a muscle, both Hinch and White had drawn their weapons. But White was just that little bit quicker. He fired first. The bullet smacked into Hinch's shoulder, knocking her back, ruining her aim. Callum kicked out and his foot clattered into her arm sending her gun clanking against the wall. She cowered and spun, and Callum was sure she was aiming for the door, to run, but White fired again and this time the bullet smacked into the wall right by her.

'Touch that door handle and you're finished,' he said.

Hinch paused, then straightened up as she turned, anger on her face as much as pain from her bleeding shoulder.

'Step away from the door,' White ordered her, and after a momentary stand-off she did as she was told.

Only a couple of beats later and Callum jolted when the door burst open and Denis was shoved inside. He fell into a heap up against the kitchen island. White's friend moved in behind him, a gun in his hand too, pointed at Denis.

'Got him just in time,' the guy said.

Denis pulled himself up, his back propped against the island. His clothes were sodden from the rain and he had bloody streaks across his face from a gash somewhere in his hairline. He cradled his left hand – broken?

'This is what he found,' the man with the gun said as he placed a flash drive onto the island.

White laughed. 'This is great. You guys are doing *all* the hard work for us.'

Goldman looked less impressed. She moved around the island until she was facing Denis.

'You know your problem?' she said to him. 'You were never as good as you thought you were.'

Denis didn't respond to her but glared at Callum.

'You really are the dumbest prick I ever met.'

It shouldn't have angered him as much as it did, but Callum lurched forward, ready to attack.

'Don't,' Goldman said to him.

And somehow the casually directed single word was enough to keep him rooted.

'Did you do it?' Callum said to Denis. 'Did *you* kill her? Or were you too cowardly, same as you were with Kozak?'

'You're so bloody lost, it'd be funny if it wasn't so pathetic. And if it hadn't got *me* into trouble too.'

Goldman took the flash drive from the island and plugged it into a tablet.

'Let's see what Lea left us,' she said.

'Just tell me why,' Callum said to Denis. 'Tell me why she had to die.'

'I didn't kill her!' Denis said. 'I would never have killed her. I *loved* her.'

'You betrayed her. And you lied to me about... pretty much everything.'

'*Lied* to you? You deserve everything you've got,' Denis said. 'She threw her life away for you. You *ruined* her life. And you didn't even know it. You didn't know the *real* her. But I did.'

Callum wanted to bite back but didn't. What difference would it make now? He turned to Goldman.

'Is it all there?' he asked her.

Goldman didn't answer for a few seconds but then a smile spread up her face. 'Oh yes. It's all here. This is exactly what we needed.'

'You fucking idiot!' Denis shouted to Callum. '*You* did this!'

'Kill them,' Goldman said, unplugging the flash drive. 'Kill them all.'

As Callum struggled to understand, the man by the door was the first to shoot. His gun had been trained on Denis the whole time and the shot hit home exactly where intended, in the middle of Denis's forehead. White was the next to open fire, aiming for Hinch. Perhaps he'd decided she was the bigger threat out of her and Callum. Perhaps she was, because she'd already been shot once but was not out of the fight. Even as White pulled on his trigger she was launching herself towards the man by the door. The first bullet missed her. The second hit her in the side before she thumped into the man and spun him around, to put him between her and White.

Callum hadn't been the target of anyone in that brief melee, but he hadn't just stood there either. As the gunfire started, as his brain fought to catch up, he'd rushed towards the island, was flying across it, arms outstretched as the two bullets from White's gun hurtled towards Hinch. He smacked into White's chest and sent him flying as Hinch smashed the other man's head into the wall before she flung open the door and disappeared outside.

White could do nothing to stop himself from falling with sixteen stone pounding into him. His back cracked off the cabinets behind him, and he and Callum landed in a heap on the floor.

Callum hoped the gun would come free. It didn't. And White was quickly re-aiming... before Callum lifted his head and sent a vicious uppercut onto White's nose. He smacked his arm onto White's arm, knocking his aim off.

The next bullet didn't hit Callum. But it did hit. Not that Callum saw *exactly* where, but he heard Goldman's shriek of pain.

White had heard too, and, surprised, it perhaps dimmed his focus just enough as Callum wrestled for control of the gun. He didn't manage it before White fired again, but he had at least pushed the gun right down beside White's head. The bullet smacked into the cabinet only a couple of inches away. Not a hit on White, but enough to leave him disorientated. Callum only compounded that when he landed another headbutt before he jumped up.

Goldman cradled a wound in her gut. The tablet... Out of her grasp on the floor. The flash drive... By the kitchen entrance. Callum rushed that way, scooped up the drive.

'Kill him!' White shouted and Callum ducked just in time as gunfire erupted again – from the man Hinch had felled?

He didn't know, because he didn't look back as he raced out of there. Raced along the corridor to the front. He heaved the door open and burst out into the rain.

Was intending to go to the car...

'Shit!'

The car was already gone.

Footsteps to Callum's left. Another armed man burst into view from the side of the house. Callum turned on his heel and ran. He dodged to the right, around the edge of the house. The barn lay further ahead in the near distance. A good place to hide? Probably not. But there'd be something in there he could use as a weapon?

If he could make it across the thirty yards of open space...

He sprinted for it before he could talk himself out of it, but another gunshot broke through the sound of the torrential rain and this time he could do nothing. The bullet thwacked into his right hamstring and even if he tried to push through the shock, the pain, the debilitation, he made it only three stumbling steps before he face-planted onto the soggy grass.

But his body didn't stop moving, and in his weary state he couldn't immediately figure out why.

He was tumbling, falling, sliding down an embankment, a deluge of rain and mud cascading with him. He scrambled with his hands, trying to grasp hold of something to stop his momentum, but couldn't manage it before he slid off the edge of an outcrop and for a couple of seconds was in free fall until he smacked down onto hard ground again.

It took him several seconds to regain his senses, for his sight to clear as rain poured down on him, filling his open mouth. He achingly turned over, coughing and spluttering and grasped hold of the leafy greens next to him to help haul himself back to his feet. Vines. He'd landed in among lines of grape vines. He looked up to where he'd fallen from. Heard shouting up there but could see no one. He went to move but winced in pain from the wound in his leg, not to mention the bumps and bruises from the fall.

He pushed through and hobbled towards the barn in the near distance. Not *the* barn – he didn't know this one, he didn't think. An in-use barn though, he suspected, given the machinery outside it, and the fact he was in an obviously well-kept vineyard.

He'd find someone. Get them to call the police.

Or would he just ask them to get in their car and take him away?

Or, if they didn't understand or were scared or whatever would he just have to steal the keys and take off and get himself to safety...?

He reached the barn, heard the voices again behind him but when he turned that way all he could see was a wall of rain and the blurry outline of vines stretching away into the distance.

He pushed open the creaky barn door and stepped into the dry interior. Drier, anyway, because water dripped down in several spots from holes in the roof. He spotted a bunch of hand tools racked up on one side, a mound of hay in another. An old tractor, no tyres, the engine taken apart, took up much of the space in the middle.

No chance he was taking that for a ride out of here.

Noise outside... Quiet voices.

They knew he was there.

Callum hobbled towards the tools, picked up an axe. He ducked when a gun boomed and the bullet splatted into the wood by his head and sent splinters flying. He looked for cover, was about to dash off behind the tractor but he spotted the movement by a side door.

'Yeah, you can stop there,' White said, coming inside, soaked through, his clothes dirtied, his gun pointed at Callum's chest.

Callum said nothing but back-stepped ever so slowly, the main door his aim.

'You're even stupider than I expected,' White said. 'How the hell did you get this far? Oh, wait. You didn't. You actually thought Denis Petit was Ithaca. That he'd killed Lea, the woman he was madly in love with. Everyone knew that. Except you, apparently.'

'How would I know that?' Callum said. 'I knew nothing about *this* life.'

'You didn't. Like I said, you're even stupider than I expected.'

Callum took another half step back but then froze when a hard object pressed into the back of his skull.

White smiled. 'What was I just saying?' he said. 'Drop the axe.'

Callum did, although his brain scrambled for an idea of how to get out of the situation. Could he duck and spin and disarm the man behind him?

Without the guy putting a bullet in his brain?

Chance probably close to zero.

Before another word was spoken the man behind him kicked the back of Callum's leg, right on the bullet wound and he roared with pain and fell down onto his knee. He took a hefty whack around the side of his head from the gun and the world swayed and he fought to stay upright.

'Where's the drive?' White said coming forward.

'I tossed it.'

'No, you didn't. Give it to me and I promise you I'll put a bullet in your brain rather than the misery I *want* to inflict on you.'

Callum thought for a moment, still struggling to come up with *any*thing.

White smiled. 'You want to know the funny thing? I didn't actually expect you to run from us like you did. But then... it quickly transpired just how useful you could be. I am curious, though... Why the hell did you think Denis Petit was Ithaca? I mean... just why!'

'It made... sense. To me.'

'Perhaps if he hadn't been so into your wife... he might have actually liked you more and truly tried to help *you*.'

'You know the problem with you people?' Callum said.

'Us people?'

'You've spent so much of your lives lying to each other... yourselves... you don't even know who you are.'

'No,' White said. 'I assure you I do.'

'It doesn't even matter,' Callum said.

'What?'

'What's even the point now?'

'The point?'

'Goldman's dead, isn't she?'

The lack of a response suggested he was probably right.

'You shot her,' Callum said, managing a laugh, which he knew pissed off White.

Although was it really wise to anger the man holding a gun to him?

'*She* was Ithaca,' Callum said. 'Right? Not you. It couldn't be you. You're not important enough. Just a dumb lackey.'

'Are you actually trying to make me hate you even more?'

White nodded to the man behind, and Callum took another crack to the head, then another and after that one he couldn't stay up at all, and his face smacked onto the floor. He choked on dirt, his eyesight bleary, his head a mess.

Then a sudden surge of adrenaline caused him to cry out in pain again when the man stood on his leg and ground his foot into the wound there.

'Ah, there it is,' White said with a chuckle and his voice, the words, brought the tiniest bit of strength back to Callum. He spotted the drive right there beside him, within reach.

He grasped it, tossed it as far as he could. It hit the far wall and disappeared into the mound of hay.

'Go... ahead,' he said. 'It's all yours.'

White stomped over and roared in anger as he hauled his foot into Callum's ribs.

'Go and get it!' he yelled at his guy before crouching down.

He grabbed Callum's collar and pulled his face close.

'I guess the longer it takes him to find it, the longer we have to enjoy some alone time.'

'S... sorry,' Callum said. 'I'm just... not that into you.'

'Same,' White said before hurling his fist into Callum's face and his head flopped back down onto the floor.

He tried to right himself, to prop himself up but this time he was drifting. Too many hits to the head. Perhaps too much blood loss from the wound in his leg.

He was only vaguely aware of White's continued taunts, instead focused on a fuzzy noise in the background. Almost like... TV static, growing louder with each second.

Perhaps the noise was only in his mind. Was this how it ended? Drifting into nothingness. The world fading and nothing left but endless static.

'There's someone here,' White said.

Not to Callum. To his friend. But the voice, the change in sound, gave Callum renewed vigour. He opened his eyes. Or his sight cleared. He wasn't sure which. He was still on the ground but a second later, when the side wall of the barn shattered into pieces, he bounced to his feet. How, he had no idea. A gun fired. Aimed at him? He didn't know. He reached down, lifted the axe from the floor.

'Callum, behind you!'

A woman. Lea?

No. Hinch.

Her voice had come from the caved-in wall.

No, not caved in. It had... exploded. Been blown to pieces. Something like that. He didn't really know.

What he did know was that a moment later a gun boomed and he felt hot pressure in the back of his shoulder. No pain at that point, just pressure. And he was already moving, twisting, nothing to stop his momentum as the axe-head swept in a wide arc...

Thud.

And then stopped abruptly, wedged deep.

He let go but the axe handle remained suspended in the air. So too the object the axe head had sunk into.

Another head.

White's startled eyes quivered a little before his body concertinaed, the axe falling with him.

'Callum!' Hinch shouted, rushing over to him and catching him just before his legs gave way.

She sat him down on a stool, his brain fog clearing, although he felt weak, disjointed, and he knew if he shut his eyes a second too long, he'd be out of it. Dead? Possibly. So he had to stay awake.

'What... How?' he asked, staring over at the other side of the barn.

Although she didn't need to answer. He could see the tractor now. Not the old taken-apart one. A newer, bigger version that she'd crashed right through the wall. Not an explosion, after all, although definitely carnage. She'd swept in right where the haystack lay. Coincidence? Who knew. But a twisted, bloodied arm dangled out of the front wheel arch of the tractor.

'Where's the flash drive?' she said. 'You have it?'

'*He* did,' Callum said, pointing to what he could see of the man.

And she went to move away but his head lolled. Had she been holding it up for him?

'Callum, for God's sake, stay awake! We need to get you out of here.'

But she did then rush off and even though he tried really, really hard, only a couple of seconds later he slid off the stool and back to the floor.

And not long after that his eyelids slid closed too.

He heard the static again.

But *was* it static? Last time it'd been the tractor.

Or had it?

His confused brain could make no sense of it. But the noise was definitely getting louder, more all-consuming as he drifted, drifted.

'Callum!'

Hinch. Back to reality again and just like that the noise was gone.

He opened his eyes. Could make out a figure above him but it was far too blurry to be identifiable.

'Callum! I got it. Come on, let's get out of here.'

He didn't respond, although he really did try.

'We have to go! Come on. For Lea. Let's do this for Lea. Let's make it all right.'

And that was exactly the motivation he needed.

A smiling image of his wife burning bright in his mind, Hinch managed to pull him to his feet.

Moments later, with her guiding him, he was stumbling to the door.

30

SIX MONTHS LATER

The sun was shining in a clear blue sky, enough to melt away the frost that had set hard the night before, at least where the rays were able to penetrate. Callum lifted the box of beer and cringed as a knot of pain pulsed in his shoulder. He did his best to ignore it and headed back out of the shed, into the sunshine in the garden and across to the back doors of the house.

'Nicely chilled out there,' he said as he walked in through the patio doors.

'You move like you're older than me,' his dad said, taking the box from him as though he couldn't manage.

Callum said nothing. He wasn't quite sure if such comments – quite frequent from his parents – were out of real sympathy or some kind of *told you so* thought process whereby they believed he'd gotten what he deserved in life.

His dad put the box down in the kitchen and within a couple of minutes pretty much every bottle had been taken by one of the guests, over twenty, and many of whom were from the rugby club and could guzzle beer a lot better than they could play the game they loved so much.

Same for Callum, really. He'd already been at the very tail-end of his playing days even before the trauma his body had suffered in Portugal several months ago. And his dad was kind of right, because even walking wasn't as straightforward as it used to be, the nerve damage in his leg from the bullet wound enough to cause constant discomfort whenever he moved.

But he'd fought through the darkest days now.

An initial month in hospital had been followed by two months of full-time 'recovery'. Recovery in the sense that he hadn't been back to work at all during that time, although he had spent many of those weeks in and out of interview rooms where he'd been grilled by the police, MI6, whoever else had skin in the deadly game that he'd been drawn into against his wishes following the killing of his wife.

Even after that initial period, when he'd finally gone back to work – a financial necessity as much as anything else, because he simply couldn't survive with no income – the authorities at large had still brought him back for questioning on several further occasions. The last of those occasions had been only three weeks ago, in fact. He genuinely couldn't remember everything they'd asked him now, the answers – the truth – he'd given in return, the names they'd talked to him about, the faces they'd showed him. The whole episode of the events leading up to the demise of Erica Goldman and Andrew White and Denis Petit in Portugal had become murkier and murkier in his mind, tainted, in a way, given the often-conflicting information he'd been fed by the people questioning him. As though one of their main intentions was to change the narrative of what had happened in Callum's own mind.

Whatever. He had nothing to hide and would only ever tell them what he believed to be true.

'It's so wonderful to see my boys back together again,' his mum said, coming up to him and holding on to his arm, nuzzling into him – something she very rarely did.

'Yeah,' Callum said, looking across the room to his brother, deep in conversation with their dad. Aaron glanced over and raised his beer bottle in salute. Callum did the same. Deena, standing next to her husband, took notice and gave a frostier glare.

She'd likely never forgive Callum now, would never welcome him with open arms, but she was here, and so was Aaron and so were the kids. It meant a lot to Callum. It was only sad that tragedy had brought the siblings closer together.

'Make the most of it,' his mum said. 'Your nephews will grow up so quickly. And...'

'And?'

'You never know... one day... You'd make a great father, honey.'

His mum squeezed his arm, and he was sure her eyes started to well, but she turned away from him and moved off, and he was actually kind of glad she did as it took him several seconds to regain his emotions and battle against his own tears.

His phone pinged.

A message. Unknown number.

Outside. Now.

He looked around the room. No one was really paying him any attention, so he moved for the front door, all manner of ominous thoughts whirring.

No, if this was something bad, a threat, there was no need to pre-empt it with a message like that. If anyone wanted him dead, they'd just do it. Probably would have done so by now.

And he had a decent idea who the message was from anyway.

He opened the door and spotted the car, the driver's window wound down, a face poking out, beckoning him over.

Jenn Hinch.

He checked over his shoulder as he headed to her car, seeing if anyone was watching him from the house.

Didn't seem to be.

He sat down in the passenger seat.

'This is out of the blue,' Callum said.

'I just wanted to check on you. It's been a while. But I saw all the cars and thought maybe it best not to go to the door.'

Probably true. How the hell would he explain who Hinch was to his friends and family?

Of course, his brother was more aware of the truth than most, and his parents knew *some* things about what had led their son to getting shot twice and beaten to a pulp in Portugal. As much as the general public knew, at least. He'd never had a formal, heartfelt apology from any news organisation for having spread the headlines about him being wanted for murder, but they had at least clarified after the event that Callum was a victim in the shootouts both in Bucharest and Portugal. And relayed a concocted story about how he'd travelled through Europe seeking answers over the death of his wife, a government liaison, only to come under attack from a criminal organisation helmed by Yuri Kozak, a gangster who'd been wanted by the UK authorities for years. A quite sensationalist story, but one that had little meat to it really, and would have been easy to pick apart had anyone bothered to try. Except no one had, and the story had disappeared from public discourse within days. The public, his parents would never know anything more. He'd signed a very clear legal agreement to that effect, breach of which would see him behind bars. Such a friendly way to thank him for what he'd done for his country.

Although the £500,000 compensation he'd finally received had been a bit nicer. A life-changing amount, even if not really enough to mean he never had to work again. Although he *wanted* to work right now, because what else was he supposed to do?

But back to the point. It *had* been a while since he'd last seen Hinch. They'd not spoken at all since his release from hospital. She'd visited him a few times during those weeks, as though she still felt some responsibility for what had happened to him, and for what would happen to him after.

'You have some news for me?' he asked, even though he knew that even if she did, it'd likely be a redacted version.

'You've probably been hearing a lot of things, but maybe it's not all what you expected.'

A strange statement, but he felt he knew what she meant. Over the last few months there'd certainly been no official news about how a senior MI6 official – codename Ithaca – had been selling intel to a foreign group from the Middle East with the intention of, among other things, destabilising international relations, and which had led to multiple deaths. Nor had there been any charges made against any surviving co-conspirators, either within or outside of the intelligence services. Although Callum felt sure that MI6 would have dealt with those people one way or another. Wouldn't they?

'So?' Callum prompted.

'Omar Yousefi is dead,' she said.

The disgraced former MP. Callum actually knew little of the detail about how Yousefi fitted into the whole thing, other than he was one of the group's key figures of influence within the UK. He'd been kicked out of the government after evidence of tax evasion had come to light and Callum had assumed that was his penance.

Apparently not.

'A motorcycle accident,' she added.

Callum raised an eyebrow.

'A little bit odd,' she said, 'as his family said he'd never ridden a bike before.'

'Did *you* do it?' Callum asked.

'No,' Hinch said. 'But the manner, the official line, does seem to be a direct *fuck you*, don't you think?'

'From who? To who?'

'From the people within MI6, MI5, who know what happened. The good guys.'

Callum said nothing.

'From what I understand, Yousefi was the last of the key players still alive. Everyone else Lea had worked to expose... is dead.'

Was that supposed to bring him comfort?

'No more bad guys,' he said.

'No, there are *always* bad guys. But I hoped this would bring some closure. And... I'm sorry I lied to you.'

'More than once.'

'But I honestly didn't do it to cause you harm.'

'No. It's just a way of life for you. For all the people you work with.'

'I swear I only wanted to help find what had happened to Lea.'

Did he believe her? He *wanted* to.

'Do you know what I think about the most?' Callum asked.

'What?'

'What was it all even for? Goldman's lies and stealing. The order to have Lea ambushed and killed in Bucharest because she'd found the truth. Kozak, Yousefi, Denis, White losing their lives, among others. So much chaos and death and pain and... what is it all even for? Because... for anyone not involved, their lives just carried on as normal, regardless, oblivious, before and after it all.'

She held his eye for a moment, and he really wished he could read her mind because it seemed like something he'd said had struck a chord.

Was she ashamed?

'The very fact that most people get to live their lives oblivious to the threats that exist? Is because of people like Lea.'

'People like you?'

She shrugged.

'Lea was a better person than I'll ever be,' Hinch said. 'The world needs more people like that. Forever selfless. Only concerned about doing what they think is right for the greater good.'

Callum sighed but didn't respond. He certainly wanted to believe Lea was that person. But was it true? He really didn't know, because he still knew so little about her life with MI6, what she'd seen and done. He only knew her as the woman she pretended to be with him. A woman he'd fallen in love with, who he'd never not be in love with, even though he now knew about the lies.

He also felt he understood some of the torment it must have caused her. He saw it now, as he looked back at the key moments they'd spent together.

If only he'd pieced it all together sooner... Could he have saved her?

'Anyway,' Hinch said. 'I'm glad you're doing OK.'

'I'm not sure I said I *was* OK, but... thanks.'

'And if you're ever in trouble, if this thing comes back to bite you again somehow... you have my number. Call me.'

Callum nodded. 'Take care.'

He got out the car and waited by the side of the road, watching her head off down the street and then out of sight.

He turned back to the house, mind churning, until he spotted his mum and Deena in the living room window, side by side, looking at him. His mum smiled. Deena didn't.

Callum took a deep breath, then headed for the door.

* * *

MORE FROM ROB SINCLAIR

Another unmissable read from multi-million copy bestseller Rob Sinclair is available to buy now:

https://mybook.to/simonpeakethrillers3

ABOUT THE AUTHOR

Rob Sinclair is the million copy bestseller of over twenty thrillers, including the James Ryker series. Rob previously studied Biochemistry at Nottingham University. He also worked for a global accounting firm for 13 years, specialising in global fraud investigations.

Download your exclusive bonus content from Rob Sinclair here:

Visit Rob's website: www.robsinclairauthor.com

Follow Rob on social media here:

facebook.com/robsinclairauthor
x.com/rsinclairauthor
bookbub.com/authors/rob-sinclair
goodreads.com/robsinclair

ALSO BY ROB SINCLAIR

The James Ryker Series

The Red Cobra

The Black Hornet

The Silver Wolf

The Green Viper

The White Scorpion

The Renegade

The Assassins

The Outsider

The Vigilante

The Protector

The Deception

Angel of Death

The Enemy Within

Burning State

The Enemy Series

Dance with the Enemy

Rise of the Enemy

Hunt for the Enemy

The Simon Peake Thrillers

Dead Reckoning

Deadly Mistake

Standalone Novels

Rogue Hero

Blind Pursuit

www.ingramcontent.com/pod-product-compliance
Ingram Content Group UK Ltd.
Pitfield, Milton Keynes, MK11 3LW, UK
UKHW041256040326
11067UKWH00007B/943

9 781837 032112